*YOU*
*FEEL IT*
*JUST*
*BELOW*
*THE*
*RIBS*

Also by Jeffrey Cranor (with Joseph Fink)

*Welcome to Night Vale*

*It Devours!*

*The Faceless Old Woman Who Secretly
Lives in Your Home*

*Mostly Void, Partially Stars*

*The Great Glowing Coils of the Universe*

*The Buying of Lot 37*

*Who's a Good Boy?*


Also by Janina Matthewson

*Of Things Gone Astray*

# YOU FEEL IT JUST BELOW THE RIBS

## A NOVEL

JEFFREY CRANOR
JANINA MATTHEWSON

HARPER

*An Imprint of* HarperCollins*Publishers*

YOU FEEL IT JUST BELOW THE RIBS. Copyright © 2021 by Jeffrey Cranor and Janina Matthewson. All rights reserved. Printed in the United States of America. No part of this book may be used or reproduced in any manner whatsoever without written permission except in the case of brief quotations embodied in critical articles and reviews. For information, address HarperCollins Publishers, 195 Broadway, New York, NY 10007.

HarperCollins books may be purchased for educational, business, or sales promotional use. For information, please email the Special Markets Department at SPsales@harpercollins.com.

FIRST EDITION

Designed by Jamie Lynn Kerner

Title page art © Credon2012 / stock.adobe.com

Library of Congress Cataloging-in-Publication Data has been applied for.

ISBN 978-0-06-306662-5 (pbk.)
ISBN 978-0-06-314307-4 (library ed.)

21 22 23 24 25   LSC   10 9 8 7 6 5 4 3 2 1

*To Mary and Will*

# Contents

# Introduction

The following manuscript was found under the floor-boards of an attic room in a bedsit in Stockholm in 1996. The proprietor of the bedsit, being possessed of no small amount of insight—or perhaps a greater than usual amount of self-importance—donated the manuscript to the Statens Historiska Museum.

At the time, the museum did not pay much attention to the manuscript, as it seemed to them to be a highly implausible personal memoir that held no cultural or historical significance—at least none that could be verified. Its author made bold claims but did not provide sufficient details to corroborate them. It wasn't until a staff member by chance learned about the body found with the manuscript that the museum began to take the work seriously.

Whom that body belonged to changed the significance of the manuscript.

The woman in question had been living under a false name for more than twenty years, so uncovering her identity took some time. Eventually, through dental records, it was determined that she was none other than Dr. Miriam Gregory.

Dr. Gregory was a prominent psychologist during her lifetime, and her work contributed to the better implementation of some of the foundational tenets of the New Society. Her understanding of how to examine and manipulate the human mind was truly staggering, and the impact her work had on the world is impossible to quantify. She was reported missing in 1975 by her wife, Teresa Moyo, after she failed to come home from work. Teresa died in 1982, so we have not been able to verify those parts of the manuscript that deal with their relationship.

Since the discovery of the author's body, the manuscript has come under intense scrutiny from a range of sources—including the central government of Western Europe and numerous academic institutions—questioning its veracity if not its very authenticity. There was much debate about the wisdom of making the document public, considering the many unverifiable claims and the outright misinformation it contains. Ultimately the Societal Council decided it was best left unpublished.

We at the Yuriatin Press disagree. While we appreciate the dangers of certain texts, we are opposed to censorship, and we have dedicated ourselves to finding and publishing those documents the Society has seen fit to hide. If you're seeing this, it is because you are familiar with our work and our ethos and have passed through our vetting process. You can be trusted to approach this material responsibly.

Dr. Gregory's manuscript did, however, pose a co-nundrum for us, given its unreliable bent. Some suggested that we publish only the sections that were able to pass unscathed through our fact-checking process, or that we simply release a summary of the book's claims rather than the entire text.

After much discussion, we decided to publish the manuscript as it was written. At least, almost as written. Dr. Gregory sometimes wrote using a typewriter, but large parts were written out by hand. There are places in which the author's writing becomes illegible or otherwise unintelligible, and a few pages that appeared to be out of order. We have edited these sections for clarity, based on what we believe to be her intent. We have noted where any text has been altered.

We have also provided additional information to add context to some of the author's statements. This ranges from correcting historical facts she has related erroneously, omitted, or even made up entirely, to including contradicting accounts of some of the personal elements of her story. We did our best to locate and interview people who knew the author while she was alive, in order to verify as much of the manuscript as possible.

Of course, when alternate versions of events are reported by different people, it can be hard to distinguish whose version is closest to the truth. We felt that, having advised readers of the conflicting accounts, they could be left to draw their own conclusions.

Most notably, perhaps, we have not been able to confirm the existence, let alone the practices, of the institute

Dr. Gregory describes. We did manage to track down one or two personal accounts by people who claimed to have spent time there, but they were far from credible and gave few details. In an interview with a fringe magazine, for example, a musician claimed to have served time in a closed facility somewhere near Providence, Rhode Island. A patient undergoing psychiatric care in Berlin asserted that they knew of a covert North American hospital. We were unable to verify these claims, so while they did alter our own perception of the text, we felt it would be unethical to include details of them. At this stage, they are little more than rumor.

We have refrained from editing the manuscript other than the small adjustments noted. Readers should be prepared to encounter the following text as a largely unaltered, highly unreliable personal account of a life. Dr. Gregory has taken no pains to be consistent stylistically or even factually. She writes at times with clarity and intention but often lets herself slip into stream of consciousness. It appears that the writing took place over the course of some years, with bursts of activity followed by long stretches of rest or disinterest. All of this makes for somewhat confusing reading at times, but we have endeavored to bring clarity where we can.

As the author is now dead, and due to the lack of firm corroborating evidence for her story, we are somewhat reluctant even to label this text a memoir. Perhaps it is simply fiction, set against the backdrop of reality.

We leave it to the reader to judge.

# Part One: The End

# *One*

I WAS BORN INTO THE APOCALYPSE.

It's probably unhelpful to throw around a word like "apocalypse," and to be honest I couldn't tell you whether it's even apt.

It looks like an apocalypse from here. Or from now. From a distance, it looks like the world ended. Maybe it did.

But—and I suspect that this isn't something people like to admit; I've seen a lot of people who lived through that time not admitting this—it didn't feel like an apocalypse.

It just felt like life.

For the most part anyway. I'm sure there were moments, you know, I'm sure there were times when the constant presence of catastrophe shook my bones, but for the most part it went unnoticed. Familiar. Like a nearby train that passes every day.

Moments pass. And it's hard to focus on the chaos about you—war and disease for miles around—when what's in front of you is so close.

I grew up at the end of the world, and all that mattered was what was for dinner.

The generations who did not experience the Great Reckoning think of it as a cataclysm with a clear beginning and end, like a curtain opening and closing on a forty-year-long epic tragedy. But the end of the world comes with neither whimper nor bang. It unfurls its blossoms slowly, majestically, one moist black petal at a time.

When I was an infant, the Reckoning was merely a war,[1] born of allies and treaties, of minor uprisings leading to fists pounding podiums across continents. The war was messy and sprawling, having nothing to do with land or resources or acquisition. It was driven by nationalist identity crises and temper tantrums. It was waged by vast families with hurt feelings and destructive weapons, standing under flags.

I was born into war, and I grew up in something much, much worse.

People tend to look at events of mass eradication as if they're simple. Finite. A pandemic kills a hundred thousand. An earthquake kills five thousand. And then it's done. We tend not to look too closely, so we miss the fact that disease, wars, and storms linger long after they're gone.

The tornado passes, and you are unscathed. Only you die weeks later because of dehydration, malnutrition. You fall ill

---

1 As with many of her generation, Dr. Gregory's birthdate is unknown. Due to the widespread bombing that took place during the Great Reckoning, many documents were lost. The New Society Records Department was established in 1943, several months after the official Day of First Peace; it attempted to reissue key documents to survivors but depended on personal recollections of the individuals themselves, which were not always reliable. Records list Dr. Gregory's birthday as the 10th of January, with no year. It seems likely that she was born sometime between 1908 and 1911. The official start of the Great Reckoning is now considered to be the July Riots in Ghent in 1912.

and seek assistance, but what medical facilities remain are overwhelmed by those with missing limbs or shattered bones.

The idea of an apocalypse is a comfort, because it makes death seem like something we can all experience together, in a single moment, a colorful firework burst. But mostly death is something you keep to yourself. In reality, the apocalypse is most likely to be you, alone in a room with the flu.

I have known death all my life. I fear it, of course. But it is familiar. Death is a stray dog I have taken in and fed—not because I love it but because I don't want it biting me out of hunger.

I HAD A FAMILY ONCE. These days no one has families, so when I tell people about mine, it is all they want to talk about. That and what the war was like, I suppose. I can't help them, though. At this distance, all I remember of my family is their deaths.

"Miri, did you love your family no matter what?" is one question people ask me. "Even if you didn't like your family, did you still care for and protect them?" is another. "Is it true that families are tribes, and tribalism is inherently violent?" is another.[2]

Honestly, I do not know. It has been decades since my family was alive. I am sure I felt something for them, but I can only recall for you my experiences. I remember being with my family. I remember huddling under the broken lumber of our home, hiding from German soldiers. Or maybe

---

2 Edited for clarity.

they were English. Maybe they were French. They were men with guns. That's all that really matters.

I remember foraging in open fields, crouching in tall grass, my mother slapping my mouth if I spoke too loudly. I remember entering our neighbors' home through a shattered window after learning they had all succumbed to illness. I remember eating their food and wearing their clothes and reading their books. I remember the books were mostly medical journals. I remember my father forbidding us from speaking to anyone. I remember hiding, mostly in silence.

I remember remembering them over and over again.

How many times can you filter a memory before it's really just a fiction? How can you tell how many times your memories have been filtered?

A strange thing to consider when you've sat down to write out your own memories. What is the point of doing this if memory is so unreliable? But there is a point. I have to tell someone. I have to—not confess, exactly, because confession doesn't require action. And I need someone to take action.

I have wanted to get the truth out for years. I have tried once or twice. Not as hard as I should have. I don't have much time left, so I suppose I'm using the time I have to write out the truth so that someone can read it and do something. But I'm selfish and I want to be understood, so I'm starting here. At the beginning. With my earliest memories. I'm starting here so I can trace the entire path that led to my greatest accomplishment. My greatest crime.

Maybe none of this is relevant, but it's mine to tell, and there's no one to stop me telling it however I want.

So. This is what happened. This is everything I remember happening. And you can judge me if you like. But, whoever reads this—I have left pain in this world. Someone needs to fix it.

I HAD A SISTER ONCE. Her name was Elizabeth. My parents were named Keith and Ewa. I do not remember loving them or being loved by them. I remember being disciplined and fed and taught. So in that way I remember familial love.

My father knew how to grow things from the earth, even after the earth was poisoned. My mother knew how to manipulate things into other things, into whatever you needed. She could craft a tent out of sofa upholstery; she could make a bed out of gathered heather and shopping bags.

I'm sure they could do more than that, of course. I'm sure they had more to them—but time reduces memories to their least complex forms. "What do you remember about your parents, Miriam?" I remember they grew things. I remember they made things. I remember they made us survive. For a while.

Elizabeth and I used to play together. She had a doll that I wanted. I had a doll too, but I had played with it too hard. It was battered and broken and barely a doll anymore. My sister kept her doll perfect, protecting it from dirt and rough play. She cleaned its face and restitched loose threads along its body.

Sometimes she would hold her doll out to me, as if to let me take it, but at the last minute she would snatch it away and run off on her long fast legs, the doll held tightly to her chest, laughing at me as I tried to keep up with her.

I remember crying as I ran after her, gasping for air, my

cheeks red in the cold, my legs aching. I remember going inside and curling into a pile of blankets—I guess we didn't have heat that year—and watching my mother cook dinner. I remember, I think, my sister coming inside and sitting beside me. I remember her reading me a story and then braiding my hair. I remember her giving me some of her meat at dinner.

It plays like a film in my head; it plays like it happened all in one day. Maybe it didn't happen at all. It doesn't really matter.

One day Elizabeth got sick. Hundreds of thousands of people got sick then,[3] and my sister was one of them. We took her to a hospital, and there weren't any beds, so she lay on a mattress on the floor and she died.

Sadness took over me, I presume. I remember a period of inactivity, but I do not exactly remember the sadness that caused this. Perhaps those feelings evaporated under the heat of time.

I got Elizabeth's doll after all, but I do not remember playing with it. I was selfish, to be sure, but I was raised in the apocalypse, and selfishness helps you survive. I was my only concern. If my parents could grow food and make shelter and keep me occupied with games, that was helpful to me.

---

3 The H4N2 influenza virus—known colloquially as the "cobbler's flu" due to early and erroneous rumors that it was caused by a foot fungus—was first reported in Salisbury, Former United Kingdom, in the autumn of 1916. Within six months, it had spread across the globe. The spread was exacerbated by the movements of the world's armies, and the virus in turn worsened the growing conflict. With a pandemic adding to the wars' burden on hospitals, medical equipment became a precious resource. This flu outbreak had largely died down by the end of 1917, although there were smaller resurgences in 1921 and 1924.

I remember moving somewhere else after my sister died. I don't remember why. I suppose the fighting came too close.[4]

I remember the new place was broken. The war had been through and left nothing behind. Nothing but battered houses and empty people.

My father made a garden there—as he made a garden everywhere. He worked in the earth with his hands, and the earth delivered life to him.

And eventually, it turned out, death. My father cut his fingers on shrapnel left behind in the poisoned soil. A deep scratch that bled for days. He bandaged it and went on working, but we saw dark veins like oak limbs grow across his hand and up his forearm. During his sleep, he gasped and clutched his breast. My mother and I burned his body in accordance with the new laws.[5]

I remember being alone with my mother, and I remember holding her. She had lost her husband and her oldest daughter, and she cried most days. She could not cook anymore, and neither of us could grow vegetables as well or as consistently as my father had been able to. She stopped crafting, and she seemed to find contentment in her sorrow. Something like contentment. Despair, maybe.

---

4 Dr. Gregory never spoke publicly about her early life, and never shared where she was born or where she lived as a child. We know that she eventually entered North America (New York, Former United States) on a ship from Trieste, but she never related how she got there. It seems likely she was from Former Poland, but as infrastructure broke down and her family moved around, it is possible they lost track of their own location. They may have even crossed borders unknowingly.

5 It's not clear which laws she is referring to. Each country had its own methods of preventing the spread of disease.

I held her whenever she felt sad, and soon, I was holding her every night. Mourning was her escape, her reason not to do anything. She regressed toward infancy, and she turned me into her mother. We were alone together for long enough for it to feel normal.

In all this war, she was the only one of my family to die through violence—although the war didn't kill her, not directly. She was outside our home, praying to a god she had either recently discovered or invented altogether, when a man approached her and asked for food. She said she could not spare any food. He asked for money, and she said she had no money. He asked for shelter, but my mother grew upset at being so needed. She was the one with needs. She no longer knew how to give, and she told him to leave.

This man was a desperate man, one of the many. Someone who had seen horrible things happen to those he loved and who, like my mother, was too broken to help himself. Bereft of anyone to help him, he was also too broken to grieve his terrible circumstances. All he had left was rage. He struck her, and she fell. She did not cry out, because she was confused. He hit her again and kicked her. And eventually she did not cry out because she was unconscious.[6]

I remember their deaths. If memory is ever true, that is how my family died.

Keith. Ewa. Elizabeth.

I did not say their names again for a long time.

---

6 Edited for clarity.

○　○　○

WHAT I DON'T REMEMBER IS how it felt to be alone. I don't remember my first moment of being just me, just Miri, all alone. I remember disciplining myself, feeding myself, and teaching myself.

I think I was only twelve, though—maybe younger, eleven maybe or ten—so I must have been afraid. Where should I sleep? How should I get food? How do I protect myself from those who have nothing left but rage?

There were still shops operating at that point, I think, but how would I get money? My parents had never seemed to use money, but they must have traded something. Their skills, perhaps. Things they had grown or made. They had taught me to do those things, but I couldn't do them as well. I couldn't do them as quickly.

I don't know how long I tried to survive like this. Tried to survive like my family, without my family to survive with. I don't know how long I tried to use their tools to keep my own life going.

Probably not long. Well, no amount of time seems long to me now.

Sometimes you get to the point where surviving takes so much work that you begin to ask yourself if it's worth it. Or you would, if you had the energy.

I'm not talking about depression, really, though I suppose there are similarities. I mean simply that sometimes, for some people, the amount of labor it takes to accrue the supplies you need to live through a day outweighs the value of the day itself. You spend each day working, striving, fighting to live—only to wake up faced with another day you have to survive.

Can we blame a person for trying to lessen that burden? For trying to redress the imbalance? For trying to make sure that the labor is worth it?

I suspect there's one child in a million who wouldn't end up doing what I did to survive, in the end. If you're alone at that age, if you have to look out for yourself, if you're in the middle of a war and there's no one around to care for lone children, you go a bit feral. You have to.

Manners are for peace. A conscience is for peace.

It started small, of course, it started cowardly. A stolen loaf of bread. A lie told to claim shelter. Promises broken. The gullible manipulated. I got better at it. It got easier—both practically and morally. I found weapons. I grew bold. Ruthless.

Sometimes in war it comes down to you or someone else, and both of you are innocent. Or neither of you are. It's the same thing, really.

The world was ending, so what good were values? What good was neighborly sentiment?

You're probably shocked, reading this. I'm not even telling you details, and you're probably judging me. "It's in times of strife that our true goodness can shine through," you're probably thinking. I've heard people say that. Countless times I've heard that said by youngsters who have never seen so much as a backyard brawl.

By idiots.

Whether you're on the battlefield or in the aftermath, no one comes out of a war with their hands clean. Not a war like that. You do the best you can, and the only morality you have to cling to is the knowledge that you didn't choose to be there. A set of powerful men, who never even knew you existed, put you there. And why? For power? For a bit more land they'd likely never even walk over?

My sins, if I have sins, can be cast at their feet—at least in part.

Those men and their nations destroyed the world. All I did was survive it.

# *Two*

I SAW A GIRL THIS MORNING WHO LOOKED LIKE MY MOTHER. IT'S strange—I haven't thought about my mother in decades, but after I wrote about her, she appeared before me. Part of me wanted to speak to her, this girl who seemed like my mother, but I didn't know what I would say. That I turned out to be so much more than she expected of me? And so much less? That I'm sorry I spent the better part of sixty years barely acknowledging her existence? That I don't remember exactly when she died?

Of course, it doesn't matter at all what I would say to my mother if I saw her again, because I didn't. It was just a girl with the same copper hair.

Anyway. Irrelevant. I have more important things to tell you.

I've read a textbook or two over the years that claimed to be able to tell students what the Great Reckoning was like, but I didn't recognize my own life there. Not at all.

Maybe it's because they were written for schoolchildren. Maybe it's because, when it's written down, when it's rendered into academic abstraction, history doesn't really bear much resemblance to real life. How could it?

History is full of dates and numbers, statistics, major events. A history textbook is a telescope's view of the universe. You can tell stars from planets from comets, but to understand the colors of rocks, the presence of water, the tiniest frisson of life is impossible.

You could read that a pandemic broke out in 1917.[1] You could note and remember how many millions it killed. You could read accounts of the chaos the disease caused in medical centers and learn that, in truth, we can't calculate how many people died of that illness, because so many of them never made it to a medical center at all. No textbook ever told the story of a girl named Miriam coveting a doll named Marguerite owned by a sick sister named Elizabeth.

If one army flings shells of gas at another, you could estimate how many are killed in that attack—but could you measure how many innocents were killed years later, when they stumbled across an unexploded shell? The impact of the Reckoning is inexpressible in mere words.

How many people buried their own dead, leaving no evidence? How many people were born and lived with no official record of their existence, only to die without ever being counted?

At a certain point, who is even left to make the tally?

History books try to clean this up, to a certain extent. Or they try to pretend it was clean all along.

I had seen a body burned on a pyre and sent out into the ocean. I had not known the person, but my mother told me

---

1 She is, of course, referring to the "cobbler's flu" pandemic, but she has mistaken the date. The disease first broke out in 1916.

he was a soldier. I had seen dozens of dead who were not counted, let alone ever removed for burial or cremation. The decomposing dead contributed to the disease. Death itself is a virus.

But what else was anyone supposed to do? Belief in an apocalypse is the belief that a greater power, a predetermined fate, has been set in motion. Once you believe that the end of the world has begun, you are complicit in its destruction.

Sometimes I wonder about the men who started our war. Those men who, from the safety of their offices in Europe and America and later eastern Asia, sent the young men of their countries out onto the battlefield to die. Who watched from on high as the fighting grew worse, who saw it spread and pushed it further. Who, somehow, were surprised when the war came back to them in the form of swarming riots. Leader after leader sent armies crawling across muddy fields, thousands of miles in all directions, and then were surprised when one came into their homes, tracking dirt across the carpet.

The assassinations that followed uprisings must have placated the oppressed, but someone had to fill the void of the dead leaders. And we all learned that the uniform one wears is more powerful than any moral dogma.

As for me, I was alone in the world. My family was gone, and there was no one left to care that my family was gone. There was no one to turn to, no authorities to take up my care.

So I did what everyone does, every single day. I woke up. I fed myself. I ran from trouble. I fell asleep. And then I did it again. I stole what I needed from wherever I could find it, I slept in whatever shelter I could get into.

That part was easy. There were plenty of empty houses.

○  ○  ○

I DON'T KNOW HOW LONG I lived like this. A week. A year. It doesn't matter. There was a point when it changed, and I do remember that.

I found a house in a city that wasn't really a city anymore. Swaths of it were completely razed; much of the rest was abandoned. There were clusters of people around, isolated from each other. It was a sequence of villages, really, within one sprawling, gutted town.[2]

There was a farm a few minutes from the house I was squatting in, and I was hungry. I climbed over the fence and dug up some potatoes and carrots, and gathered handfuls of greens. But I guess I was more desperate than cautious, and someone saw me.

I heard a yell and ducked behind some tall tomato plants, shoving what I'd gathered into my bag. Given the robust condition of their gardens, there was no question that the farmers were armed, so I ran. After a few moments, I heard gunshots but did not turn to see how close they were.

I ran without looking until I found myself in a neighborhood that appeared to be completely empty. I found a house with an open window and slipped inside, ducking down

_____

2 There are several possibilities for the city Dr. Gregory mentions here, though she fails to give any clues that would narrow it down. She clearly spent part of her childhood near the Baltic coast, but there is no way to know how far or in what direction she traveled, either with her family or after their deaths. In describing this city, she doesn't mention the surroundings—whether she was near mountains or ocean—or indicate any landmarks. Some have speculated that it was Leipzig, which had seen catastrophic damage early on. Frankfurt is also possible, but it remained relatively populated even later in the Great Reckoning. The third most likely location is Cologne.

and listening to see if I was still being chased. There was silence.

Eventually I stood and peered outside to double-check, but it was getting dark and no one was there. I decided I might as well stay where I was for a while, at least for the night, so I washed off a couple of the carrots and some of the greens, sat at the dining-room table, and began to eat.

I don't know why I used to do that. I was living like a rat, scampering about in search of food. I would grab bread or apples and run, find an empty house, and sit at the dining-room table to eat. As if I was still a person, still a member of a family.

I don't know why. I would like to know why. Is it strange that even now, after all these years, I don't fully understand who I was as a child? I suppose I don't really know who I am even now, as an adult. As an old person.

Anyway.

I ate my scavenged meal and went to see if this was somewhere I could stay. Finding shelter was always easy, but finding a place to sleep inside that shelter was another story. You never knew when you were going to find a bed with a body in it. You never knew how long it might have been there. A lot of people had been sick, and often there were no hospitals for them to die in.

Looking for a bed was risky.

The house was small—a tiny shingled hut, really—behind and perpendicular to a row of tenements along the main street. It was out of immediate sight, which could indicate either that it had long been coveted by scavengers for its privacy, or that it was private enough to not have been discovered. I stepped tentatively into each room, bracing myself for the stench of strangers, but there was nothing to find. No one to find.

The rooms were all tidy, the beds were all made. There wasn't even that much dust, considering the circumstances.

I picked the biggest bed, obviously. Is it strange that I don't want to be judged for that? I've done a lot of things I could be judged harshly for, but I don't want anyone to think I was wrong for sleeping in the biggest bed I could find.

I fell asleep quickly. I always did in those days. I slept soundly and fully while mortar shells fell across the world. It's peace that's kept me awake. I slept while the world was destroyed; I lie awake now that it's rebuilt.

But as quickly as I fell asleep, I was awakened—suddenly, sharply, with a resounding slap to my face. I woke up breathing hard, terrified, to find my bed surrounded.

"Who are you?" I heard someone say. "What are you doing in our house?"

There were eight or nine girls standing around the bed. They were around my age, some of them much younger.

I told them I'd thought the house was empty, and I offered to share the food I had left, which is as effective a method of crowd control as any. Plus, I was not armed.

Three of them held me down while two more asked who I was with.

"No one," I repeated to half a dozen variations of this question.

"Where are you from?" asked one girl, the shortest of the group, but before I could answer, I heard two girls whispering from the back.

"Quiet," the shortest girl ordered. "Take her food."

The girls took my satchel and rummaged through it, pulling out apples and spinach and even a half-eaten loaf of bread I'd taken from one of the wealthier, more fortified areas of town.

They shared and devoured all I had in nearly the same time it took them to pull it from my bag.

"You're alone," the shortest girl said. She didn't intone it like a question.

"Yes," I said. "My family is dead."

The girl seemed to relax. There was a long silence. I could still hear chewing, as a girl in the back of the room ate the last piece of the apple core.

"Am I free to go?"

"Yes, but you don't have to," the short girl said. "But if you stay, that's not your bed."

We moved to the kitchen. Its cupboard doors gaped open, revealing sacks of grains and piles of fruit, not stored neatly like a family's pantry but with the haphazard density of a squirrel's buried stash. In the corner there was a wood-burning stove, and in the center of the room was a table. Pails of what looked to be fresh water lined the walls.

A couple of the other girls sat me down and started grilling me. Where was I from, how did I find their house, had I taken any of their stuff, that kind of thing. They asked a lot of questions before they considered letting me ask some of my own, but eventually what started as an interrogation became something more like conversation. How did your mother die? What's the most disgusting body you've found?

I learned that they had all lost families, although two

of the girls were cousins. I learned names: the girl who first spoke to me, the shortest of the group, was Margot. Margot was the de facto leader of the group. I don't think it occurred to anyone to mind this; it felt natural. She was loud and caustic, with long thick hair that seemed to sway slightly even without a breeze.

And Naija, who had traveled further than anyone else to get there. She was tall and quiet. At first I thought that was because she didn't speak the language well, but I was wrong. She spoke five languages, I think, at least five fluently. She would stand in a corner, not speaking but taking everything in.

The gang was what you might expect to happen when the world ends, and no one is left to look after the children. They had found each other, helped each other, banded together into an awkward unit. They had found a house that looked empty, that was surrounded by other empty houses, that they could keep coming back to without anyone knowing they were there.

It's basic evolution. Your chances of survival are stronger when you're part of a group; we all know this instinctively. We may not like it but we know it. You're more likely to live if you're part of a group—and here I am now, alone and dying.

The girls didn't exactly welcome me with open arms at first. That's evolution as well. Outsiders are dangerous. They can't be trusted. If the group is to be safe, you have to protect it as much as it protects you.

They never asked me to join them, but they said I could stay for a few nights. It was cold that night, and a storm was looming; they wouldn't push me out into it. So I stayed for a few days. For a few days I helped scavenge food, I mended torn clothes, I joined in with their games.

Then, just when I'd told them I would move on, snow started to fall.

I thought at the time that I was an outsider moving in on an existing group, a finite and complete unit. But now that I understand more about the world, more about how people work, I realize I was just one in a sequence. Every single one of those girls was once a loner who stumbled across the group, who was treated with caution but allowed to stay. I don't really know how it happened with any of the others. Is that strange? Have I just forgotten or did I never bother to ask?

Well.

For me it was a snowstorm that lasted two days and left snow in piles for weeks. That's all it took to make me part of the gang. Obviously there were no street cleaners, no one to shovel the drifts aside, no one to salt the roads so they were safe to walk on.

By the time roaming the streets alone seemed safe again, the idea of my leaving had disappeared.

I don't know if that's beautiful or sad. That you can find a family—for a while—by simply being thrown together temporarily and coming out the other side, not bonded necessarily but committed.

Or maybe it's just evolution again. You're stronger in a group. The group is stronger, the larger it is. We are all just trying to survive.

# *Three*

I HAVE BEEN TRYING, FOR THE LAST SEVERAL DAYS, TO REMEMBER more details about this small segment of my life. It's hazy—it shifts and changes, and I can't be sure of it. Perhaps because this time was so short and so much in flux. I'll tell you what I remember, and I'm sorry it isn't much. Things will get more certain as we go along.

I don't think I was naive enough to think the gang could become a stand-in for a family. Perhaps that's why this is all so indistinct to me. I didn't believe it was permanent. No one was naive enough for that, not in those days. Naivete is a luxury.

So I was never under the illusion that I had a family again, after I found the gang. I would have been an idiot to feel that way. But it's difficult to spend all your time with a group of people and not become a little too comfortable with the situation.

Comfort is dangerous. It is the illusion that nothing will ever change even when things are changing constantly, right in front of you. And this personal conservatism is seductive.

Everything about our group was always in flux. We rarely

stayed in the same place for long—we'd move on after a couple of weeks, a month maybe, trying to avoid being tracked by militias, army recruiters, or police. We sought out reliable sources of food and orbited them for as long as they stayed reliable. Which sometimes wasn't long.

Food was the focus; clothing and shelter came second. Food was hard. Clothing and shelter were easy. So our priorities often went sideways.

We had a routine, of sorts, although it seems odd to call it that now. A routine today means coffee at 8:30 every morning while you read the paper, lunch at the same deli at 1:00. No part of struggling to survive a barren, war-torn world looks like a routine when you compare it to that.

But in its own way, it was.

We would find a new place to stay, and Naija would spend a day or two outfitting it with candles, cooking equipment, and beds made of rags, towels, and scraps of clothing she stole from nearby homes. I say "stole," but many of these homes were abandoned, or at least unburdened by living bodies who would take umbrage with her stealing a few necessities.

Some of the girls felt like this was a wasted effort—at best, the houses we stayed in were irredeemably dirty, and we knew we'd only be there for a few weeks. But Naija persisted, corralling anyone who was willing to join her cause.

We would dust and clean as well as we could. I would mend curtains and bedspreads, doing my best to make them feel cheerful, making my best approximation of "homelike." I could not sew as well as my mother, of course, but I managed to patch things together.

When she found homes that housed human remains,

Naija wouldn't allow anyone else to handle the bodies—she would do that herself. She would wrap them carefully in whatever blankets we could spare, bundle them into a wheelbarrow, if she could find one, and take them away.

I asked her about what she did with them, but she never told me. All she would say is "They are human beings," giving me a strange look, as if I was wrong even to ask the question.

I assume she buried them. I don't know where. There were cemeteries, of course, but they tended to be full and unkempt.

Wherever she took them and whatever ceremony she used to observe their passing is lost now, with her. But the process was weighty, important, and extraordinarily personal to her—she wouldn't allow any cleaning to start until she'd finished. Looking back now, I wonder . . . If I had shown more interest in and sympathy for the corpses of the Reckoning, demonstrated even a modicum of understanding of spiritual rites, maybe Naija would have welcomed my help. But she was the only one willing to even look at a body for long, let alone touch it, and the disinterest of the rest of the group put her off inviting us to assist.

After the bodies were gone, there was the smell to deal with, as well as the need to destroy whatever bedclothes or furniture they had been found in. We all helped with that. We couldn't burn those things, as we wanted to draw as little attention as possible, so we threw them into a river or barn or any other nearby structure.

This too became routine. It only takes a few times before expunging corpses from their homes becomes ordinary.

Although—you know, I think that was only ever true for some of us. I don't think it ever really was that way for Naija. I remember now, she would be even quieter than usual for a couple of days, every time we moved. And Margot made it clear that the rest of us were to leave her alone when this happened.

Not all the girls were adept at picking up on other people's moods. Maybe that's to be expected. Maybe moods are a luxury. Or maybe they were just insensitive kids.

Whatever the reason, Margot and I often ended up running some kind of interference to protect Naija from the rest of the gang during those early days after a move. We never acknowledged what we were doing, and I don't know if Naija ever knew the lengths we went to.

I'm sorry. I'm suddenly struggling with this. With Naija. I haven't thought about her in so long, and somehow it's only just hitting me that she lived through the Reckoning too. Or maybe she didn't.

I wonder what she did with her life, if she survived. I wonder if she was happy. Despite what she did to us later, I hope she was happy.

AFTER I HAD JOINED THE gang—I can't remember how long after, probably not very long—one of the girls left. I don't remember her name, but I remember she had long, wild, blond hair. At least, I think she did. I think she's the one that left first.

I don't know. It's not important.

She got recruited, I think. One of them got recruited at some point. There were still some efforts being made to recruit people into the army. None of us really knew what the war was about—probably by that point it was about nothing.[1] Probably it was about nothing from the beginning.

But every so often, some recruiter who was traveling around what was left of the country would spot us and come talk to us. To those of us who looked old enough and well enough.

We always listened because they always had food, but none of it really made sense. None of the things they told us had anything to do with our reality.

The recruiters each had vaguely threatening smiles as they wooed us with fresh water and chocolate. We were—or at least I was—keenly aware of the game being played, and I knew that in war there was no safety, no protection by or from authority. If a member of the army wanted to arrest us or even shoot us, they could, without repercussions.

But then one of the girls—I think, I'm almost sure it was the one with the long, tangled, blond hair—joined up. I was devastated. For a moment. For me it was the breaking up of our group, and the group was the only reason I felt safe. But of course she wasn't the first to go. Far from it. Girls left almost as often as they arrived—she was just the first for me.

I was devastated for a moment, but then I saw that no one else was devastated, and now I don't even remember her name.

I learned to deal with the constant flux of the group, girls

---

1 Dr. Gregory is not far wrong in this assertion. There were reasons for conflict, of course, but not many of them really justified the scale of the violence, so dismissing them as "nothing" isn't entirely inapt. The initial clashes were driven by nationalist identity disputes, escalated by a domino stack of treaties that drew successive countries into war. There was also an element of experimentation. In Europe, at least, there had been peace for some time, but the development of war machines continued. The first battles were a chance to test them.

joining and leaving, revolving around the nexus that was Naija, Margot, and me.

Because we were the nexus. Somehow, even as young as we were, we had realized that if we wanted security in the gang, we needed to have order. And to have order, we needed to be unassailable. We had to appear calm and confident; we had to be trustworthy and authoritative.

But everyone needs an outlet. If we had to be perfect to the rest of the girls, we had to be imperfect with each other. We had to let ourselves bend and breathe with each other, in order to be immovable to everyone else.

We would take days together, apart from the group. Tell the rest that we had to do some kind of crucial reconnaissance, scout out a possible new food source, spy on another group to see if we should be afraid of them. But really we were just getting away. Going to the nearest wild place we could find—woods, rivers, lakes—to be wild ourselves.

It's not accurate, but I see those days in permanent twilight. The sun hanging low, sending golden beams through long grass. Like some kind of saccharine coming-of-age movie, the kind that's full of slow shots of some teenager's eyelashes, hesitant kisses, and an ending that leaves everything ultimately unresolved.

Some kind of intolerable nonsense like that.

There's a particular color palette to films like that. The look of nostalgia. Maybe that's how we all remember our adolescence—whether we grew up peacefully, surrounded by meadows, with competent adults having a care for our future, or alone in broken cities as war raged all over the globe.

Maybe that's beautiful.

The world was in chaos, but I still got to have long, aimless days. I got to have first kisses. First more-than-kisses.

I got to have a little taste of a sweet, tender innocence that, when you look back at that time as a whole, seems entirely absent from the world.[2]

So that's nice.

I don't know how long this continued. A year? I don't think much longer than a year, but a year feels eternal when you are young. The three of us, surrounded by an ever-changing circle of half-formed girls who looked to us for leadership, even though we were in exactly the same position as them.

We traded what we could for what we needed from the people around us. There was one in particular. A gruff, broken man who somehow always seemed to have fresh meat and bread, and who wanted nothing from us but to talk.

He never asked us anything that would make us uneasy. He didn't want to know our names; he didn't want to know where we were living. All he wanted was stories.

He would tell us his own tales of what he'd seen as he walked the world, and ask us for our own in return.

He had an accent we couldn't place,[3] and a store of unfamiliar fairy tales that delighted us. We liked to think we

---

2 Edited for clarity.

3 While we are reluctant to claim complete confidence in this, it seems almost certain that the author refers to Josef Hinter, a mercenary spy. He traveled throughout Europe disguised as a beggar—he had lost a leg and was blind in one eye, which made the deception easier—and collected information, which he would then sell to the highest bidder. Among other crimes, he sold information that led to the catastrophic bombing of Edinburgh in 1919, and the deliberate release of disease-infested rats in Rome in 1921—attacks which led to hundreds of thousands of deaths. He was executed by the Austrian government in June of 1922.

were independent. We liked to think we didn't need or want anyone else, but we flocked to him like birds desperate for a scrap of bread.

I think we just loved knowing an adult who wanted to listen to us. We told him everything we could remember. Everything we could imagine. And he drank it all in as if we were telling him the secrets of the universe.

Naija spoke more to him than she did to almost anyone else. I think she was drawn to him because he had also come from so far away. Not in the same direction, of course, but he reminded her that the world was bigger than the collection of towns and cities near us. He reminded her that she'd had a home somewhere else. Somewhere wildly different from where she now found herself.

We would come across him every few months. Somehow, no matter where we moved, we would find him again and tell him stories we'd collected in the meantime.

There are stories I struggle to recount now—it seems so fantastic that such things could have happened—but back then they were bright and alive and real.

Like the cult we stumbled upon that believed this really was the end of the world—that it had been planned by a group of divine beings thousands of years ago, and that the only way to survive the cataclysm was to journey to the deep, frozen north and pledge allegiance to the beings—who would then take the faithful to paradise while the rest of us burned.

Four of the girls left us for that group.

There was the group that claimed they were building an unassailable city, using plans given to their leader in a divine vision, where they would wait in safety until the fighting stopped. Two girls went with them.

There were guerrilla groups determined to disrupt all military activity on all sides, wherever they could find it.

There were dozens of reasons to leave our little cluster, and eventually everyone did.

Because one day the army came. Not some recruiter—a commander, with a battalion.

They came for us. We were traitors, they said; we'd been trading secrets. We'd been colluding with spies.

I don't know where Margot went when this happened. She was there when they came down our street. She was beside me at the window when we saw them appear. But by the time they were at the door, she was gone.

The commander questioned all of us, one by one. Some of the girls he dismissed when he was done with them, letting them wander back out into the street to find their own way. Me he questioned over and over again, but I didn't understand what he was talking about.

He didn't believe me. "I know you're lying," he said. "You deliberately traded information about military movements to a known spy. Your Indian friend told us everything. She told us it was all you."

I never saw Naija again.

# *Four*

I KNOW HOW LONG I SPENT IN PRISON. OF COURSE I KNOW HOW long I spent in prison. It's an odd thing, but when time has ceased to matter almost everywhere else, in prison it remains scrupulously marked.

So I know that I entered prison on the twenty-first of March, 1922. And I know that I left prison on the fourteenth of September, 1925.

I believe that means I was twelve or maybe thirteen when I was arrested. I was so young.

I was . . .

When I picture myself in prison I picture—well, myself. My adult self. Why didn't I realize how young I was?

Why didn't I realize I was a child?

I HAD TO STOP FOR a while after writing that last. I had to stop, and it took me a few days to start again. I'm trying to keep my emotions in check while I do this. I'm trying to keep a clear head, to make sure that I give an accurate account, but sometimes it's difficult.

The memories are difficult.

Anyway.

I was imprisoned from 1922 to 1925. I wasn't sentenced to that length of time—in fact, I wasn't sentenced to anything. Trials were a luxury the world couldn't afford[1]—I had been marked as a troublemaker and put somewhere out of the way. That was all that mattered.

The government's priority[2] was, of course, the war effort. I'm not sure if there was conscription[3] of female soldiers at this

---

1 Dr. Gregory is exaggerating here. While the criminal justice system wasn't operating as efficiently as it does today, trials and legal sentencing were still carried out throughout most of the Great Reckoning. There is no record of Dr. Gregory standing trial. Nor is there a way for us to determine whether that is because she was never tried, as she claims, or simply because the records of her trial were lost. We do know that she was held for some time at Gevangenis van Antwerpen, in the north of Belgium, because her name appears on a record of inmates present during a brawl there in 1924. We have been unable to verify the dates of her incarceration because the prison itself was bombed in 1931, and most of their records were destroyed. The records that were recovered from the site after the bombing were badly damaged, and in many cases only a few words or names could be made out.

Naturally, from a modern viewpoint, Dr. Gregory's incarceration looks unusual, even inhumane, given her age at the time. It's important to remember that laws around juvenile offenders were still developing at this point in history. In addition, the extensive bombing that Europe suffered in the early years of the Great Reckoning left a dearth of suitable buildings for confinement, so often detention centers specifically for young people were simply not available. However—since it was common for incarcerated people to be given the option of cutting their sentences short if they were willing to serve in the army—there would have been few adult prisoners left behind bars at this stage.

2 It is not clear if Dr. Gregory was aware of the country she was in at this time. As stated earlier, she was incarcerated in Belgium, but we have been unable to determine where she was at the time of her arrest. From 1917 until 1932, Belgium was occupied by the German army, as was much of the Netherlands and the eastern regions of France.

3 Conscription of able-bodied men between the ages of eighteen and forty-five was imposed across Europe by the end of 1915. Conscription of women for front-line combat was never universal, though several countries

point, but those women who were of suitable age and ability were deployed to more important areas. They were nurses, they were mechanics, they were farmers. Prison guards were important only if they were overseeing POW camps—the rest of us were overseen by whoever was left.

So the guards tended to be elderly. That didn't exactly make them pushovers—they knew what they were doing and more than one had a genuine cruel streak. But most of them could be easily outrun, which made breaking the rules for something you wanted a reasonable bet.

There was also not a lot of money to spare for the upkeep of the prison, and it was in a bad state of disrepair. There were loose windows and broken doors, enough that if you wanted to get out of the building, you could find a way without too much trouble. It was still risky, of course; there were guards on surveillance, and whatever other shortfalls the prison had in terms of equipment, it did manage to keep them well armed. So you could get out of the building fine, but that didn't mean you'd get away without being shot.

Still, occasionally someone would try. I don't really know why. The prison had a roof. It had heating and freshly laundered clothes and hot showers—if not consistently, at least more often than the outside world.

It had regular meals. It had a doctor and a dentist. It had a library. What was there in the outside world at that point that could make up for the loss of all that?

---

did implement it during the late 20s and throughout the 30s. However, as Dr. Gregory points out, most women were already working in crucial areas and could not be spared, having taken over for their male counterparts as the men were called up to serve.

As soon as I arrived, I had two rotten teeth removed and three fillings put in. I was given inoculations I should have had years earlier. I was given medication for the asthma that troubled me from time to time.

On top of all this, I was learning new things for the first time I could remember, and nothing could have stopped me. There were so many books to read—there were schoolbooks, instruction manuals, reports of psychological studies. Novels.

I read them all.

I read everything I could get my hands on, whether it interested me or not. It was the most peaceful existence I'd known.

For a while.

And then I met Elsa.

ELSA HAD BEEN WATCHING ME, she said.

"Watching me?" I said. "Why?"

"I don't know," she said. "I was interested."

"In what?"

Elsa was fascinating. She held her head at a slight angle, looking up at me from under her lashes, a small smile always playing across her lips. She seemed to me somehow slightly out of focus with the world around her, but like everything she saw was completely clear. It was intoxicating.

"You read a lot," she said. "I mean, you really read a lot. You read all the time."

"I like to read," I said.

She leaned in a little, her eyes glinting. "Why?" she said.

"I don't know."

"Yes, you do," she said, "if you think about it."

I tried to think about it, but it was a bit distracting to have her staring at me.

"I don't know why," I said again. "I just like it."

"But think about it," she said. "Close your eyes and let the thought come."

"Why do you even care?"

"Just try, please. I want to know."

I sighed and closed my eyes. I could feel her face close to mine, but I tried to ignore it. I breathed. In. And out. And after a moment I began to speak.

"I think it makes me feel quiet," I said. "Relaxed. Like I'm not here. Like I'm not in prison. Not in a war."

"You feel peaceful? When you read?"

"Yeah. More peaceful than I do any other time, anyway."

At this, a real smile spread across her face, slowly, broadly.

"You don't know what you're talking about," she said. "I can show you."

She led me through the prison, across a recreation room and down a corridor, around corners and through doors, until I had no idea where we were. I was nervous. We were expected to be at our own cells by five each evening, as there was an inspection before dinner. I worried that I'd wind up alone somewhere with no idea of the way back.

Eventually we came to a battered-looking door. It had an imposing lock, but the lock was rusty and brittle and, as it soon became clear, not functional. Elsa gave it a shake, and it slipped from its moorings, dangling off the door by one screw. She pushed the door open, and I felt damp air across my face. I could see a stretch of concrete and then the prison wall. We were outside. Through one of the rotted outer doors that led to the possibility of freedom and the risk of death.

"No," I murmured instinctively, drawing back from the door.

"It's okay," Elsa said. "We won't go far enough for them to see us. And even if we did—I mean, look."

She had a point. The day was misty and damp. Anyone would struggle to see us in our gray prison uniforms against the gray stone through the gray air.

She stepped through the door, and after a moment I followed her. She turned immediately to the left and moved along the side of the building. It felt foolish to follow her, but still, I did. A little way along the wall there was a patch of ground where the concrete was cracked and covered with moss. She turned to face me before sitting down, settling in cross-legged on the ground, and directed me to sit across from her.

"Do you come here a lot?" I asked.

"Hmm," she said, "sometimes. I don't really need to anymore; it will work for me wherever I am, but I thought it would be helpful for you."

"What do you mean?"

"I've never shown this to anyone," she said. "I don't know why, but I want to show it to you."

"Show me what?"

"You said reading gives you peace. This will give you more."

She said that she could help me find peace beyond anything I'd ever thought of—peace that would survive fire and knives, let alone a damp patch of ground.

Years later, I tested her theory. She was right.

I didn't quite get there that day, though.

I sat across from her, as she had told me. I unfocused my eyes but I didn't close them. I didn't breathe so much as I let the air around me go where it would, the dampness of it filling my lungs until they felt like a pair of lakes. My heart rate slowed. And I let her introduce me to her kind of peace.

She didn't have a name for what this was, but after a while I started calling it the Watercolor Quiet. It was—it is—both serene and colorful. A soft drip to stain the mind, gentle shades absorbed into the consciousness. Like painting over your thoughts with what you wish them to be, instead of accepting what they actually are.

The Watercolor Quiet begins with eyes closed. There is breath, then speech. What is said is unimportant, as long as it is an interrogation of memory, of experience, of self. Each interrogation digs beneath the one before, until language dissolves into a hum, and words burst into colors. And in your mind, you can reshape and change the colors into anything. Inside the Watercolor Quiet, you are alone and active, and your world is full of light and thought. The name is deceptive, really, but honest too. It is not a state of calmness, but intense energy. It is like the ocean on a still day—smooth on the surface but with a universe of life and action underneath. It looks like inaction but it's anything but.

And I did feel peace. It was like finding a secret corner of the brain, a magical spell, a missing piece of space-time. I felt like I floated, a little bit. Just not quite enough to forget how cold and wet I was.

I started going to that patch of moss with Elsa every day, whatever the weather.

Snow. Thunderstorms. Blazing sunshine.

It felt like nothing else mattered. The world was burning around us, but it couldn't touch us.

We believed it couldn't touch us.

I believed it couldn't touch us.

I'VE SAID THAT I KNOW exactly how long I was in prison, and that is true. But I only know this because I know the dates. I don't remember the time passing. I'm not always sure when things happened. It seems reasonable to assume that they were relatively spread out over the years, but they feel like they're piled on top of each other.

I suppose it doesn't matter. I suppose prison doesn't matter.

At some point after Elsa started teaching me—maybe it was a year later, maybe it was the next day—Helen intruded into our lives.

It was simple at first. Childish. I suppose everything we did was childish, really. We were children, after all.

The first thing—at least the first thing I noticed, the first thing I remember noticing—happened as we were walking to the cafeteria for lunch. A couple of other kids were walking in the other direction, and one of them walked into Elsa. Nothing too serious, just a shoulder banging up against another shoulder, but when I turned to look, the girl's face was twisted into a scowl.

"Watch where you're going, spacehead," she said.

Elsa didn't say anything, just smiled slightly. That seemed to make things worse.

"What are you leering at?" the girl said. Then, after another moment of silence, "Empty-headed loser."

She glanced at me and gave another scowl before turning and continuing down the corridor.

"Are you okay?" I asked Elsa after she was gone.

"Oh, yes," she said. "That's just Helen. She came here on the same day as me. We were friends."

"What happened?"

Elsa looked puzzled. "Nothing happened. Time passed. I haven't spoken to her in a while."

"Why is she so mad at you?"

"I'm sure it's nothing," Elsa said. "She's probably just having a bad day."

Helen must have had a lot of bad days.

After that, I noticed her a lot. Sometimes it was nothing, or almost nothing. I would spot her staring at Elsa and me from across the room, something hidden and brutal in her eyes. Or that's how it seems to me now, but hindsight is half projection.

Sometimes she was more confrontational. Once she upended Elsa's tray as we were walking to our table in the cafeteria. A book I'd told Elsa to read went missing from her cell and turned up two days later, ripped to shreds. At some point, Elsa got a black eye and wouldn't tell me where it came from.

And Helen was never alone. She had a set of cronies, acolytes even, although perhaps that sounds too grandiose, who were always a few steps behind her whenever she did anything particularly aggressive. She must have relied on their support a fair bit—whenever she was on her own, her attacks were reduced to glares and whispered insults.

"Shouldn't you do something?" I asked Elsa, after a while. "Shouldn't you fight back?"

She looked at me, a little puzzled. "Why?" she said. "What would it accomplish? Helen's feelings aren't my responsibility."

"But she's hurting you," I said.

"No one can hurt me," she said. "Only I am responsible for my own pain."

I should have done more myself. You will probably think that I should have done more myself. But I was so young. Still a child. And though I'd had to learn to take care of myself, I still looked to others to lead me. When I could find someone who would, that is.

I was deferring responsibility, I suppose, but isn't it the right of a child to defer responsibility? I didn't think of it in those terms at the time, naturally. Mostly I was distracted. Helen was worrying when she was there—at least, she was to me—but most of the time she wasn't. Elsa didn't want to talk about her, and I wanted to talk to Elsa.

Is it strange to have been so happy in prison? I had never known anyone who made me feel the way she did. It was like the world had been askew, slightly tilted on its axis, and she set it at its right angle.

It wasn't romantic—that's not how we related to each other—but it was more than mere friendship. It was kinship, perhaps. She simply understood things in a way that made them make more sense to me. She made me look at myself differently, see myself differently.[4] So I don't remember loving my family, but I remember loving Elsa.

I thought for a moment I had found someone who would see me through. I wonder if things would have been better if she had.

I DIDN'T SEE IT COMING. I wasn't fully aware, I don't think, of the environment we were living in. The psychological environment. Looking back at things now, with a greater understanding of how people operate, I should have noticed. But I didn't.

I don't know, to be honest, if I didn't notice, or if I ignored it.

Discontent is everywhere. It's a constant. And discontent left to brood becomes bitterness. Anger. Fury, even.

There must have been conversations I overheard. Whispers that I walked past. I guess I just dismissed them.

It was prison, yes, but it had its benefits. It was safer than the outside world, removed from the conflict. There was food.

There was routine.

You don't know, most people can't know, how valuable routine can be.

But there was discontent.

There was discontent, and it brewed, and in the end some people were looking for a fight.

---

4 Edited for clarity. This paragraph was smudged, and the paper appeared to have water damage.

I've thought about this a lot in the years since. No other part of my life has caused me so much confusion.

What was there to win?

Life wasn't good in there, of course it wasn't. But it was much worse elsewhere.

I don't know how to communicate that to people who weren't there. When you look back, you see the magnitude. You don't see the detail.

The everyday, gray detail.

You don't know how something can be deeply traumatic and yet somehow incredibly boring.

This interminable stretch of disaster.

And there was no escaping it, not anywhere. It overwhelmed us all, as we worked to get through each day. To find food and shelter and safety.

In prison those needs were met. It made things simpler.

But people don't always want things to be simpler. They want a say. They rail against authority if only to assert their own existence. So occasionally someone would mutter some of their bitterness into the world. If a guard shut them down for some broken rule, they'd say, "Just you wait," or, "I could make you say that out of the other side of your mouth."

Silly things like that.

Helen was one of the people I heard say things like that. I didn't take her seriously because, as furious as she looked most of the time, she didn't seem like a particularly intimidating person. Once I saw her screaming into a guard's face that he'd regret ever mentioning her name, and she had to crane her neck all the way back to do it.

I would have told Elsa so we could have a laugh about it, but I didn't think she'd enjoy the joke.

Elsa didn't enjoy jokes as a rule.

So there was discontent and bitterness. Helen was discontented and bitter.

And Elsa and I continued to head for the little patch of moss just outside the walls every day. By this point, I had become much more comfortable in the Watercolor Quiet. Comfortable enough that I almost thought I'd be able to enter it at will, just like Elsa, even in the crowded prison. She could be in the middle of a fire or earthquake and completely at peace.

But we were doing more than just finding peace by this point. We'd started experimenting with how we could affect each other when we were meditating.

One of us would transport herself away, and the other would take control of what the first was feeling.

A few murmured words could change a prickling drizzle into a warm sunbeam.

Silence could become a cacophony, a circus, or an orchestra.

I read everything I could find on meditation, but there was nothing that came close to describing what we were doing.

Of course, the prison library was hardly comprehensive. But I've searched in the years since. I don't know how Elsa came across the Watercolor Quiet, and I don't know how we developed it. But it's certainly been useful.

I wonder sometimes if it would have become even stronger if we'd been able to keep practicing together.

But there was discontent. Among some of the prisoners there was discontent.

Looking back from this great distance, I think there was more logic to it than I had appreciated at the time.

The discontent wasn't about where we were, or why we were there.

Those prisoners—those young, young prisoners—they just wanted control.

Someone I barely knew muttered to me that if we wanted to, we could take over. Kill everyone who wasn't a prisoner.

Or maybe she wasn't really muttering *to* me so much as near me. Either way, I heard her. She said that if all the prisoners banded together, we could run things ourselves.

I asked what they would do to the people who didn't join them.

They would stay prisoners, I was told. Those who fought would rule. They would have earned that right.

It's funny how often that assumption arises.

That you can earn the right to control other people.

I asked how prisoners could fight back when the guards were the ones with guns.

"Not the only ones with guns" was the response. "Not the only ones with bullets."

And maybe you're thinking that I should have told someone. Reported this person to the guards. But the truth is, I didn't really take her seriously. It all seemed like bravado.

What would you have done, I wonder, if you were faced with what comes next? Whoever ends up reading this manuscript.

A rebellion breaks out, and you have three options.

You join the rebellion, and if it succeeds, you become part of the ruling class. If it fails, you die, probably.

You tip off the guards and potentially end the rebellion before it starts. And if it does start, and it succeeds, you die, probably.

Or you do nothing. You wait to see whether you'll continue to be ruled by the state—a state you're not sure exists anymore—or you'll begin to be ruled by the sort of people who engage in violent takeovers.[5]

What would you do?

What is the right choice?

Is there one?

Is there ever a right choice?

---

5 Edited for clarity.

# *Five*

DISASTER COMES ON ORDINARY DAYS. IT'S ONE OF THOSE THINGS that's obvious when you say it, but somehow you never really believe it to be true. But it is.

Disaster comes on ordinary, nondescript, boring days. The law of numbers. Most days are ordinary, so when else would disaster come?

So this is how the next disaster of my life came.

I'd had an ordinary night's sleep, an ordinary morning shower, and an ordinary breakfast. Elsa and I were walking along an ordinary corridor, and Helen was walking toward us. I wasn't worried about her, though, because a guard was in the corridor as well.

Looking back now—thinking about Helen, about her psychology—part of me wonders if something had happened to her that morning. Some kind of catalyst, some kind of upset. She'd been stewing for a fight all those months, planning even—stealing weapons, sounding out allies. A whispered insurrection. But in the end it all felt petty and of the moment. She was ready, and no one could hold her back, and Elsa was just the boot to strike the match on.

"Look at this," she said to no one as we walked toward her. Or rather, toward the door at the other end of the corridor, which was on the far side of her. "The sleeping beauty herself. And her little stooge. What, are you off to play in fairyland? Off to pretend you don't live down here with the rest of us, just as dirty, just as poor."

Elsa said nothing, just looked down for a moment, the smile that was always floating on her lips never faltering.

"I'm talking to you, princess," said Helen. "I'm talking right to your face. Don't you have anything to say to me?"

"Good morning, Helen," said Elsa, and Helen punched her in the face.

HELEN GOT A FEW HITS in before the guard got to them, and Elsa was bleeding from the corner of her mouth.

"Hey," said the guard. He was younger than most of the prison staff, mid-fifties or thereabouts, but he had trouble walking after being shot in the knee in the first waves of the war. He'd also had an eardrum blown out at some point, probably by a bomb dropping a little too close. "Hey, settle down."

More people were coming into the corridor now, from either end. A wave of people leaving the breakfast table as another wave came to replace them.

Helen didn't seem to even notice the guard until he got close enough to put a hand on her shoulder. He grabbed her, and in one motion she pushed Elsa away and turned on him.

I've never seen anything like her fury.

She was small, but she was much stronger than she looked. She threw the guard against the wall with astonishing force.

He banged his head and seemed dazed for a moment—and a moment was all Helen needed. She punched him again, making his head bounce again against the concrete. Blood started pouring from a wound on his head.

She grabbed the truncheon from his limp hand and swung it at him, again and again, until he slipped to the floor, blood streaming down his face.

I'd like to say there was a moment of shock. I'd like to say I saw dismay cross Helen's face at that moment, fear and regret, maybe. And perhaps I did, but I can't be sure. I can't be sure that's memory and not creation.

And even if there was a moment of shock, it was only that. A moment. Then there was elation. Triumph.

Helen pulled the guard's gun from its holster and shot him once in the head. I'm pretty sure he was already dead. Roberto. I think his name was Roberto.

"Who's with me?" she cried.

There was a beat of stillness, like all the air had rushed out of the room, and then a growing roar. Helen pulled a big ring of keys from Roberto's belt and threw them to one of her cronies.

"Release everyone who's still locked up," she said, "as long as they're willing to fight. And someone do something about the dream-weaver here."

I had been so shocked by Helen's brutal attack on the guard, I'd forgotten it had started with Elsa. By this time, she had slid to the floor and was sitting cross-legged, her back perfectly straight, her eyes half closed and unfocused.

She was in the Watercolor Quiet as violence ignited around her.

"Elsa!" I cried, kneeling beside her. "Come back. We have to get out of here."

She didn't answer me. Suddenly she was thrown back against the wall. Helen had struck her in the shoulder with the truncheon.

"No!" I yelled. "Leave her alone!"

"You're either with her or with us," said Helen. "And look at her. She's not with you."

She was right. Even after being hit so hard that she fell back against the wall, Elsa stayed in the Quiet.

"Please," I said. "Please leave her alone."

Helen smiled a little. "Fine," she said. "I won't touch her. But I won't protect her either."

She stepped back, and the crowd flooded past us. I was knocked over and had to claw my way back up, using the wall for leverage against the tide of people. Someone shoved me, and I fell back, bumping my head hard against the wall. I did not feel pain, I felt nausea.

I tried to get to Elsa, to stop her from being trampled, but the crowd continued to surge past, pushing me farther away from her.

I saw her hand lying pale on the concrete floor. I saw a boot come down upon it hard. There were too many people, and they were moving too fast, and I could not stop them crushing her beneath their fury.

"Get up," snapped Helen, still standing amid the flow of rage, watching me. She had incited a battle that was raging around us but was taking the time to single me out. I don't know why. "What are you going to do, stooge? You fight or you die."

She held the truncheon out toward me, an offering and a threat. I could hear gunfire from somewhere else in the prison. I knew that if I didn't satisfy Helen, she would kill me then and there—there was still a weird, gleeful light in her eyes—but all I could manage was to nod slightly.

That seemed to be enough for her, at least to decide I wasn't worth the trouble. But she clearly didn't trust me either, because she didn't give me the truncheon. More shouts and gunshots came from just outside, near the courtyard, and she joined the moving tide, a weapon in each hand.

I pressed myself against the wall and looked around for Elsa. She was slumped against the wall, completely still. I could see a trickle of blood on the side of her face. I moved toward her, but someone grabbed my arm and began to drag me away. It was the girl who had bragged about having guns, and she hadn't been lying. She pressed a pistol into my palm and pulled me along the corridor.

"You heard," she said. "You fight with us or you die with her."

I looked mutely at the girl. Was she right? Was Elsa already dead? Trampled beneath the feet of our fellow prisoners? Or was her death inevitable, no matter what I did? If Elsa was unconscious or lost in her own mind I could not help her. I wasn't strong enough to carry her, and I wouldn't be able to wake her up.

I let myself be dragged along until the girl was satisfied I wasn't going to go back to my friend. She let go of my arm. We came into the cafeteria, which was mostly empty, though it hadn't been for long. There were bodies crumpled on the floor, five or six prisoners and two guards,[1] blood still pooling beneath them. One of the guards moaned, and my erstwhile captor pounced, beating him in the head with her pistol. It would have been quicker and kinder just to shoot him.

I left her to it and headed down a different corridor, past a row of cells. Someone called out to me from one of them. She knew my name, but I didn't know hers. Or maybe I did at the time and I've forgotten.

"Miriam!" she called.

In the cell to my right was a young woman, shaking her door. It wouldn't open.

"They wouldn't unlock it," she said, tears in her eyes. "They said they'd be back to deal with me. Don't leave me here, Miri. Help."

I told her I would try to find keys, and she pleaded with me not to leave. "They'll kill me!" She was crying and shouting at me.

"Stop panicking," I scolded. "I can't help you if I don't leave."

And I left her. I had no idea what I could do to help her. Ask Helen if I could borrow the keys she stole from the guard she murdered? If I could even find her. I knew that if she saw

---

1 There are records of a fight at Gevangenis Antwerpen during Dr. Gregory's time there—as we have said, it is the only record of her presence. But it was merely a fistfight involving seven or eight inmates that was quickly put down, with two instigators spending time in solitary confinement. There is no record of a riot on this scale—but, as we have also said, this might have been one of the many records that were lost when the prison was bombed several years later.

  If such a riot did happen, we can assume it was unsuccessful, as the prison ran normally up until the bombing.

me do anything other than joining the fight, she'd kill me too. So I continued on my way.

I sped down corridor after corridor until I came to a battered, broken door. I checked over my shoulder, but no one was around. The fighting had moved to the yard on the eastern side of the building—I could still hear it, but it was muffled.

I opened the door and stepped out, and the noise grew louder. I knew that if I turned right and walked along the side of the building, I would enter the brawl, and if I turned left, I would find the mossy spot of ground where I had spent so much time with Elsa. But I didn't want to do either.

I stepped out from the wall. I was hesitant. Nervous.

No, terrified. I looked up at the guard tower nearest me. Surely there was no one there. Or if there was, they would be looking in the other direction. I would have to take my chances.

I took a breath and sprinted across the grounds.

The pop of pistols and screams of prisoners followed me as I ran, but I kept my attention in front of me. Every moment I expected to feel the sudden heat and pain of a gunshot wound, but there was no turning back.

Even when I made it to the prison wall, I didn't look behind me, just searched for a weak point. Running my eyes over its bricks and its mortar, looking for cracks. I moved along the wall, frantically running my hands over its surface. What if I couldn't get out? What if they found me here trying to escape? Neither the guards nor Helen would show me mercy.

And then I found it. One loose brick, just over five feet

from the ground. I gripped it with the tips of my fingers and wiggled it until it came free.

If the mortar had weakened around that brick, I reasoned, then maybe there were others. I searched for more, closer to the ground, but they all seemed solid. It wasn't going to work, I thought. Would I have to risk the gate? If any guards had stayed at their posts, it would be to man the gate. I looked around in desperation, and then I saw it. A little way back toward the prison—the guards must have been using this as a dumping ground—there was a pile of broken equipment. Maybe something there could get me up to my foothold. I ran over, and yes! There was a table with one leg broken off. I dragged it to the wall, one ear still listening out for someone approaching, but all I could hear was fighting.

I propped the table against the wall to make a kind of ramp, and scurried up it. It was a bit of a stretch, but I managed to get my foot in the hole and push myself up. Suddenly, there I was. On the outside.

Free again, for the first time in years. Responsible for myself again. Alone again.

# Six

I HAVE LITTLE MEMORY OF WHAT I DID WHEN I LANDED ON THE
other side of the wall, except that I know I twisted my ankle.
Not surprising, really—it was a high wall. I suppose I drifted
for a while. I had drifted before; I knew what I was about.
And look at me now—drifting again in my twilight years.

I suppose that for a while I returned to those habits of
my life the last time I was alone. Always moving. Finding
what shelter I could, what food I could. I think I did this for a
while, but it was harder than before. There was more danger,
more damage, less food.

Eventually I decided to try to return home. My real home,
where I had lived with my parents and sister before we'd started
moving, always moving. The last place where the world had
felt a little bit safe. I didn't expect to be safe there again, of
course. I just wanted—something. Something hard to define
but necessary. As a mourner views a body one last time, perhaps, hoping to bring closure, to place the wax seal on the
envelope. I suppose what I was looking for was a gesture of
finality.

But it was fruitless, of course. I had not marked the route

my parents took me on, or the path I forged alone, or the passage I traveled with Margot and Naija. I had not noted the direction of travel when I was brought at last to the prison. So why I thought I'd be able to find my way home is beyond me now.

There were times, as I traveled, that things did start to feel familiar to me, but I could not trust my own perceptions. So maybe I found home and maybe I didn't. Even now, I can't tell you.[1]

If I had found it, I could not have truly recognized it. Trees change. Landscapes change. Neighborhoods and streets and memories change. I would see an oak tree I thought I recognized, but I would talk myself out of its being familiar at all because the context was removed. And how unique can an oak really be?

I remembered one from my childhood, at the end of our parents' property, with unusually straight branches. They weren't perfectly rodlike but enough so that it stood out to me. Elizabeth and I read books under that tree. Below the tree was a steep ravine leading down to a wide creek, where we would catch frogs and collect river rocks.

---

1 It seems highly unlikely that Dr. Gregory did manage to return home to her birthplace at this time. We have no way of tracking her specific movements, of course, but the little we do know suggests that she moved in a different direction.

Although there are no records to confirm it, it is possible that Dr. Gregory was born in Former Poland. From there, though her movements were probably not direct or consistent, she must have traveled west through Former Germany until, at the time of her arrest, the nearest appropriate prison was Gevangenis Antwerpen in Former Belgium.

The location of the commune she describes in this chapter is known—it was near what used to be the French-German border. Therefore it seems probable that, rather than turning eastward to Poland, she turned south.

The oak I saw after escaping prison had some straightish branches, but it was much taller than I remembered, and next to it was a narrow creek. There was a gentle slope down to the water, but nothing as dramatic as a ravine. Perhaps time had distended my visual memories. A few steps down a rocky path to a creek as an adult, a virtual cliff to a child.

I lost trust in everything I saw. I lost trust in myself. I didn't understand how only a few years away erased my instinct for home, for family? Surely the human body, like some animals, retains its sense of direction, its homing nature.

But blame could also be placed on the soldiers and scavengers who populated the land. There was much more rubble and ash than I remembered from before prison. Even the most fortunate roads were overgrown with weeds and brambles. Others had been broken apart by tank treads, gunfire, and explosives.

Every so often there was a spark of awareness, a moment where things seemed familiar, but the fire never ignited. I was in darkness. My home was gone. The world was gone.[2]

But what had I expected to find, anyway, in returning to where I was born? If it had been possible to return to where I was born. Would there have been an epiphany, a great idea about how to undo the disease, the mistrust, the earthquakes, the wars? The only realization left to me was that humanity had turned against itself so utterly as to destroy everything around it. It seemed right somehow that the earth

2 Edited for clarity.

would immunize itself against humans with volcanic ash[3] and raging seas.[4]

Standing in a fallow field of chopped gray cornstalks, years old and barely recognizable, I glanced back over my shoulder one last time, a final attempt to glimpse even a slightly familiar sight. A house, a tree, a doll. But even the rocky path I had followed to this forsaken place seemed to have vanished.

Was I just trying to distract myself? I had left Elsa behind. I didn't know if I had left her to die, or merely left her dead. I have no memory of what I thought about this at the time. But looking back, considering myself as a child, it seems likely that I dedicated myself by trying to find my own home because I needed a goal. A project, however impossible.

Maybe I shouldn't try to psychoanalyze my past self.

At some point I stopped believing I could find my old home. But I continued on because I had nothing better to do than keep moving. I did not know where I should go, or what I could make of the rest of my life. What was there to be made, in all that chaos?

---

3 It seems likely that Dr. Gregory is here referring to the 1921 eruption of Mount Etna and the 1923 Yellowstone mini-eruption. The events themselves had a combined death toll of over 30,000 people, and the ash released into the atmosphere caused a volcanic winter that lasted until 1927, devastating crop harvests and leading to a sharp increase in the cost of food.

    There is no evidence that either eruption was caused by the Great Reckoning or any other human activity.

4 There were several tsunamis during the years of the Great Reckoning, occurring across the globe. Former Japan, Norway, Canada, and Mexico were among the countries hit by devastating tidal waves. In truth, earthquakes and tsunamis were no more common during the Great Reckoning than they are at any other time.

○  ○  ○

EVENTUALLY I FOUND MYSELF ON the outskirts of what had once been a village. It looked like it had been bombed at some point, and many of the buildings that remained had fallen into severe disrepair.[5] It had been several days since I'd found food, and I was getting desperate.

Night arrived bearing the unpleasant gift of rain, and I searched for shelter. There were a few houses still standing nearby, but I saw lights around them, and something in me shied away from the idea of being near other people. Despite my weeks alone on the road, despite my loneliness, I still wanted solitude and peace.

I wanted to spend some time in Elsa's Watercolor Quiet and restart my memories. Clean out the cobwebs and crumbling boxes that filled the attic that was my mind. Like the whole of Europe—like the whole of the world—I needed a new beginning, a new way of thinking, a fresh approach to how to be human.

But first I needed to get out of the rain. A leafy-enough tree helped a bit, but I knew I'd catch cold if I stayed there too long. The lights from a short row of crumbling stone houses flickered in the drizzle and mist, and in my discomfort I began to question my goal of living completely on my own. I did not want to return to prison or be shot by a stranger or be welcomed happily into some cult or commune. I simply wanted a roof.

---

5 The town mentioned appears to be Clervaux in Former Luxembourg. It suffered damage from heavy artillery in 1913, and its survivors fled. It appears to have remained completely uninhabited until two or three years prior to Dr. Gregory's arrival.

So I decided to get a roof. At around midnight—I couldn't be certain as I didn't own a watch, and maybe that was fine, maybe the world had moved away from numerical time—I saw the lights go out in one of the homes, and I crept toward the fallen neighborhood. I stayed low, occasionally hearing what I thought were voices but were more likely the huffs of foraging deer behind me.

The houses were about three hundred meters from where I was, and there was nothing to hide behind. Fortunately, clouds obscured the moon, and I moved more confidently. In the alley behind a brown stone cottage—I say *alley*, but the houses behind it were completely razed, so it wasn't much of an alley anymore—I found a doorless shed. Inside was some rotted lumber, a handleless spade, dirt, and stones. I grabbed the spade tip and wedged it between two planks on the shed wall. The boards pried apart easily, and I pulled them away, setting them down behind me.

I listened carefully for people, but at first there was no movement or sound. I attempted to wrench a few more boards from the shed, but this time found more resistance from the rusty screws and nails binding it all together. My palms began to bleed from the pressure I was exerting on the spade's head. I laid all of my weight onto the small curve of steel, but the wood did not shift. What did shift was my grip on the spade. I lost my balance and my contact with the lever and fell hard against the far wall.

I held my breath, and within a few seconds a dim light in the house came on. I saw the light moving about in the rear window, and then I heard a door open. Standing on the back step was an old man, years lining his face. In one hand was a candle, in the other a pistol.

He was only a few feet from me. My head throbbed from the fall, and my hand was on fire from the cut of the spade. I wanted to cry out, but I did not. He shouted something in a language I did not know. And then the candle went out, drowned out by the rain.

I closed my eyes and breathed. In. And out. I concentrated on the pain in my hand. I let that pain become the only thing I knew. I embraced it, welcomed it. Allowed it to be part of me. I did not think of Elsa, because it would have ruined the exercise. But this is what she taught me. And I was good at it.

I ignored the footsteps and the unintelligible grunts from the old man coming toward the shed. I thought only of the pain, and soon the pain in my head and in my hand was everything. It was my world, my life, my love, and I would accept nothing else. My breathing slowed to nearly nothing. All was silence, and soon the old man's suspicions were defeated by his frustration with the rain, and he returned to his home. Or the home he was occupying.

I don't know how long I was in my trance state, but by the time I became conscious, the rain had stopped. The clouds had ceded the sky to the gibbous moon. The pain was gone—or not gone. The pain was so much a part of me now that I did not notice it. The way you do not notice your heart beating or your fingernails growing.

The boards I had pried from the shed still lay on the ground, and I started to pick them up—but, realizing I no longer needed shelter from the rain, I decided to leave them.

Returning to the tree I'd originally taken shelter under would be difficult without the cover of rain and clouds. The moon lit up the empty fields in an icy blue; every shadow of every reed, every twig, shone in stark black contrast. If anyone was awake and watching, I would be seen.

I had no choice but to hope for unanimous sleep. I walked back to the edge of the forest. I did not run, though I wanted to. Walking would be quieter, more natural. I did not look back to see if any lights returned to windows. I only listened for voices, for footsteps. I heard none.

I walked at least a mile into the woods before finding a soft place to rest among some ferns and falling asleep.

THE NEXT MORNING, I KEPT walking—roughly south, I believe, though it's hard to be sure. I ate berries where I could find them. I tried fishing but had no equipment or training for it. Still, I crouched half-frozen in a small river, thrusting my shaking hands into the water and grabbing at nothing.

Sometimes when writing becomes too exhausting for me, I go downstairs and watch my landlady's television. Recently I saw a program that showed people fishing with their hands. There are different methods for different fish, it turns out. You can tickle trout until they go into a daze, or you can slice your hand so swiftly and accurately through the water that the fish has no chance to escape. Of course, I knew neither of those techniques then, and instead rummaged in the shallows like I was looking for car keys in a handbag.

In the late afternoon, starving and lightheaded, I crouched

near some brambles for more than an hour, until a rabbit emerged without noticing me. I grabbed it quickly and broke its neck slowly. It screamed. It shocked me that it could scream. I apologized to the creature for my inexperience with humane hunting. Would a hawk or a wolf also feel sorrow for causing harm? I doubted it and moved on. I would need to get better at killing prey—not because of empathy but because I would need to get better at survival in general.

But I did not get better, and the human body cannot go for weeks without food. Even a day without food hampered my ability to hunt, to focus, to meditate my way out of discomfort. My hunting and foraging abilities were not improving at the same rate as my body's need for nutrition.

My resolve of isolation and self-sufficiency was waning like the moon at this point, but I did not know how to approach anyone for help. I wanted help, but I had nothing to trade for it. I had not seen a coin or a bill in years—and in any case, who even knew the currency anymore or if it had value? No, the payment for help would be emotional indebtedness at best, and enslavement at worst.

If my freedom was to be put at risk, I would need to make the danger worth it. Stealing is survival. It is a crime and a sin, of course, but uniformed men had imprisoned me without crime, and god had forsaken me for lesser sins.

BEING WILLING TO STEAL IN order to survive means nothing if you cannot find anyone to steal from, of course. But I had my target.

A farmstead—in part old stone buildings, in part make-shift shacks—nestled between two verdant hills.[6] There were people about at all hours of daylight—watering crops, tending livestock. At night there were always two people with rifles on guard over the fields. The dark of the new moon protected me the night I arrived, though, and I crept into the fields as quietly as I could. I was not able to distinguish carrots from turnips from potatoes, so I dug up whatever I could and shoved it into my satchel.

I concentrated on the task, working quickly, not look-ing up but carefully listening for human movement. I heard no steps, no breaths, no voices. I did, however, hear a click, just behind my right ear. I did not have to look to know the sound of a gun being cocked. I froze. I considered attempting a swift escape, but my body was too weak to make it far. And even if I had been fit, I could not evade a bullet. So I dropped the satchel and raised my hands. As I rose up from the soil, my knees quivered. I thought I might fall, but I managed to get myself upright.

Two guards trotted toward me. This third guard I had not seen, had not attempted to even find. In my hunger, I had failed to perform a proper study of the place.

As she approached, one of the farmhouse guards spoke. She said something in Russian, which I did not speak, and I shook my head. She repeated herself in French, and then in English, asking, "What's your name?"

---

6 We know the location of the farmstead mentioned here, as it corre-sponds with other accounts of this time. It is in Former France, near Mal-brouck Castle.

"Miriam," I said, but my throat was parched, so it came out as a pinched whisper. I swallowed and repeated my name more clearly.

"You look hungry, Miriam. Is that why you're in our field?"

I nodded.

"Bring her in," the guard said, and we began walking.

After a few steps, the guard told the person behind me, who I still could not see, to lower their rifle. Then to me: "You can put your arms down, Miriam. We know you're not dangerous."

I couldn't tell if she said it with pity or derision.

Inside the house, at least a dozen people were gathered in a large living room. A fire was lit, and a tall woman with long black braids was reading from a book to a semicircle of others listening attentively. This was not what I wanted: another survivalist camp, another set of outlaws. A tribe, however gentle and small, dreaming of aggression and expansion, imposing their own ideals on anyone they came across. Safety becomes violence when mixed with fear. And closed groups feed off collective fright.

The guard who had asked my name told me hers: Ekaterina. She took me through to the kitchen and sat me at the table. She held up my confiscated satchel and began to rummage through it. "Ah, carrots. They're very good this year. And some radishes. The radishes are not so good. Keep the carrots, Miriam, but I will trade you radishes for some chicken stew. You will like it better."

She was correct. I liked the chicken stew very much. Buttery, soft flesh in rich, salty stock with white beans and potatoes and yellow squash. In my desperation I ate too fast, and my belly hurt. I tried to breathe through it, but I felt nausea overtaking me.

"She's going to vomit," said someone.

Ekaterina replied, "Of course. She ate too fast. How long since you have eaten meat and fat, Miriam?"

I asked, "Can I leave now?" There was a brief pause before I added, "Thank you, by the way."

"You may leave anytime you want," a voice from behind me said. It was the woman who had been reading in the living room. "You may also stay as long as you want, with some supervision, of course. I think you will find our farm friendlier than the woods, though. Who found this girl?"

"Rohaan did," Ekaterina said, a proud smile on her face as she looked toward the person who had taken me by surprise. I turned my head to see this Rohaan.

In the corner stood a boy no older than ten, with bashful eyes. He was holding a toy rifle.

# Seven

I WAS GIVEN SOME BREAD TO CALM MY ROILING STOMACH AND offered a bed for the night. I was too tired to say no. I slept late the next morning—the combination of my first real meal and first real bed in weeks, I suppose.

After I woke, I ventured out into the small garden, still hesitant, still unsure of myself. But the tall woman from the previous night spotted me.

"Ah," she said. "Good morning. You'll need some break-fast, I expect, and then why don't you and I take a walk? Get acquainted."

I did not want to get acquainted, but I decided if that was the price of breakfast, then on balance it would be worth it.

She introduced herself as Nora and told me she was from the United States—from Philadelphia.[1] She left during the

---

1 The woman described here is Nora Bostwick, who, of course, needs no introduction. One of the leading voices in the post-Reckoning political re-construction effort, she was elected to the German Provisional Government in 1941 and joined the Global Council upon its establishment in 1945. After she retired from politics in 1963, Ms. Bostwick released a memoir about her time on the farmstead, which she established in 1921, and the impact it had had on her later career, titled *A Farmhand's Throne*.

flu pandemic to come to Europe. It was not the flu that cast her out, as the same influenza that ravaged America ravaged the rest of the world. But, the Great Reckoning was not just plague, nor war, nor the charcoal skies of volcanoes. It was racism, xenophobia, misogyny—fear ingrained in every system of government, every nation, every economic system, every religion.

"At that point, the States was one of the safer places to be," she told me as we walked through the paddocks and gardens. "There was no fighting yet on American soil;[2] we were just sending soldiers to France and Greece and Russia to support those fighting there. So it seemed crazy to my friends that I would want to leave. And then it was only a few months after I did that America became as dangerous as anywhere else."

"But why did you come?" I asked. After all, as intelligent as she was, Nora was not psychic. She could not have known about the violence that would come to Philadelphia after she left.[3]

She gave a smile. "The same reason most people moved to new places before the war," she said. "Work."

---

2 The United States government declared war and officially entered the Great Reckoning in September of 1914, but did not impose mandatory conscription. Rather, able-bodied men were called on to volunteer. The government claimed that it was vital to join the war to defend democracy. President Taft, who had promised not to enter the war during his successful campaign for a second term, became increasingly unpopular as American lives continued to be lost, even as the causes of and justifications for the war became muddied. In mid-1918, after repeatedly delaying the overdue election, Taft was assassinated. His death led to riots that blossomed into a second civil war, which ultimately was subsumed by the spread of the Reckoning.

3 Philadelphia was the site of some of the first violent outbreaks on American soil. Extended riots toward the end of 1918 escalated into the Battle of the Bell, which raged for two weeks over Christmas and ended with the sacking of city hall.

"Work?"

"Mm-hmm. I was a teacher's assistant at a university.[4] And while I was there, I was taking as many classes as I could, studying psychology. My boss would let me sit in on courses and even graded my work, but I wasn't allowed to earn credit toward an advanced degree."

"Why not?"

"I'm Black. And a woman."

"Why should that matter?"

"Miri, I have never known. But it does. Or it did to them. But after a few years, I had all the education of any other doctoral candidate and not a single diploma to show for it. So I came here."

"Did you find it? Work?" I asked.

Nora threw back her head and laughed. "Oh, absolutely not. While I was right to leave Philly, it was a bit naive of me to come here. I overestimated how many schools would still be operating."

"What did you do?"

"I got lucky. Universities shutting down means a lot of academics finding their way on their own—for the first time in their lives, in some cases." She laughed again. "I ran into Alice—you'll meet her eventually—and we decided to find a place to camp out. Alice is a botanist. She was working at Oxford when it was bombed,[5] and after that she was in much the

---

4  Ms. Bostwick worked and studied at Temple University from 1910 to 1917.

5  Oxford University in Former England was bombed in April of 1919. Around 60 percent of the buildings were destroyed, though there were only a few dozen casualties. The university had already paused almost all teaching activity and was largely conducting research by the time it was destroyed.

same position as me. We wandered about for a while, just the two of us, and then we stumbled on this place.

"For the first couple of years, we didn't do much more than squat here. But no one turned up to kick us out, so we settled in, started to work the land properly. Invited others to join us. Help us."

"Help you how?"

"First it was Rory. He's an engineer, specializes in electronical science. We asked him to rig up some kind of lighting system that would help our crops grow, even when ash season lasts for months. Then Efia. She was a professor of zoology and was able to help us set up safe and productive livestock.

"Alice is a scientist. She knows a lot of other scientists."

"So everyone here is a scientist?" I asked.

"Not at all," said Nora, "but most of them are academics of one kind or another. We have poets, psychologists, historians, philosophers. All highly educated people with skills the world doesn't want right now. Skills the world needs perhaps—but not ones it's ready to use."

"What do you all do here?"

"We talk. We debate. We contemplate the future."

"The future," I scoffed.

"According to Willem, one of our sociologists, at least thirty percent of the world's population has been eradicated in the fifteen years since the war began. If things continue as they are—and there's no sign of them stopping—he estimates that number will double before it's over."

"Sixty percent of all people?"

"That's the estimate. When this all comes to an end

there'll be a lot that needs rebuilding. It's hard to know what use there'll be for a professor."

"Is anyone here not a professor?" I asked.

"Sure," said Nora. "Max was a banker, I believe, and Cassandra owned a millinery store. And there have been other people who've come through but chose not to stay. I imagine we can be frustrating to be around sometimes. Our debates can get, well—over-involved, perhaps. And not everyone is keen on lectures about Ivan Pavlov or Frederick Douglass."

"There are lectures?"

"Of course, Miriam. What else is there to do with the time?"


As it turned out, I enjoyed them, the lectures. I hadn't had much of a formal education in my life. I didn't so much leave school early as it left me, and while I read voraciously in the years when I was in prison, there was never anyone to guide my learning. I had simply picked up whatever book appeared interesting to me at the time.

Nora taught me about psychology, about how we make decisions, about the connection between biological need and emotional need.

And, in turn, I taught her about the Watercolor Quiet. Initially she was skeptical about the usefulness of these exercises, thinking of them only as rest or reflection, a calming gesture. But Elsa's meditations were anything but calming. They required you to acknowledge every part and feeling in your physical body, to micromanage every fiber, every cell. They were mentally exhausting to perform and even more so to teach.

But I was given my time for lessons. Everyone participated with attention and sincerity, though many were just not cut out for this work. They confused meditation with upright napping or extreme emotional focus with intellectual vacancy.

It wasn't a nap or meditation or hypnosis. In the Watercolor Quiet, my mind was completely active—alive with colors and visions. But I had difficulty finding the right words to help others achieve the states I could achieve. I had begun to take the Watercolor Quiet for granted, and trying to explain it was like trying to explain thought itself.

I kept working on it, as I kept working on all things. We all were journeying toward our best selves—teaching each other, learning from each other, and trusting new people to adapt well to our way of life.

So, over time I improved as a hunter. "Improved" is a generous term here, I suppose, as it suggests I had some skill to begin with. I gained a base level of competence, would be more accurate.

Ekaterina taught me to use a rifle, showed me where to aim to kill the animal quickly and painlessly. Ruth taught me hand-combat maneuvers for self-defense.

We all had to learn these kinds of things because, as isolated as we were, on occasion outsiders arrived to harass us. Sometimes they wore uniforms and brandished weapons, but when we refused to let them enter, they would leave, which suggested that they had little authority and few bullets.

Sometimes they wore suits and claimed to represent a banking or government interest, demanding loan payments or taxes. Again, when ignored they would eventually leave.

Sometimes they wore next to nothing but dirt and desperate faces. More often than not, these were the ones we actually had to fight. We tried not to do serious harm; we tried not to resort to weapons. We wanted neither to hurt anyone nor to waste bullets. But if they attacked first, we fought back. Usually it was just a matter of holding them off for long enough to ask if they needed help. Most conflict was resolved just by offering food and a supervised night's sleep in the barn, much like my own first night on the farm. Sometimes these guests would be waved off without comment the next morning. Others would be invited to stay, just as I had been.

IT WAS COMFORTING TO KNOW that we all shared similar paths in life. Families dead. Opportunities vanished. And nowhere else to turn. This was, of course, nearly universal to all survivors of the Reckoning, but it felt good to talk about it. To share. To be heard and acknowledged. No matter how much worse someone else's story was from my own—Nora, the granddaughter of American slaves, for example—there was always a gesture of shared sorrow, of empathy.

But this group of scientists and philosophers talked about more than just personal experiences. They were determined to root out the causes of the world's pain. What leads us to attack each other, when so much of our lives are spent facing the same struggles, the same fears?

On top of the lectures, the practice sessions, the sharing of knowledge and experience, there were debates that ran late into the night. Fervent discussions by the fireside that continued into the next day, as we hoed rows and planted crops.

"There's always division," Ekaterina would say. "No matter what is shared, there's always a way to separate groups of people into one tribe or another. You belong to a collective, and you feel driven to protect it."

"Yes," Alice would chime in, "and that drive leads you to see threats that don't really exist. And if you act on them, you spark a reaction, and it all billows out into more violence, more threat."

"Then it's hopeless," Rory would counter. "It's human nature to form tribes, and the natural result of that is tribal rivalry, with each group set against each other. We'll always have conflict. This war will end, eventually. All its death and destruction will be behind us—we'll have peace for a time, perhaps, and then we'll fight again. Probably over what we've done to each other over these decades."

"If we could only break down the idea of tribes altogether," Nora would add. "Or convince the world's people that they are all part of the same one anyway."

At this point Willem would laugh and scoff. "Yes, exactly. All we need is to tell people there are no borders between us, that we're all one."

It was baffling to watch. I'd never seen people talk like this, disagreeing but not arguing. I would watch them debate late into the night, energized by their differences. It was a heady environment to be in. Rich. Exciting.

It might seem hypocritical to decry borders, fences, when we ourselves defended our land from outsiders. And perhaps it will be odd for you—whoever's reading this—to consider that removing borders was an absurd suggestion. Today a borderless world is the norm. It is much more difficult now to envision a Europe, or a world, carved into hundreds of distinct sovereignties. These are the fantastic, ancient tales grandparents would tell you, if there were such a thing as grandparents anymore.

Well, we are all the descendants of societies we cannot understand.

While some in the group seemed to approach these debates as purely academic, as theories and studies, Nora was a true believer. An idealist. Hopeful. She would talk about what she called a "new society," with no nations, no flags, no armies. A centralized government with satellite "capitals" on each continent. And she would talk about this in practical terms, as if it were something that could really happen.

We owned guns for hunting and protection, Nora reasoned, but we should not be allowed to do so. Or rather, we should have no need to do so. Wealth exists somewhere, and it must be found and shared. Wealth cannot corrupt if it is not consolidated. Violence cannot operate without tools. And above all, tribalism begets fear, which leads to aggression.

I agreed with her ideals, but I must admit I was with the cynics as well. Nora's dreams were beautiful, but putting them into practice seemed beyond impossible. How could humanity ever rid itself of nations, let alone families—whether blood-related or connected through interests, like our little farmstead?

To Nora's credit, however, she lived out her ideals in the small setting of our farmstead. Rumors and distrust within the group were quashed with open debate and thoughtful discussions. Fear of outsiders who came into the region was put to rest through communication and generosity. Utopian ideals weren't just bandied about over dinner and around lectures—under Nora's direction, they were translated into lists of objectives and tasks.

It wasn't until much later that I would recognize these lists for what they were: manifestos. The first drafts of an insurgent constitution.

AND SO I BECAME A part of things. I arrived at the farm as an adolescent and I left it as an adult. In the intervening years, I learned as much from my companions as I could, and taught as much as I could. But more important to me, of much more interest, was how I could incorporate what I learned at the farm with what I had brought with me.

I spent those years developing the Watercolor Quiet well beyond what Elsa had ever imagined it could be.

We grew in number over those years; people came from all directions to help grow vegetables, participate in lectures, and contribute their skills to our betterment—despite the fact that we had run out of beds. I considered myself lucky to have arrived when I did. Soon the empty houses and fields that surrounded us were commandeered and merged into our community, and we began to refer to ourselves as the Arboretum.[6]

We took in families, outsiders, fugitives (myself included). Some among us left eventually. The goodbyes were always amicable.

Some left because they felt they had gotten as much from

---

6 Several founding members of the New Society Council had ties to the Arboretum.

being with us as they needed. But some left to start their own branch of the Arboretum[7] in some other place: Oslo, London, Tripoli, even America. It felt like we were spreading a new philosophy, a new religion even. The dying world willing to try any experimental medicine to heal itself, all conventional attempts having failed.

My contribution to this effort was the Watercolor Quiet, but though I was developing my own practice in exciting new directions, it still rarely connected with others as anything more useful than a relaxation exercise. I was appreciated, certainly, but never fully understood.

There was one exception: Rohaan, the orphan boy who at just ten years old had caught me in the garden with his toy rifle. Rohaan did not talk much. He chose his words carefully and spoke more with adults than with the other children.

I was in a strange position in those early years that I was on the farm. I had long since stopped tracking my birthdays—or the passage of time in general—I was no longer a child but wasn't really an adult either. Thinking it through now, I must have been around fourteen or fifteen when I arrived. Maybe sixteen? I don't think older than sixteen.

Anyway. The specifics are irrelevant; all that matters is that I had the independence of an adult but still had plenty to learn. I was still growing, still developing, still becoming my own fully formed person. I suppose because of this—because

---

7 The spread of the Arboretum would have far-reaching consequences for the world, once the Great Reckoning ended. While the group started as a philosophical society, many of its members moved into politics when the rebuild began. Several headed up local and regional councils in the 40s and 50s, following in the footsteps of their founder, Nora Bostwick, who played such a crucial role in shaping the New Society.

I fit partly into both areas and wholly into neither—I became the unofficial child-minder of the farm.

Most of the children that ended up with us—most of the children in the world, I'd imagine—had lost one or both of their parents, like I had. Most of them had witnessed horrific things, like I had. I could understand them, but I was old enough to hold some sway over them as well, and I was trusted by the adults to look after them.

It was the first time I had really spent observing other people. I became fascinated by the various behavioral quirks of the children. In the few that had a parent on the farm, I spotted consistent behaviors and opinions. When Willem's daughter, for example, heard her father mention that one of the boys needed to bathe more often, I noticed her start to sniff at him and make a face, even though he smelled no worse than he had the day before.

Cassandra's son developed a habit of asking his mother to confirm his every opinion. "I like blueberries, don't I, Mama?" he would say. Or, "Do I prefer the blue jersey or the red one?"

I marveled at the connection they had. I could not remember acting that way with my own parents.

Rohaan, I had learned, was the son of Ekaterina's best friend, Brigitte. Brigitte had died when he was two, leaving him with his father, who had died a couple of years before I arrived at the farm.

When I first met him, though he was not generally unruly, Rohaan was prone to occasional outbursts of violence and aggression. I remember catching him in the barn one afternoon, assaulting a feral cat. The cat was cornered, hissing and trying to get around the boy. But Rohaan's swift kicks were too rapid for the cat to break free, not to mention that he had severely injured the poor animal.

I made him stop, but it took the better part of an hour to calm him down. I didn't know at the time—it took a year or so before he would talk about it—but this was behavior he'd learned from his father. To strike out at something that annoyed you, use violence to control those smaller than yourself. That's how Rohaan was treated during the years between his mother's death and his father's, and now this was how he dealt with his anger, his guilt, his fear and frustrations.

Nora, Ekaterina, and the others had not known about the severity of Rohaan's aggression, because he had learned to not demonstrate these behaviors publicly. But I saw him, and I helped him.

For the next two years, I would sit with Rohaan in the woods each afternoon, as Elsa had done with me. We would breathe together, count together, then fall silent as we individually felt and acknowledged each part of our bodies, each electrical charge, each cell dying, each cell dividing. He was reluctant at first, only pretending to participate in my exercises, his face contorted into a sort of grimace. It did not look like a face of cynicism or pain or sadness. It was simply a darkness that shaded his thoughts, manifested in the twisting of his lips and cheeks.

I allowed Rohaan his own space and time to choose to engage, and after the first few months, he did. The strange expression disappeared, and I could see full relaxation, an uncaged mind. Eventually I began to speak to Rohaan of his father's abusiveness and his mother's absence. I began to offset the history of those people to help him separate from them. To help him become his own autonomous entity. To learn from the world rather than from a family that could not, alone, provide him with the breadth of knowledge and morality required to be a good human.

I kept my eye on Rohaan as best I could, and I saw real progress. He began to speak more, though still with the same considered tone. He still experienced bouts of rage, but rather than leave the public space to spend his violence on animals or even himself, he began to speak openly of his emotional experience. He made himself vulnerable, and in doing so made himself stronger.

One afternoon, as we walked back to the farmhouse, I mentioned Rohaan's father—a mistake, really, as I tried to keep discussion of his past within the confines of his hypnotic states. I immediately regretted saying something in full conscious conversation, fearing a relapse of his horrible memories, that he might be forced to revisit his trauma. But he said simply, "I have no father."

I did not want to confirm this untruth, but I also did not want to pursue this subject. I said, "You once did but not anymore."

"Did I?" Rohaan asked.

I thought he was being sarcastic, but when I looked at him, I saw that he meant it.

"I don't remember him," he said.

I skipped lunch to write down this fascinating development.

# Eight

IT'S STRANGE TO THINK ABOUT THESE THINGS NOW. LOOKING back from this vantage point, it appears that my life has been defined by solitude. There are times during which I'm surrounded by others, and then they inevitably come to an end and I am alone again. Even now, as I write this, I don't believe I've spoken to another person in some days.

I wake in this small, chilly room, I read here or I write—mostly this account, sometimes not. I go for my walks. I do all of it alone. Sometimes I stop to have coffee or a pastry, and I talk to people then. Sometimes I come across my landlady in the corridors, and we greet each other.

But those interactions aren't real companionship. They're merely chitchat. And then I return to my solitude.

I suppose it is my natural state. I wish it had been otherwise. Anyway. Irrelevant.

You might have noticed that—as when I was with Margot, Naija, and the rest of the girls—I was becoming comfortable in the Arboretum. Not necessarily secure, not quite, but comfortable. There was a presumption of a certain day-to-day stability.

And I suppose I was again allowing myself to grow close to people. To the children I worked with every day. To Rohaan with his serious, studious face. And to the adults who, for the first time, were giving me examples of living to aspire to. To Nora, with her blazing ideals, her wry optimism. To Ekaterina, who protected those dear to her like a tiger.

It is hard to stop yourself from developing affection for people, even when all your past experiences have taught you how dangerous it is.

So.

I continued to look after the children of the group as I grew out of my teens and toward my twenties. My work with them and the Watercolor Quiet became more focused after my breakthrough with Rohaan and his memories. I began to piece together objectives beyond mere exploration. Was it possible, I was wondering, to build a person better? To equip them better for the world around them with the Watercolor Quiet?

Since my early success with Rohaan, I had been working more on how the children reacted to the Watercolor Quiet. They were more open to it than adults, which is not surprising. They had no preconceived ideas to layer onto it. They did not dismiss it as simple meditation, because they had no experience with meditation. They took their cues from me, and I took our sessions seriously.

I was beginning to wonder if, rather than just dampening traumatic emotional memories, I could reorganize them. Detach them completely from the earlier pains of war and smoke and disease.

Elsa's practice had been predominately ameliorative, but

I was reworking it toward internal psychological repair. Elsa hadn't been teaching me to heal myself, only to normalize an affliction, calm the noise of the past, so that I could function better. She used the Watercolor Quiet to temporarily escape her existence. I believed there was more within it to unlock.[1]

With Rohaan I had added an external voice, a passive psychiatrist of sorts to guide him. I believed I had found a way to undo emotions attached to specific memories, and I was finding that the process, in some cases, altered the memories themselves. It was unpredictable and appeared random to me, but I was hoping that I'd be able to pin it down. To establish what was happening within the Quiet that was having this impact, so I could wield the tool more deliberately.

As an example, I had a small session with Rohaan in the early afternoon one day, just after lunch. As we made our way to the small clearing, near a barn, that I used for such work, we saw two adolescent does. During our session, while Rohaan drifted into semiconsciousness, I explained that a doe was a female deer, and that young deer were red but the adults were brown. In a couple of months, those deer would be much taller, with dark brown coats no longer spotted with white.

Rohaan sat for a moment, letting my words seep into him, a strange expression on his face—somehow both still and alert. But alert to something I could not see, something within his own mind. He repeated back what he was learning and began describing what he was painting in his own mind. When the session ended and we stood, the deer spotted us

---

1 Edited for clarity.

and ran quickly into the nearby trees. Rohaan laughed at their startled prancing, and I laughed too at his delight.

On the walk back, I asked Rohaan what he had seen and learned today. He said that we saw two bears eating corn. One was red and the other was brown. I asked him when we saw the bears, and he said it was at sunset.

It has always been true that memory is changeable, unreliable, but Rohaan's response to the Watercolor Quiet was beginning to make me wonder if it was controllable. I needed to know more.

I suppose this stage of my work could be called blind research—I knew little other than that there was something to be learned. I went in search of it in every way I could, but I did not yet know how to direct the search. I was really just writing down the details of each exercise and the changing behaviors I observed in my subjects.

It was clear to me that the Great Reckoning would still be doing damage even after the fighting had come to an end, even if the volcanic ash clouds opened like curtains on a stage play. The conflict would end one day, inevitably, and the world would rebuild, but people would continue to suffer.

I was hopeful that the Watercolor Quiet could help children left broken by the Reckoning. We are creatures built on a foundation of our experiences, but if we could control our memories, we could control how much impact each experience had.

I was careful with my experiments, of course. I didn't want any child to wake up only to forget how to do basic arithmetic or the names of their friends. I purely wanted them to be able to own their pasts, to be active creators of all that they had already experienced rather than passive participants in an inevitable fate.

And my work did not go unnoticed or unappreciated by the adults of the Arboretum. Although they themselves had not moved beyond simple meditation, they could see that things were working differently in the children. They could see that the child whose fear of water had caused a meltdown every time she was asked to bathe was now happily learning to swim. They could see that the child whose nights had been punctuated by terror and panic was sleeping peacefully.

I appreciated any praise I received, but I must admit there were times I wished I could have the kids all to myself. It was a selfish impulse, born not out of any kind of maternal instinct but out of simple scientific curiosity. And it was foolish in retrospect, though I was too young and inexperienced to realize it at the time.

For the first time since I'd lost my own parents, I had the chance to observe the tiny, infinite ways people interact with their children. I saw a mother carefully brush her son's hair from his face as he lay in her arms, tired from a day's play, and I saw him repeat the action with a kitten he'd befriended.

If I'd been a better scientist back then, I would have recognized the value of the data I was gathering through seeing the children relate to their parents. The repetition of beliefs, mimicry of behaviors, passive ideological acceptance.

Oh, I was so young. Still a child by modern reckoning.

Anyway.

My issue was that often, when returned to their parents, the children would regress in their behaviors. A day or two away from the Watercolor Quiet, and they would return to crying or bed-wetting or acting out violently. It seemed that the Quiet could only pacify them for a short time and would eventually wear off, the way one might scrub a bathtub only to see it collect grime again over the next few days.

I began to theorize that these kids' traumas and bad memories were linked directly to their parents, if not through abuse or neglect then through the Reckoning itself. Even the most perfect mother or father, in the early 1900s, could not truly protect their child from hunger, from gray winds, from the nomadic militias that had cropped up following the entropy of war. I began to wonder how each parent had reacted to each individual trial of the past decades. What impatience, frustration, anger, helplessness their children had witnessed in them, in the people who were supposed to be their unassailable protectors. Every time they watched their parents fail, I believed, their feeling of security in the world and their place in it was eroded.

On top of this, every faulty impulse, every bad habit, every prejudice their parents carried, the children would inherit.

Familial nationalism. That's how I came to think of it. Families, like nations, generated a sort of patriotism as a protective measure. I hadn't thought before about the effects of families on children, though I remembered my own parents' drive to protect me. The way my mother would throw out an arm to herd me behind her when we came upon a stranger we couldn't trust. The way my father went hungry when food was scarce, so Elizabeth and I could eat. Yes, the benefits of family are obvious and innate. Nurture, education, love, nourishment, and basic care are the responsibility of any parent, whether human or deer.

But was that universally true? Biologically, insects do not require mothers beyond birth or fathers beyond fertilization. A damselfly in a swamp does not need to be held or fed or even taught to fly. And beyond biology, other elements of parenting point to child-rearing as a detriment to children's development. Verbal and physical abuse, the teaching of bad habits, and a kind of tribalism that limits expansion of the mind by limiting the physical and spiritual distance a child can roam from their family.

I was not there yet, but I was on the cusp of something. I know now what it was, of course, but then it was all ahead of me.

I was energized, optimistic. And, as we have discussed, I was comfortable. So we know that things were going to change.

IN THE ARBORETUM, WHILE NORA preached against tribalism and division, we put in place careful measures to protect ourselves, our crops, our children from interlopers. We had rifles for hunting and knives for butchering, and though ill-meaning intruders were rare, it was implicit that these tools could also be used for protection. So we were a fortress of loyalty and respect for one another against outsiders who meant us harm.

We were our own tribe.

And we became a tribe without any real, credible knowledge of what threats there were to us. Postal services had all but broken down; occasionally there were telegrams, but they were too brief to give detailed information.[2] When people

_____

2 The degradation of communication systems was one of the most corrupting influences in the later decades of the Great Reckoning. Several

joined us, for a night or forever, they might bring stories of roving militias and raiding parties.

But they were just stories. Of course there had been militias, I'd encountered them as a child, we all had. But at this late stage of the Reckoning,[3] we had little evidence that violent skirmishes and marauding were still taking place anywhere near us. It was easy to believe, though.

And stories, like damselflies, populate and spread in the right conditions. In the humid haze following a storm, eggs hatch below the water, and soon thousands of exotic insects color the dense air like floating jewels. They are beautiful, with bright bodies, kaleidoscopic eyes, and wings like stained-glass windows, so we appreciate them. We allow them space in our ecosystem, because they stimulate the surface of our imaginations. We accept them because, unlike wasps or ants or bottleflies, they cause no harm.

But order requires balance. Nature is an eclectic mobile, and if one side overwhelms its partner, it can throw off the entire precarious system. This is true of storytelling too. We allow stories of criminal invaders to grow unchecked. But are these stories damselflies, or are they termites?

---

devastating assaults, including the razing of Dar es Salaam, were directly caused by the loss of urgent command messages. The communication breakdown was equally due to the loss of personnel to operate the systems and to the destruction of crucial infrastructure.

3 Dr. Gregory is incorrect in placing these events at a "late stage" of the Great Reckoning. Although she has not specified a date we know, based on Nora Bostwick's account, that her time with the Arboretum came to an end in 1931, more than a decade before the global cease-fire was signed. But it is true that this area of Europe had seen more violence in the early years of the Reckoning. By the mid-1920s the fighting in Europe had moved farther east, while it increased on the American continent and in Asia.

○  ○  ○

A WHILE INTO MY COMFORT, into my routine came the Jacobs family. Intact families were a rarity, so they stood out.

Nathaniel, the father, was an entomologist from Cambridge. The English Cambridge, not the American one. His wife, Lana, was a professor of literature. Their two daughters, Alicia and Ellen, were around six and nine, with matching blond braids. There were also three adult cousins, three men just a bit older than me, whose names I have thankfully forgotten.

Alicia and Ellen folded into my crowd of children easily, and their parents seemed happy to let me take care of them. I tried to explain the work I did with the kids, but they didn't seem to understand or to want to. They viewed me, I think, as an elevated nanny. But for me, of course, the family presented a unique opportunity for study.[4]

There were a handful of children with us who had one parent, but until this point we'd never had a complete family, with both parents still alive, still around, still involved in their children's lives. It was an exciting development for me.

I thought it would be an exciting development for me.

And at first, it seemed like their arrival would be good for all of us. Nathaniel had always been a gun hobbyist, it turned out, having gone on hunting trips with his father since his early childhood. He was able to repair some of our rifles and train us to use them better and soon took over as our hunting coordinator.

A couple of weeks after they arrived, Lana asked me about my trips into the clearing with the children.

---

4 Edited for clarity.

"You shouldn't be taking them alone," she said. "You should have people with you for security. That's the problem with this place—none of you take security seriously."

"We have patrols," I said. "There's always someone on guard."

"*Pfft*," she said. "Two people. That's not enough, and the rest of you just relax. You're not ready to go. If someone attacked, you'd all be butchered in your beds."

"Who's going to attack?"

"That's just the thing—it could be anyone. The Russians, probably."

"We've had a couple of Russians come through, actually. They do what everyone does. They eat, if they need to eat, they stay for a few days if they need the rest, then they move on. Most of them, that is—obviously Alexei stayed, and Sofia and Ekaterina."

"You can't trust them. You can't trust any Russian."

I laughed a little, nervous, unsure. "You can trust them as well as you can trust anyone, I suppose. Which is cautiously."

Lana glanced at me and looked away. She muttered something under her breath, something like the word "savages."

I wondered if I should say something to Nora, ask her to better explain to Lana what the Arboretum was about, but I didn't want to offend anyone, so I let it go. I hoped that, as Lana spent more time with us, she would calm down a little.

But fear is more contagious than calm.

A while later, I overheard Hugo—a young former soldier who'd lost a leg in battle and been abandoned to his fate by the army—speaking to Ekaterina. There was a flush in his cheeks, and he was stumbling over his words.

"I'm sure of it," he said. "They've been scouting us; they're getting ready to attack."

"Who is?" she asked.

"I can't be sure—I haven't seen anyone's face, but Nathaniel thinks it's the Africans."

"The entire continent?" she asked, mildly.

"Nathaniel has good instincts about this kind of thing, and I saw boot prints near our farm. I know someone's watching us."

I moved away at that point, not wanting to be seen.

Slowly our cautious tales of outsiders began to metamorphose into conspiracy theories. Soon the fears of our little collective focused not on common, desperate thieves, but on armies of displaced Turks or Americans coming to claim the land as their own. The more we farmed, the more we hunted, the more valuable our land grew. And if we were to survive, we needed to band together as a farm, as a family, as a nation.

For a while, Nora did her calm best to soothe these fears, but when she saw Lana sewing a flag, she'd had enough. She threatened to remove the Jacobs family—their children and cousins included—from the Arboretum if they continued to sow fear and tribalism. Lana complied and put the flag away, but with tight lips and chilly voice she said: "It's a slippery slope, don't you think?"

A slippery slope runs downhill in both directions.

A flag is not just a flag. It is a symbol of a step forward into aggression. It's a slippery slope. A commune is a collective, a selective family connected by common cause rather than genes. It's a slippery slope.

Lana fed back to Nora what she saw as her own hypocrisy.

But it wasn't hypocrisy—simply a lack of nuanced definitions. To stick with rhetorical clichés, the flag was not, in fact, a slippery slope but a thin line separating family from nation, collective from clan, commune from militia.

And I saw on Nora's face that she did not have a response to Lana's amateurish retort of "slippery slope." Nora could intellectually spar with great academic minds. She could give and take counterarguments, allowing their rightness or justification time in the sun to grow or wilt. Nora knew that truth is a tree. It is sturdy and strong, but only after it has fully matured and weathered the brutal critique of nature.

She had no weapons against brittle, determined ignorance.

And in Lana's cold voice, I heard something else. Lana Jacobs would fight and fight hard against anyone who would harm her family. And by extension this included those who would not adequately protect her family from harm.

I DID NOT ENGAGE WITH Lana and Nathaniel or with their brutish-looking, silent cousins. They were worrying, but they were not my responsibility. Their children were.

Lana and Nathaniel did not show much interest in my work with the kids. They only knew that, since their children met me, Alicia stopped hitting her sister and Ellen stopped waking up in the night screaming. I welcomed the Jacobs parents' lack of interest in my work. I knew it would be difficult to win parents over to the idea of using children in scientific experiments, even if those experiments were centered on making the children happier and calmer.

And Alicia and Ellen had responded well to the Watercolor Quiet. Often it took new children a while to adapt to the technique, but both of them seemed to have a natural gift for it. They attached themselves to me more than any other child had done, and I enjoyed their company.

During a treatment session with the girls, about four or five months after they arrived, Ellen started responding differently. Her shoulders began to slump, and her stiff, deliberate voice began to quiver. At first it shook like a sob, but then her words sped up and became erratic, a vomiting of nonsense that crescendoed into a scream.

I sat beside her, trying to pull her out of her state. Her face was red, almost like she was choking, but the words came faster and louder.

Alicia was still sitting calmly, eyes closed, unmoved in her own Watercolor Quiet.

"Ellen," I said, almost shaking her. I repeated her name louder, firmly holding her shoulders. She didn't respond to me. She just kept vomiting words. But the seeming illogic of what she was saying began to take some narrative shape.

So I took a step back, keeping a hand warm on her back as I listened to her. She named off colors and shapes, then places and names, eventually reaching Nathaniel and Lana.

Then Ellen said: "They took me. Papa and Mama. They took me."

I gave a start.

"Who took you?" I asked, shaking Ellen lightly.

She stopped speaking. Her red face lightened, and she opened her eyes. Her pupils immediately constricted in the afternoon sun, revealing the deep green of her irises.

"Nathaniel," Ellen said, calm now that she'd vomited out the poison. "Lana," she added.

"Are they not your parents?" I asked.

I waited for a response, but Ellen offered none. Her green eyes were unblinking and not quite fixed on me, seemingly looking at a point just beyond me.

"Ellen," I pleaded quietly.

"She's a liar." I heard Alicia's voice behind me. "A liar!" Alicia shouted. She lunged over my shoulder and dug her fingers into Ellen's face. Ellen shrieked as Alicia landed two digits in her right eye and a thumbnail in her upper gums.

Ellen thrashed, heaving her body onto the grass, and tried to roll away from her sister. Alicia thrust herself after Ellen, but I grabbed her before she could get to her.

"Alicia. Alicia. Alicia," I repeated over and over, each iteration longer, quieter. Alicia's breaths went from a heaving pant to slow, deliberate inhales and exhales. I lowered my head to catch her eyes. She tried to look away but eventually gave in and looked at me.

Her eyes were dark brown, almost black, unlike the vibrant green of her sister's. Alicia's nose was wide at the bridge and her chin square and handsome. Looking back at Ellen, who was lying in the grass, but looked ready to run at any moment, I took in for the first time her narrow nose and delicate, pointed chin.

They weren't sisters at all.

# *Nine*

I WENT TO NORA IMMEDIATELY, OF COURSE.

She and Ekaterina and I sat on a small balcony in the early evening, looking out at the forest, discussing what had happened.

"So you think one of the girls is not theirs?" said Ekaterina.

"I'm not sure either of them are really their daughters," I replied. "I'm not sure what we should do about it."

"But why should there be something to do?" Ekaterina asked. "It's likely these girls were left orphaned, like so many of our children here, and Nathaniel and Lana decided to look after them."

"But why wouldn't they tell us that? Why pretend? And Ellen's outburst sounded like she had parents living, that she was taken against her will."

"And Alicia said she was lying."

I didn't respond.

"I understand you're feeling uneasy," Ekaterina went on, "but I think you may be overreacting."

"Nora?" I said. "What do you think?"

Ekaterina had been unconcerned about the situation, but

she was interested in it. Somehow Nora seemed detached, though. As if she was observing from afar. But when I spoke her name, she pulled herself back a little and looked at me.

"I think you're right to be concerned," she said. "If you're right that Nathaniel and Lana stole these girls, then that suggests they're people we should keep an eye on. But we're not really in a position to adjudicate on who should be responsible for which children. No one is in their right place right now, and they won't be for a long while."

"So you don't think we should do anything either?" I said. I admit I was disappointed in her.

"I think we should watch," she replied. "If it becomes apparent that the girls are being harmed by the Jacobs, then of course we will intervene."

"Or we could kick them out now and prevent them doing harm in the first place."

Nora smiled. "Yes, that is always the temptation. But we don't really know anything, and we cannot punish people on suspicions alone."

The three of us sat in silence for a while.

"I've upset you, Miri," Nora said eventually.

"No," I said, quietly, unconvincingly.

Nora smiled again. "I know the girls like to stay close to you, so keep them close. But not every problem is yours to solve. And you have no more right to decide for those children than Nathaniel or Lana do. And perhaps less."

I didn't respond.

At the time, I was hurt and confused by Nora's inaction, but I have more patience now, more understanding. Things had become more and more complicated for Nora and the Arboretum over the years. Those that stayed with us and then moved on told other people we were there, sent us those they came across who needed our help.

And we were glad to help where we could, but eventually the need started overwhelming our resources. We had limited space, limited food. We could have expanded—there was nothing but space around us, nothing but land—but that would have taken people with the capabilities for that expansion. Better builders to construct more shelter, better farmers to increase our crop yields.

Nora had had to start turning people away. Some offered money, but money had no value anymore. Neither did gold, nor did anything other than food or shelter.

"You're doing good work, Miri," she said, eventually. "I can't say I fully understand what it is you do, but the effect you've had on the children is astounding. You're helping as many people as you can. That's all anyone can ask—it's more than anyone can ask."

I was silent.

"And you're researching?" she asked.

"Not really," I said.

Ekaterina scoffed. "Not researching, my eye. I've seen her at it," she said to Nora. "This one writes everything down, piles of notes she has. She pores over them when she should be sleeping."

"That doesn't count," I said.

Both of them threw their heads back and laughed at that.

"Doesn't count!" said Ekaterina. "This idiot!"

"My love, what do you think research is?" laughed Nora.

"But it has no point," I said. "I don't know how to pull it all together, to learn something from it."

"Yes, well," said Nora. "Ideally you'd be at a university by now. You're what, twenty? You should be working in a lab, with professors, with everything at your disposal to forge a proper path for yourself."

"There's not much I can do about that now," I said.

"Not right now," said Nora, "but you might want to start thinking about when you could. This war can't last forever. It's a wonder it's sustained itself for as long as it has, to be honest. There's probably only a few more years left in it."

"We don't know that."

"I think we do. It could drag on, but every year it becomes harder and harder for the world's governments to keep sending soldiers, weapons, money. It'll end. And when it does, what will you do?"

I was stunned by this question. I had never thought about life after the war, or when I had, it had seemed like an unreality. An impossibility. The Reckoning had made everything else temporary. It hadn't occurred to me that it would be temporary too.

My entire life had been about trying to survive. I had never imagined that I could make an active choice about what I wanted to do. About what I wanted my life to be. I never thought I would be able to stay still for long enough to figure that out.

"You should think about it," Nora said again. "I could write you letters, recommend you to universities. Those that are still standing. Temple wouldn't give me a doctorate, but there are people there who'll take my endorsement seriously."

"Are you going to go back to Philadelphia?"

She gave a short, bitter laugh. "Never."

"But then, why would I?" I said.

You see, I was comfortable. I had not learned from my mistakes. I had begun to assume that I would always be part of the Arboretum, always with Nora, with Ekaterina.[1]

"Miri," Nora said gently, "this place isn't serving me anymore. And I'm not serving it."

I sat perfectly still.

Nora went on: "You haven't been thinking about your life after this. And that makes sense. No one thinks ahead when they're twenty, even if they don't live in a burning world. But Ekaterina and I have been thinking. There's work that needs doing out there and we believe—us and a few of the others—that we could be the ones to do it."

"When are you going?"

"Soon. It feels like it needs to be soon."

"Why?"

"There's a difference between being a leader and a tyrant. Do you know what it is?"

I shook my head mutely.

"It's in the people. As long as they want to follow you, you're a leader. The longer you stay in place, the more dissatisfied people become. You grow stagnant. You become a tyrant. And I have no appetite for that."

---

1 Edited for clarity.

I swallowed hard. "Where?"

"Munich." Her tone lightened a bit. "Initially. There's someone there with similar ideas—he was a politician in India before the war; his name's Anand Balakrishnan.[2] I've had a copy of a treatise he wrote on government for years, and we've managed to get a few messages back and forth. He thinks I could help him, and I'm eager to do more than just sit here in safety trading ideas."

"Why can't I come with you?"

"This isn't your work, Miri, and I think you know that. And for the moment, you're needed here. But promise me one thing."

"What?"

"I don't know what it will be like here after I leave. I can't control that. I don't know who will step up to lead, who everyone will want for that. There might be tension. I want you to promise me that if things go badly, if it becomes unsafe, you'll get out as soon as you can."

"But—"

"Don't worry about Rohaan," Ekaterina said. "He's coming with me."

"I know you'll want to get the children out too—do that, if you can," said Nora. "But if you can't . . . it's okay not to sacrifice your entire self."

I didn't know what to say to that, and we sat in silence for a moment.

---

2 Anand Balakrishnan galvanized broad support around himself during the final years of the Great Reckoning, and was ultimately elected the first Global Council Chief in 1945. He served for five years before declining health forced him to retire.

Ekaterina gave an awkward laugh. "Well, this has been fun," she said, "but I think we all need something in our bellies."

She and Nora headed downstairs to dinner, but I stayed up on the balcony for a while.

Alone. Worried. Devastated.


So THIS IS HOW IT ended.

Meals, gatherings, everything seemed to grow less convivial over the next few weeks, though that might have been just me. Perhaps they'd been getting quieter for some time, and I was only just noticing.

But as many of us grew more restrained, the Jacobs family and those that had grown close to them got louder. They walked with a swagger, they leered at those they saw as weak, they carried guns and knives everywhere they went, prepared to defend themselves against a nonexistent memory.

I was alive with anxiety, dreading the moment Nora would leave me there alone. I tried to get her or Ekaterina alone—to talk more about their plans, to persuade them to take me with them, to persuade them not to leave at all—but it was impossible. Someone else was always around, and this started to feel deliberate. I simmered in my fear, waiting for the moment Nora would announce her departure.

But that moment never came.

It was a cold morning in early winter, and I heard someone shouting Nora's name. There were other shouts as well. I went to see what was going on.

Alice and Rory, two of Nora's oldest friends on the farm,

were on the deck outside the kitchen, asking if anyone had seen her.

"I saw her last night," someone said. "She and Ekaterina were checking on the food stores, making sure they were keeping cold enough."

"Ekaterina?" said someone else. "I've been trying to find her too. She's not around."

"I haven't seen Efia or Willem this morning either," said another, with a laugh. "Have they all run off together?"

A few people laughed at this but quickly stopped.

"They could be hunting," Alice said, but she didn't sound convinced, and I wasn't either. Nora never went hunting—she accepted the need to kill animals for food, but she didn't like to see it.

There was a harsh laugh from behind me, and I spun to see who was there. It was one of the three Jacobs cousins. The eldest. The other two were a step behind him.

"She abandoned you," he said. "Got bored." It was the most I had heard any of the cousins say in their time with us.

"Fuck you," Rory said, and another cousin laughed.

"Mama's left you, and she's not coming back," he added.

Rory was leaning forward, as if ready to advance on the Jacobs men, but Alice held his shoulder gently.

"Alice?" I said, cautious at this stage, not wanting to give anything away. "What's wrong?"

"We don't know," she said. "Nora's gone. But all of her belongings are still here."

"That's strange," I said, but it made sense. Nora would have wanted to travel light—some water, a few clothes, toiletries. She could not have dragged a trunk of clothes with her, or her massive collection of books, if she was in such a hurry to leave.

"I think those Jacobs boys did something," Rory whispered, turning away from them with his shoulders hunched against them.

"I don't think they did," I said, keeping an eye on where the three men were standing, watching us huddle and talk. "I think she's left. I heard her talking with Ekaterina about maybe leaving."

"To where? When did you hear this?" Alice snapped at me.

"I don't . . . It was a while ago. I wasn't sure she was serious." I didn't want to say too much, especially with the Jacobs cousins paying such close attention.

"Alice," Rory said, "we need to call a full meeting. If Nora's gone for good, someone's got to step up."

"Would that be you or me?" Alice asked.

"Both of us."

Alice nodded curtly.

They called for a meeting that night, but only about eight of us showed. The seven members of the Jacobs family and twelve others did not. Alice talked about reconvening the evening salons—partly to return the Arboretum to its intellectual roots but also as a way to bring us all closer together again. A form of family bonding.

While she was talking, it seemed like everything could be okay, but as the conversation proceeded, the cracks started to show.

"What do we do about . . . ?" someone said.

"About what?" said Alice, with the air of someone who knew exactly what.

The woman who'd spoken—I don't remember her name—rolled her eyes. "Come on. You don't think . . . There are people who are going to challenge this."

"If you're talking about the Jacobs family, they know the goals of the Arboretum and agreed to abide by them when they arrived."

"They will not, and if you think they will, you're a fool and not fit to lead any of us. Haven't you noticed how few people even turned up for this meeting? We're outnumbered. And those people are violent—they'll hurt us if they have to."

Another voice joined in: "Why aren't we asking the obvious question? The Jacobs could have killed Nora." There were several shouts against this extreme idea but more than one cry of agreement.

The worried stir spiraled on for a few minutes until Rory stood, bringing the group to silence.

"Okay," he said. "While I like your plan of inclusion and togetherness, Alice, it's too little too late. We have a crisis, not just of disunity but of violence." He spoke dramatically, his manner almost statesmanlike. "Our way of life is no longer just under threat of attack. It has already been attacked. We are Nora's intellectual descendants, and this is our home, our farm. If we are to return to our old ways—to shun aggression, fear, and tribalism—we must remove those that stand in our way."

"We'd have to do it by force," someone said after a moment of quiet.

"We do not," Rory countered. "We will have to do it by diplomacy. The Jacobs, for all of their differences, have worked hard on this land. We cannot ask them to leave without recompense.

"We will take our time and negotiate what is rightfully ours and theirs. Alice, you'll be able to handle that, won't you?"

From the look on Alice's face, I could tell she had not discussed this with Rory previously.

"I will talk to Nathaniel and Lana," Rory said. "I'll talk to them tonight. And if they agree, we can begin the process of divorce and divvying up of goods. It's most important that we keep the house and the land. Anything else in the farmstead, including crops and stored food, is open to negotiation."

There were murmurs of trepidation.

"If they do not agree to go," Rory continued over the nervous chatter. "Then we'll ask that they, in good faith, participate in our salons and our gatherings. We appreciate the hard labor they have put in, but the Arboretum will fail if we cannot all stay together. We can't allow things to continue as they are, but we can give the family options. Stay, if they are willing to stay entirely, or leave."

It was nearly 10:00 P.M. when Rory accepted the unanimous blessing of our group to talk to Nathaniel. He left the den of the main house and headed toward the barn, where the Jacobs family slept. Alice went with him.

"Do you think they'll agree?" I heard someone ask.

"I think they'll take everything from us," someone replied.

AND THEN IT WAS QUIET for a moment. We began to stand up, one by one, to say our goodnights. Some would stay up to see how Rory and Alice's conversation went with Nathaniel. I chose sleep.

As I stood, I noticed something in the window. I thought

it was a bird, based on its quick movement. But birds wouldn't be landing on sills at this time of night.

Then I heard a gunshot.

Then a scream. And another gunshot.

Gunshots were common, but not this late. I looked out the window again, and again saw the movement. It was not a bird but a man. He was crouching, moving swiftly along the front porch of our farmhouse. It was his head I had seen bobbing along the bottom of the window.

"Run!" I shouted. "Out the back!"

The front door swung open with a loud crack, and almost immediately there was another gunshot. My ears rang.

I heard a scream, but I did not stop. I scrambled for the back door. Another shot. Several more. I did not look back. I ran. And I ran.

I ran out the back door and across the rocky, empty cornfield, long since harvested. It left me no place to hide.

I heard more gunshots and something swished past, close to my head. They had seen me. I ducked instinctively but I did not look back. I ran.

I ran.

I ran and I heard thumping steps running behind me, gaining ground. I ran even when the hand of the man behind me crashed down on my neck, toppling me forward into the cold, hard ground, my legs still thrashing even as my center of gravity tumbled ahead of my feet.

I heard the dark laughter of one of the Jacobs cousins above me. His body on top of mine, pressing the air from my lungs. My hands slapped at him as he tried to pin my arms down. He succeeded, and then he rolled me over, holding my wrist tightly as he pulled my forearm up my back. Every muscle from my shoulder to my fingers burned.

I wondered why he was hurting me rather than killing me. Perhaps they wanted me alive because they still wanted my help. Perhaps they wanted me dead, and this man just wanted to torture me first. But when I finally opened my eyes to see who my attacker was, I saw that his head was turned. He was looking at something several feet away.

It was the rifle. He had dropped it when he tackled me, and it was lying out of reach. He stretched his free hand toward the gun, keeping his other hand on mine, still pushing hard my twisted arm up my back. I was crying. Not in pain but reflexively. My eyes watered and my throat croaked. I could not stop it.

I wanted to run. I was desperate to be moving—not to get away, not for my safety, not consciously. It was deeper than that. A visceral primal urge to run as fast and as far as I could.

I needed to run.

And so I did. I ran nowhere.

Flat on my back, I moved my legs, kicking back and forth in a horizontal sprint.

My flailing destabilized the brute holding me down. He turned around and pulled tighter and tighter on my wrist. The pain was unbearable, but I kept running, prone in an empty cornfield, beneath the weight of my assailant.

He worked his knees onto my thighs, trying to pin my legs down, and as he did I saw my escape. Every one of the Jacobs family carried either a gun or a knife on their person at all times. This one carried both.

I shifted my pelvis like a sprinter making the final turn

on the track. My legs now kicking upward to his left. I caught part of his inner thigh and, I believe, his testicles. He winced and let up momentarily but not enough for me to break free.

I did manage, however, to get my right leg out from under his left. I wrapped it around his leg, twisting us both onto our sides.

With my right arm still pinned by his thick hands behind my back, I used my left—now freed from my own weight—to grab at the knife sheathed on his belt. My free arm was tingling and numb, so I couldn't feel for what I needed. I had to watch my movements and move quickly.

He countered as soon as he felt my hand at his waist. Letting go of my other arm, he throttled my left wrist with both hands, sending the knife flying out of my grip into the dirt, several feet past my head.

He laughed, then pulled back his arm and punched me across my temple. I couldn't see anything, hear anything, think anything for a moment. I wanted to vomit. Maybe I did vomit. Later I would find stains on my shirt that looked as if I had. But I don't remember.

What I do remember is the cousin scrambling off me, stumbling quickly toward the knife he had knocked from my hand. Reflexively I pulled myself up and began to crawl, in a daze, back toward the farmhouse. From behind me, I heard his feet stop. I knew he had found the knife. My hands kept clawing through the dirt. I could feel the skin on my knuckles breaking in the rocky autumn soil. Then I felt something else and stopped.

The cousin was running back toward me. But I had what I needed.

I picked up the rifle he had dropped earlier, turned around, fired.

He was only a meter or so away from me, the knife at his side, prepared to plunge it into my chest or neck or face. His body jerked to the side, and from his hip I saw a burst of skin and denim fly away. He shouted in agony, and his momentum carried his body just past mine, until he landed face-first in the dirt.

I stood over him, cocked the rifle, and pointed it at his head. He was crying, trying to speak. He may have wanted to plead for his life, explain the actions of his family. I didn't care. I shot him quickly at the base of his skull, ending him immediately.[3] I'd butchered pigs before.

I turned away from the farmhouse and ran. I ran more slowly now, exhausted and limping. But I ran. And I did not look back.

---

3 It is difficult to verify this account. There are numerous reports of murders by militias in the 1920s and 30s. So while it is not unreasonable that this particular story could be true, Dr. Gregory's execution of this unnamed "cousin of the Jacobs family" reads more like a crime thriller and feels out of character with the more controlled persona she has constructed in this book.

# Interlude

There is a gap at this point in the manuscript that it seems important to address.

Nora Bostwick's account of her time during the Great Reckoning and the early days of the Arboretum puts her move to Munich in spring of 1931. We have no reason to doubt Dr. Gregory's claim that her departure occurred immediately after Ms. Bostwick's but we have not been able to verify it. While we have found several accounts of people who, at one time or another, lived at the farm while Dr. Gregory was there, none of them remained there beyond Ms. Bostwick's tenure.

There is a record of Dr. Gregory as a passenger on the SS *Conte di Savoia* in 1941. The passenger liner departed Trieste on the twenty-seventh of October and docked in New York on the twenty-second of November. This means there is a gap of some ten years, between 1931 and 1941, in which Dr. Gregory's activities and movements are unknown.

If we assume that she journeyed in a consistent

direction during these years, she would have kept moving southeast after leaving the farm, through Former Germany and Austria, before arriving in the northeast of Italy. Of course we do not know when the doctor arrived in Trieste or how long she was there before she set sail for North America. In the following section Dr. Gregory discusses her determination to travel to Philadelphia, but she does not disclose why, if this was her aim, it took her a decade to leave Europe.

It's possible she traveled to Trieste via Switzerland, which wouldn't have taken her too far out of her way. This is assuming she was traveling to Trieste intentionally—a big assumption, given what we know of her life in Europe.

It seems likely that she continued to move around with no goal other than meeting her immediate needs, crossing borders without realizing it, and eventually found herself in a port town with an opportunity to leave the continent entirely.

It's fair to suppose that she continued to live as she had before—simply trying to survive as the Great Reckoning continued around the globe. This part of Europe had seen intense fighting during the 1920s, and much of it was demolished, but by the 30s the focus of the war had shifted to new areas. The most violent and significant battles of that decade were happening in Africa, Russia, and the South Pacific, though the American continent was also home to intense fighting, particularly in the southern states of the Former United States and in Central America.

This does not mean that Dr. Gregory's travels during this time were entirely safe. While the world's armies might have been deployed elsewhere, the ravaged lands they had abandoned still contained plenty of dangers. Desperation breeds danger, and this was a desperate world.

We do know that, by the time she arrived in the Former United States, Miriam was referring to herself as Dr. Gregory. This could shed some light on her activities during the missing decade. Perhaps she found a place to safely pursue more formal studies, earning the qualifications she needed to continue her work. She could have journeyed to Vienna, perhaps, and sought out the remnants of the Wednesday Psychological Society—or even Freud himself.

We cannot know if she would have been successful. By the early 30s, the destruction in Austria was almost absolute, and though the fighting had moved on, the region was too damaged to be functional on a large scale, and therefore precious few records survive. As for the Wednesday Psychological Society, little is known of its members' movements during the Great Reckoning.

As the world was rebuilt, there were several psychologists who claimed to have become members during this time. One or two even claimed to have been directly taught by Freud himself, but their claims could not be verified.

During her life Dr. Gregory was not known to make any such claims, perhaps preferring to cement her status through her own demonstrable expertise. It seems strange now to allow someone to use the honorific *doctor* without providing some kind of proof, but we must keep in mind the turmoil of the era. It was simply not possible during that time, in that part of the world, for Miriam to be awarded a doctorate by a respected and certified institution. Whether she earned hers through study under a qualified professional—Wednesday-affiliated or otherwise—or simply decided that she had earned a right to the title on her own, her work proved that it was apt.

It is unfair to speculate about why Dr. Gregory elected to omit these ten years from her account. It's possible that nothing of note occurred during this time, so she saw no point in addressing them at all. It's possible that she elected not to share certain events from that time; without knowing what they were, naturally we cannot give any opinions as to why.

It's possible that there's no need to look on this omission with any suspicion at all.

It's also important to note that we, as readers of this work, should be ready to question the motives and understanding of its subject and author. It's tempting to consider a contemporaneous view of political developments as more valid than a modern one. It is easy to assume that someone's day-to-day experience of life would give them a keener understanding of their political climate than an outside observer, but this is a false premise. Indeed, people tend to have a narrow view of their world—political movements are of concern only as they affect them personally. They cannot take the wide view that we can when looking back on history—and, of course, they cannot predict outcomes that we know in hindsight were caused or prevented by events of the time.

During the latter half of the Great Reckoning and the years that followed its end, there was widespread discussion about how the world would rebuild itself. It's easy to assume that this discussion must have happened with some urgency and haste. The breadth of destruction was, of course, immense and the longer it took to rebuild a safe world, the fewer people would survive it. Indeed, global population levels have not fully recovered even today.

But it would be a mistake to look back and assume that because the reconstruction was chaotic, it was thoughtless. The steps taken to rebuild the world, the decisions made about how to do so, were the result of lengthy consideration and comprehensive scientific study.

The writer of this manuscript seems to believe, or to be trying to make us believe, that the current structure of our world was put in place simply by those loud enough to demand it. That the rules we follow were invented by opportunists. If she were right in this, it would follow that the society we live in is little more than a global cult.

While we accept that some patrons who choose to access material from this press might subscribe to some skeptical thinking when it comes to the Society, we want to urge readers to resist ascribing undue weight to the author's conspiracy theories. Aside from the thorny issue of treason, it is a fool's errand to attempt to divine the motivations of persons who worked to rebuild our world. Many of the statespeople and activists from that time are no longer with us, so we can no longer ask them how they felt at that time. They did give frequent and comprehensive interviews during their lifetimes, and we would humbly suggest that these are a better resource than one woman's dubious screed, when it comes to researching our history.

The treaties that were signed in the wake of the Great Reckoning and the laws that were put in place are, of course, open to scrutiny and criticism. Like any other laws and treaties, they were written by people, and people are fallible. But it is absurd to suggest that they were not thoroughly considered and debated. That the conclusions drawn by our founders were based on whim and an excess of credulity.

It is one thing to engage with critical material, but it is quite another to take everything such material suggests as objective truth or wisdom. We invite readers to level the same skepticism advocated by the author at the work she herself has done. Question the Society, yes, but also question the questions themselves.

*Part Two: Manifest Destiny*

# *Ten*

AND SO I ARRIVED IN A NEW WORLD.

I had heard stories of Ellis Island, the point of arrival for most European immigrants, but of course by the time I arrived in 1941 it no longer existed. Liberty Island was still there, as were the twisted remnants of its once great statue.[1] There were no huddled masses. We had been reduced. We were just the stragglers. Those left behind. The few who, by luck or misfortune, had escaped the apocalypse[2] and who would maybe have been better off dead.

I had no plans for New York other than to simply debark and immediately seek transit to Philadelphia. I didn't know if the contacts Nora had offered me so many years earlier would

---

1 The precise date of the destruction of Ellis Island and Liberty Island is disputed, but it is generally agreed to have happened sometime during the bombings of 1928 and 1929.

2 What Dr. Gregory terms "the apocalypse" was not quite over by this point. The official end of the Great Reckoning was in 1943. It is true that by the time Miriam arrived in the Former United States, the violence had ebbed across most of the world, as various nations declared cease-fires. The first global cease-fire was signed in December of 1942, though it did not hold into the new year. After two more attempts, the Day of First Peace was declared on the twenty-first of April 1943, and the decades of war came to an end.

still be helpful, but I had no other goals, other than to try to improve my work. Going to Philadelphia gave me direction. It gave me the illusion of direction.

The trains were no longer running, either within New York City or without. There were few employees left to operate or maintain the vehicles. So I set out on foot, hitchhiking where I could and walking when I had to. It took a full week, and I hardly ate except what food was given to me.

The Americans were kind but not welcoming. They introduced themselves and smiled. They tipped hats and commented on my excellent English. This friendliness suggested to me a readiness to bring me inside, let me warm by a fire, cook me some food. I would, of course, have offered to do some work around any house or farm that offered hospitality. But I found that in America, kindness stopped at speech.

Occasionally someone would see me on the road, ask me where I was walking to. I would point to my map—I had found it at an abandoned shop near the port in Manhattan. The length of my journey usually surprised people, and if they had food with them to give, they would give it to me. Sometimes they gave me money, though the value of the dollars varied dramatically from town to town. I did not turn down any gifts, but what I wanted most was water. There was plenty of fresh water on my route, but I did not trust it. Swamps and still ponds with an iridescent sheen, a sign of pollution from industrial waste, either deliberately dumped or dispersed through destruction or abandoned factories nearby. Small rivers and creeks were my only source of water. But water was difficult to carry and not always clean.

Much of the soil on the East Coast of America was still

gray and black, almost two decades after Yellowstone.[3] I did not know if the land was unusable or simply unused. Perhaps smiling greetings were all the Americans had left.

I did not think at all about where I had come from. Over the years, I had perfected not thinking about it.

The years before my arrival in New York or the years since. In writing all this down I am facing memories I would prefer to leave in the shadows.

I sat down to write about the Jacobs family some months ago. I don't know how long exactly. I sat down to write about them, and while I did, I held it all at arm's length. Lana and Nathaniel and their brutish cousins.

The children: Ellen. Alicia.

I ran away from them. I ran away from all thought of them, and now I'll never know their fate. I'll never know what happened to those girls.[4] I'll never know what happened to Rory and Alice, to Alexei and Sofia. To the children.

It's difficult, what I'm doing. It's harder than I thought it would be. I knew it would be laborious; I knew it would take time and energy. But . . . thinking about the past, thinking about the people—I wasn't expecting it to hurt quite so much. I have had to put all of it aside—put all of them aside—for so long. I had to survive. And to survive, I had to let them all go.

But writing about them brings it all back. I can see them. I can see Rory, squinting through glasses that were ten years out of date. I can see Alice bent over tomato plants, trying

---

3  The Yellowstone eruption of 1923.

4  Edited for clarity.

to make them flourish through an ashen summer. I can see Margot and Naija. I can see Elsa.

I am haunted as I write this. Surrounded by people I spent the best part of my life trying to forget. Would it have been easier if I'd kept them with me? A little bit of pain every day instead of the flood all at once now—now, when I need focus more than I need regret?

It's too late to ask these questions. I lived the life I lived, and as I recount it, the ghosts appear around me, and they don't leave. And there are more to come. By the time I reach the end, I'll be crowded out of my room.

Anyway.

Nora had given me a list of names before she left the Arboretum, and after I got to New York, it was all I thought about. All I thought about was the work I had to do and those who could help me do it. But when I arrived in Philadelphia, I found none of Nora's colleagues at the university.

I wasn't so much surprised as disappointed.

I'd had a few letters from Nora over the years, and I knew that she'd been trying to get in touch with her old friends but hadn't had replies. The Reckoning wasn't over by this point, but the fighting had eased enough for the mail to be a little more reliable. Still, it was difficult to track people down. It was difficult to know who had survived.

I spent two days asking around the campus for the various people she'd mentioned before I found someone who knew something. Before I found someone who knew someone who knew something. Before someone recognized one of the names.

Harold Olson. Eventually someone recognized the name

Harold Olson and told me that he was retired and living near campus.

Harold was old, eighty, maybe eighty-five. He was tall and thin with only a few silver hairs drawn straight back over his scalp. Despite being retired, he answered his door in a button-down shirt, tie, and black slacks. He did not wear shoes in his home, but I could see a perfectly polished pair sat next to the front door. I wondered if he'd wanted to retire at all or had simply left for lack of students. Like many I had met in America, Harold asked me how I was doing and smiled as I spoke. And like the others, he kept his body rigid and forbidding. He did not look ready to welcome me into his home.

But when I told him that Nora had sent me, he went from nice to magnanimous. He made coffee and sat me in his living room. I told Harold about the Arboretum and Nora. I told him about the uprising of the Jacobs family and my narrow escape.

"Did Nora . . ." he asked fearfully.

"She was gone by that time," I told him. "She went to Munich, but the last time I heard from her she was in Geneva.[5] That was a year or so ago. Do you have any food?"

The coffee was causing my hands and knees to shake. My empty stomach could not bear caffeine as a replacement for food. I was too exhausted to feel shame for such a direct question.

---

5 By this time, Ms. Bostwick had been elected to the German Provisional Government. While news of this might not have made it back to her friends in Philadelphia, it seems unlikely that Dr. Gregory herself wasn't aware of it. It seems strange that she wouldn't relate this news here, but perhaps we can put this down to a lapse of memory.

"Of course," he said, expressing shame of his own. "How rude of me."

He went to his kitchen, where his cupboards were filled with boxes of grain, cans of soup. He cut slices of soda bread and heated some tomato soup on the stovetop for me.

"Nora was my brightest student," he said.

"She said she was not offered a doctorate at Temple," I retorted, a little bluntly.

"There have always been white people," he sighed, "in every institution in this country who are threatened by Black people. Her dissertation—it was called *Anti-tribalism in a New Societal Methodology* or something to that effect— was brilliant, if a little idealistic. I fought for her. But her oral panel was a row of old white men—like me, but I hope in looks alone. They corrected her grammar, her presentation, what they called her 'unprofessional appearance.' Everything but the ideas themselves."

"She told me about her thesis," I said. "She was still idealistic. She and a few others were planning to work toward reshaping the world after the end of the war."

"I'm too old to see the world recover," he said matter-of-factly. "But if it does, I hope she's in charge."

We ate soup and bread. I told Harold about the Watercolor Quiet and my work with the children at the Arboretum. That Nora had encouraged me to continue my studies at a university. That I desperately wanted to learn more and develop my techniques. I was uncertain what college would do for me, but if it provided the resources and safety for my studies, then that's what I wanted.

"You can stay here," he offered. "For a time. The university is not the same as when I worked there, and I don't think I have the power to get you what you need. But I have food and a guest room. And this part of town is safe. Nora was like a daughter to me. Any friend of hers is family."

But I did not want or need another family. I'd had a family who gave birth to me, but they were too vulnerable to live. I'd had a family who helped me scavenge food, but they were easily dispersed by soldiers. I'd had a family in Elsa who taught me to center myself, but she was too willing to abandon life in the face of conflict. I'd had a family who encouraged me to learn and grow, but they were overtaken from within by the very tribalism they eschewed.

Each of them provided something valuable, but they were innately fragile. I was tired of starting anew every few years. Sitting across from Harold in his quiet, cozy home, looking into his deep brown eyes and withered face, I trusted him. I did. He was sincere, but I needed a place to work, to grow—within a formal institution, not under the guise of family. I was beyond communes and gangs and tribes. I wanted a place to do my job, whatever that job would be.

"Thank you, Harold," I said. "I cannot, though. As Nora would have said, 'Break from the family nation, and become who you are.'"

He smiled and nodded and said, with a touch of disappointment, "That's Nora."

Harold knew a program in St. Louis that was working with children. One of his former students had taken over an orphanage there and directed its focus toward helping children recover from emotional trauma.

"It's not a university," Harold said. "But you may find it

more beneficial to you, anyway. And I believe you could be beneficial to them."

So this was it. The moment Nora had told me to prepare for. The Reckoning was ending, the world was about to be rebuilt, and I had to decide where in this new world, this new society, I would fit.

I could have taken a different path. Ignored Harold's offer and knocked on other doors. Found a place at a university, perhaps, put my research into laboratories and libraries. But that life appeared lonesome to me.

All things considered, I think the loneliness would have been worth it. A different path would have been worth it. But we all have regrets.

THE ORPHANAGES WERE NOT ORGANIZED at this point. The world was not organized.[6] The New Society still resembled the academic salons of the Arboretum more than it did an actual government. Much of the violence of national wars had ended by the late 1930s, but violence in the aftermath of nations cannot be cleaned up so quickly. For a time, we were peaceful but collectively unstable—no concerted recovery effort, just a globe full of survivors trying to do the work that was in front of them.

---

6 Dr. Gregory seems to suggest that the years following the end of the Great Reckoning were something of a free-for-all. But this implies that there was no government-mandated recovery effort, which is clearly false. While it is certainly true that many private facilities were established in the rubble of this postwar period, they were far from the only help available. There were, of course, state-run facilities throughout the Great Reckoning and beyond it, which provided care for orphaned children. Any attempt to suggest otherwise is an affront to the people who carried us through this time of trial and rebuilt the world we live in today.

I joined the staff of the orphanage in St Louis: the Gateway School for Wayward Youth. Our building was mostly stable but not suited for the purpose. It had once been a school, but the gym had been bombed at some point, and the grounds were overrun with weeds. Saplings sprang up through what had been floors. None of the rooms were suitable for sleeping, so we rigged up makeshift dormitories.

The children were a mixed bag. They came and went a lot. For some, the promise of a bed, food, an adult to make decisions for them was all they wanted. For others, used to living independently, the school's environment was too cloying and restrictive. We had a lot of runaways. We were not a prison, and we had no state mandate to keep anyone there. We did our best, but if children wanted to leave, we did not force them to stay.

And of course they were all—we were all—still suffering. We had what would now be called PTSD. The teachers, the cooks, the doctors. The children.

We were trying to recover from lives lived in conflict and fear, but recovery requires rest. A building full of the traumatized is not a restful place.

But then, this is how I found my calling.

I had been counseling the children for several months before I felt that some of them were ready to try a more concerted and intentional regime of therapy. When I fled the farmstead that had once been the Arboretum,[7] I had left

7 The farm that housed the Arboretum, and at which Dr. Gregory began her research, became a site of much interest after Nora Bostwick's ascendence to the Global Council—but by the time it was rediscovered in 1946, it was much altered. Whoever took over after Ms. Bostwick's departure had

behind every word of research I'd collected, but in the years following I'd done my best to commit it to memory.

I decided it was time to continue my work, to expand on the Watercolor Quiet with these American orphans. Elsa's technique had centered me from the start. To her it had always been a personal and intimate practice. And my own use of the technique still closely resembled hers: a way to calm troubling emotional ties, to keep painful memories in check. In my work with Rohaan and other children at the Arboretum, however, I had begun to shape it into a promising methodology, which I continued to develop and strengthen over the years since. Why keep something so healing and grounding to myself?

I started with a young girl named Florence. She was thirteen, and at first refused to speak to anyone at the facility save for me. That kind of thing was not unusual. She had been alone when we found her the previous year, and badly malnourished. There is nothing to be gained in comparing the experiences different people had during the Reckoning—suffice to say that we had all seen and done horrific things. Florence carried a particularly heavy weight with her, though, since her memories would eventually cease to have any relevance to her, I see no reason to relate them here.

Like Elsa, I preferred to work outdoors, away from other

---

clearly abandoned it several years earlier, perhaps seeking out the renewal of civilization that was developing around them. Since the events of 1931, most likely, there had been squatters in the buildings but no long-term inhabitants. None of the research materials Dr. Gregory mentions were found there, and it is impossible to know what happened to them. Perhaps the Jacobs family and their cohort destroyed what was left behind, or perhaps they took it with them when they left. There is simply no way to be sure.

people and artificial light. I don't know if this was a natural inclination or just force of habit. I had learned the Watercolor Quiet outside, and I had practiced it with the children of the Arboretum outside. After all that, four walls and artificial light felt constraining.

There was a general effort to recultivate the grounds, and I had commandeered a small area for myself. It wasn't completely wooded over, but young trees were growing there, and the ground was covered in soft heather.

I started by teaching Florence general meditation, which she mastered faster than I expected. I believe it was a relief to her to be able to separate from herself. It afforded her rest. And her speed was incredibly helpful for my studies. I was glad to move on to the Watercolor Quiet.

Once she was adept with my technique, I began to explore her past. To this day, I'm unsure of the extent to which she was aware of how much I learned about her. But what I learned about her doesn't matter. My goal was to make use of the meditative state in order to clean away the trauma of her past. To cauterize her wounds. It was even more successful than I thought it would be.

One by one I explored Florence's most painful memories. I walked through them with her, carving gently at their contours until each one broke away.

The system worked in alternating sessions. One day we would use her meditation practice to excise the wounds of her past, and the next we would talk through the memory we had detached. In this way, she was able to talk through her past without feeling its trauma.

And without the burden of a family—which, as I learned

in the Arboretum, could easily undo all progress—slowly Florence transformed before our eyes. She began talking to her classmates and instructors. She became an enthusiastic participant in games and athletics. Her academic performance improved steadily. She started telling jokes.

Having succeeded with Florence I expanded my practice among the other children. One after the other, they grew more trusting, more assured. Better able to cope with the demands of life. Indeed, I was so successful that some of my colleagues asked me to treat them as well.

For the first time, I felt comfortable and useful in my role in society. I was doing good. I was contributing to something tangible and real. The Gateway orphanage was soon able to do more than just care for children—it was able to help them become productive. It was able to prepare them for the world outside. People from across the Midwest started taking notice, and we began to employ more staff. I hired assistants and taught them how to conduct my process.

Still, I felt I could be doing more.

While the children and their caretakers were leading happier, more comfortable lives because of my work, the results seemed to me imperfect. No one felt fully whole. At times, I would see someone drop back into themselves, draw back from those around them, as if an unutterable sadness had suddenly blown across them like an unexpected change in the wind.

There were limitations to the Watercolor Quiet. I studied and developed the approach as a science, but it seemed to work more like a spell that allowed children to package and store memories. It was positive and groundbreaking, to be sure, but still far from perfect.

I wanted to free people entirely from the trauma they had suffered, but it seemed to me that all I had done was open a door to a garden. They could not stop themselves from venturing back into misery from time to time.

At this point, I started to do wider research, outside my own practice. I wanted to know what others had learned before me. It was not easy—I did not have access to many of the resources I needed. But the recovering postal service did give me greater access to textbooks and other resources; in combination with my own experiments, this led me to establish a new goal.

Clearly it was not enough to remove someone's emotional connection to their memories. Repackaging trauma was not enough. Unopened boxes demand opening. But what if I could remove painful memories entirely?

# *Eleven*

WHEN YOU LOOK BACK ON YOUR LIFE, VERY LITTLE OF IT IS SIM-
ple. This is a generalization, of course; I can't be sure that it
holds true for people whose lives were different from mine.
Not everyone comes of age during the apocalypse. Perhaps
people born now will look back on their lives to find very few
complications at all. I'm not sure I believe this, though.

But perhaps I should avoid generalizing. Looking back
at my own life, most of it is complicated. But this period of
time . . .

For once, I think, things really were simple. Straightfor-
ward. Not easy—I don't think anything was ever easy—but
clear.

I had work in front of me to do, and I knew that it was
good work. I saw the impact of it around me every day. I made
people better. I made them happier. I helped them rebuild.

In my first days at the orphanage, the focus was on stability. Getting everyone through another day. Making sure
people were fed. Clean. As physically healthy as we could get
them. Emotional health seemed like a luxury.

And my task was nearly impossible. Sisyphean. Each day

wrung me out to the bones, and the knowledge of the coming day robbed me of rest.

The only help we provided in those early days is that the children in our care ended each day as alive as they'd begun it. For the most part.

Once I started my work with Florence, though, there was more than just getting through the day. More than just getting the children through the day. There was purpose. There were goals.

Eventually, as I began working with more and more children, we were able to give them structure. And once we gave them structure, we began to be able to teach them.

Ours was a much more complicated version of teaching than Society-run Childhood Development Centers can give now, naturally. Some of our children at Gateway had no prior education at all. Some had picked up strange scraps of knowledge here and there, but they had no way to put them in context. Some had an expert understanding of mechanics but had never learned to read.

But having to individually cater to each child's educational needs was easy compared to managing their individual traumas.

It took a while. Probably a couple of years. I don't know, really; maybe it was a few months. Maybe it was a decade. Trying to pin down time from this distance is like looking through a kaleidoscope. It doesn't matter anyway.

Maybe none of this matters. Why am I bothering to write all this down? I don't even know who I expect to read it. Am I doing this to keep myself occupied? Old, alone, with nothing better to do. Spending hour after hour spilling out my memories onto paper with no real reason to.

No. There is a reason. I'm just not sure this is enough. I'm not sure writing it down is enough.

I'm tired. And demoralized. How am I supposed to complete a task this big when I don't even know if it'll have any impact? What good is my story after I'm gone, anyway?

But then again, why not? I'm old. And alone. And I have nothing better to do.

Anyway.

We developed something like a routine at Gateway. We had calm. We had happiness, even, and who would ever have thought we could get to that?

The world around us was still struggling to build itself up again, to put the fear and desperation of the previous years more firmly in the past. That's a tough thing to do. They keep intruding. Interrupting.

Behind our doors, though, we were growing. Other orphanages in the area started asking me to work with their children. People started coming from nearby towns. Hundreds of people heard about what we were doing, what I was doing, and came looking for the help only I could provide.[1]

So I suppose this is when I learned that things are never simple for long.

I am not by nature a teacher. I lack the skill of divining a path from someone else's ignorance to my own level of

---

1 The author talks about herself in wildly inflated terms here, suggesting an unrealistic self-image in the extreme.

knowledge. I cannot see where the first step is on the journey, because I have left it so far behind. I don't know how to distill what has become second nature to me—the organically consolidated knowledge of a lifetime—into a replicable set of instructions. I second-guess what I'm telling people—not because I worry that I'm wrong, but because I'm unsure if it's truly possible to communicate what I mean.

Language is rich and vast, but with all its breadth, it's insufficient. Every word, every turn of phrase, every variation of tone is liable to be misinterpreted. When we speak to each other, how can we know what has shaped each other's view? What unknown connotations they bring to our words? It is overwhelming. If you think about this for too long, it is terrifying. But I found myself having to think about it.

I did not know then how important my techniques would become,[2] but I knew that they were helping the people around me. I also knew that there were more people around me than I was able to help on my own. I had no choice but to pass on my knowledge.

I was cautious about it. Perhaps that was a mistake. I took on one apprentice at a time. I wanted them to develop their own practices before I began training them to work with others. They would observe me with subjects for weeks before I let them work with the children themselves, at which point I would observe them, for weeks.

---

2 The technique Dr. Gregory calls the Watercolor Quiet has been developed into a crucial part of the Society's operations. We have all been through a process developed over the decades from her starting point. But while her innovation was important, the state-sanctioned process that all children go through at the age of ten is the culmination and advancement of work performed by many dedicated scientists and researchers.

I thought it was best to be careful. But others thought it was better to be efficient. And I didn't notice what was happening. How could I? There was too much to do.

I kept one student at a time, and they were with me constantly. We worked with as many children as we could. I was completely focused on my work and didn't notice that a certain impatience was growing. It's understandable, I suppose. People were suffering, and they saw suffering end for others.

It's funny. I'm only realizing now how naive I was in this moment. I had thought that any innocence or credulity in me had long since been burned away. If it ever existed in the first place. But thinking about it now, I was so trusting. I told my students that I expected them to use the Watercolor Quiet with children at their centers, but not to pass it on. I was the only one, I believed, who could do that. And I never questioned that they would follow my guidance. They all seemed to have faith in me. They all seemed loyal.

But one of them—or several of them; I don't really know, I don't really care to know—chose to ignore me. I don't know who it was, and I don't know how many of them there were, because I didn't realize it was happening for several months. Possibly longer. But some of the people I'd trained began sharing that training with others. Who, in turn, passed it on to yet more people.

I have a lot to regret from my life. We'll get to all of that. But this is the first time things really went wrong. When the actions I took—or didn't take—caused irreparable harm.

I had developed a methodology for separating people from their trauma, for allowing them to live more peaceful lives, and I thought I would be able to keep control of it. It was mine, after all. Who would be able to use it but me?

But it escaped my control and ran rampant. It spread and spread, iterated many times, and each iteration was one step further from where it started.

Today, if someone developed a medical or psychological treatment like mine that treatment would be put through a rigorous assessment process before it came close to being used with the general public. It would be tested and tested again in multiple, controlled, peer-reviewed studies. It would be verified by the Society and by an independent medical or scientific body.

It would take years to be approved. Because it takes years to know that a particular treatment is truly safe and effective in achieving the desired result. It would be carefully codified, and its use would be strictly regulated.

We would be horrified if something so powerful were unleashed on the world without that kind of process today, and yet we accept without question a now-ubiquitous treatment that never had any testing at all, except for my own experiments.[3] I am not saying that the Society is wrong to use my technique as it does, necessarily—after all, we have created a peaceful world. But if I had known the lengths to which it

---

3 The author is being both exceptionally arrogant and alarmist. She sounds like a conspiracy theorist. The Age Ten Protocols and the treatments relevant to them were not "unleashed"–they were carefully and thoughtfully developed. It is foolish to suggest that they were implemented without proper vetting. Our world was almost destroyed by violence caused by inherited hatred and prejudice. By removing the ability to inherit, we have achieved a truly peaceful and equal world.

would be taken, I believe I would have kept it to myself and found another way to help those children.

My work was shared around the area, and within a year or two it was officially endorsed by what would turn out to be the short-lived government of the United American Continent,[4] and eventually by the North American Regionality of the Societal Council. From there, I suppose it was only a matter of time before it spread worldwide.

And I received praise. Nora and Ekaterina wrote to me of their pride at my accomplishments. "We always knew," they said. "We always knew you'd do something great with your life, but even we couldn't have imagined this." They told me I was "helping not just rebuild the world but make it better." They said, "The Reckoning was a high price to pay, but you are helping make recompense."

I drew warmth from their praise, but I knew it was misplaced. They were wrong. The world was wrong.

Even as it spread, even in my dismay at how far and how quickly my work moved outside my control, I did not realize what the Watercolor Quiet would become. I was trying to heal trauma. That was all. Was I not right to try to heal trauma?

Was I not right in that, at least?

---

4 The United American Continent was established in 1944 and lasted just ten months, after which it was subsumed into the new Global Society. There is no record of its government officially endorsing Dr. Gregory's technique during those months, although American representatives on the Global Societal Council were vocal early supporters of the Age Ten Laws that developed from it.

# *Twelve*

It was my assistant, Rosemary,[1] who first told me about Secretary Marshall.[2]

Rosemary had been working with me for about a year. She had initially come to me for training, but it became clear quite quickly that she was not suited to treating people herself. She did not have the patience for it. She did not even really have the patience to go through my full program. She claimed she didn't need it, but she wasn't a very good liar. At that time she wasn't a very good liar.

Anyway. Irrelevant. At this moment, it is irrelevant.

Although Rosemary was ill-suited to providing my treatment

---

1 It appears that the woman here called Rosemary is in fact Dr. Rose Haverstock. No doubt readers are aware of her groundbreaking work over the latter half of the twentieth century. Dr. Haverstock is a world-renowned physiologist and researcher, whose influence cannot be underestimated. She has often spoken of her time with Dr. Gregory at the Gateway Center and is open about the affection and regard they had for one another.

2 Edith Marshall was the Society's first Secretary of Education, beginning in 1945. Her position evolved in 1949 to Secretary, Department of Childhood Development. Previously, Marshall was a popular poet and traveling actor. Her fame and charm made her one of North America's most beloved politicians during the founding years of the New Society.

to others, she was invaluable as a researcher and scientist. While her coldness sometimes upset me, she kept me from becoming too sentimental about my work.[3] She took little personal interest in the Watercolor Quiet, but she saw value in it.

She could see the effect it had on the children—but, looking back now, I think there was more to it than that. Rosemary was fascinated by the impact we could have on other people and was interested to know how far we could go. Because the impact we were having was positive, at the time I didn't question her input. No, I welcomed it. She helped me improve the process. She pushed me to refine my craft.

With her help, my work grew more precise. More powerful. I had never had a relationship like that before. I had known people who had something to teach me. I had known those who had something to learn from me. But this? We were not teacher and student; we were not looking up or down at each other. Neither were we true equals. We, with our entirely different attitudes to life and to work, our complete lack of similarity in how we worked and what we valued, were able to create what neither of us could ever have created on our own.

We pushed each other. We bounced off each other and found more than we could on our own. Looking back, I don't know why I considered her my assistant, to be honest, but at the time we never questioned it.

But this is not what I was talking about. I was talking about Secretary Marshall.

---

3 We have combed this manuscript from start to finish several times and have failed to find any evidence of the author having even an iota of sentiment toward her work.

Rosemary came to me as I was doing my meditation practice in one of the private gardens. I found myself needing to devote more time than usual to my own sessions those days. Keeping myself on an even keel was essential, and sifting through other people's trauma is not conducive to a clear, unbiased mind.

Rosemary waited over by the trees—tall, serene sycamores—watching me, fidgeting, chewing her lip until she was sure I was finished, but I could tell this was hard for her. Having no patience for meditation herself, she could not understand my reliance on it. She recognized it, though, and maybe that's enough.

I took a final breath, retreating into my body, and looked over at her. After having to wait for me to finish, she seemed suddenly reluctant to talk. I cocked an eyebrow at her, and she walked over and sat on the grass beside me.

She looked away for a moment before speaking. "I should have spotted this earlier," she said. "I haven't been paying close enough attention."

"To what?"

"To Secretary Marshall."

"I don't know who that is, Rosemary."

"How do you not know Secretary Marshall?"

Rosemary was incredulous, but I have never had much patience for politics. I understand that they are a necessity in forming any kind of cohesive society, I understand there must be structure in order to have peace and community, but I don't operate on the same wavelength as politicians. I knew the broad strokes of what was going on; I knew how the world was being rebuilt—that much was unavoidable. But I didn't bother with the minutiae. With the people or the policies or the campaigning. I didn't have the time. I would like to say that I regret this now, but I'm not certain I could have done anything to alter the course of events, in any case.

Rosemary, on the other hand, seemed always hungry for news. She tracked everyone, constantly reading up on who was moving through the ranks of government, or trying to. We were very different people, she and I.

"Marshall has a column in the paper,"[4] Rosemary explained. "It's not a big deal, just a few inches every other Thursday. She talks about her vision for the region and the Society in general. Usually it's a lot of hot air masquerading as idealism and opportunity."

"But—?"

"But there's been a strain of thinking in her columns that seems to be getting more and more prominent. It started with a vague comment here and there, asides about value of counseling for children, that kind of thing. But today's column goes a lot further. She mentions you by name, accuses you of conducting illicit medical experiments. She even suggests that you could be hurting the children you treat."[5]

It took me a moment to process this, but I knew that I couldn't change my course based on criticism from a low-level

---

4 While it is true that Secretary Marshall had a column in the St. Louis Post-Dispatch in the mid- to late 40s, it is misrepresented here. It ran monthly, rather than biweekly, and had little to do with her political career; she wrote memoir-like accounts of her time in the theater. She occasionally wrote humorous poems and short stories.

5 Again, this sort of story, if it ran at all, would not have been authored by Edith Marshall.

stateswoman. "I'm not concerned about gossip columns," I said.

"It's not a gossip column. People listen to her." Rosemary paused again. "She's quite charismatic, the kind of person whose ideas seem to spread over great distances and blossom overnight."

"But it's not true," I retorted. I felt like a child deflecting a playground accusation.

"It's not about truth, Dr. Gregory. It's about what people believe."

"Well, what do you suggest we do about her?"

"We have to write our response, and it has to happen quickly," Rosemary said. "We know she's wrong; everyone who works here knows she's wrong; we have evidence where she has conjecture. The longer we let her speak about this unchallenged, the harder it will be to stop her."

But I wasn't so sure. In part because I wasn't quite convinced that Secretary Marshall was a threat to us. But also because I didn't feel that I could categorically claim confidence in the system I had unleashed. It had morphed and moved and grown beyond me, and I no longer knew how it was being practiced outside the Gateway Center. I knew I had not harmed the children in my care—but how could I say the same for someone practicing my method who had learned from someone who had learned from someone who had learned from me? I had no idea what was happening with cases three times removed from myself.

I asked for time to think. A week later, when Rosemary brought it up again, I asked for more time.

"The story is getting out of hand," she said. "But I won't do anything until you say to."

She lied. The next week, the paper published Rosemary's own response to the column. She refuted Secretary Marshall's claims and suggestions point by point, citing case studies from our orphanage. She praised the work of those who were carrying my method further into the world, claiming that it was the only way to bring peace and stability. She even invited Marshall to tour the facility in order to address her concerns. She was careful, though. She suggested no malice on the Secretary's part, leveling her ire instead at commentators who were broadcasting ill-informed opinions as fact. She stressed the need for careful research, for respecting the experts, and she offered herself as the expert in question.

So it was done. Within a few months, Secretary Marshall had visited our facility numerous times. She publicly repudiated her earlier opinions about our practice, and she became a champion of the Gateway Center and the many other facilities practicing some variation of the Watercolor Quiet.

I really don't know how to judge the impact this had. Everything was changing so drastically and quickly.

It's probably strange for children born now to imagine this, but until the end of the Great Reckoning, there was no universal income, no universal education, no universal career guidance. Wealth was kept within the tightly guarded borders of nations, of governments, of businesses, and of families.

We were an orphaned people in the Reckoning. We had all been surviving alone, by our wits and gambles, for so long. But as the New Society gained traction as a philosophy, and later as a fully realized world government, that began to change. Soon, whatever need we had could be addressed by some newly developed agency.

What a luxury.

These days it doesn't seem like a luxury, of course. Such a system seems essential, basic; it's taken for granted. The state is everyone's parents and it will see to everyone's needs—whether those needs are nourishment and support or discipline.

There were revolts against the formation of the New Society throughout the 1930s and 40s. But they usually burned out before they spread too far. They would lose momentum because it's hard to rise up against a government that's giving people everything they need. Even if that same government is taking something away in the process.

Anyway. Irrelevant.

I still can't decide if Rosemary was right to do what she did. Her counter-editorial seemed to suffocate the flames ignited by Secretary Marshall, but I had not authorized her to write it. Rosemary chastised me routinely for my silence and apolitical nature—she did not understand. She claimed that political engagement was a moral imperative, but I think for her it was really just love of the game. She was good at speaking, arguing, maneuvering to get what she wanted, and she liked to win.

I never liked speaking out. The squeaky wheel gets the grease. Unless the squeaky wheel is removed and replaced, discarded into the junkyard of unremarkable history. To stage a public fight only draws more attention to oneself. I always felt that way.

I always used to feel that way.

But not anymore. I don't have much time left now. I can feel my energy waning, and the last thing I need to do before it's my time to walk on is to speak. To tell the truth about things. Where I was at fault. Where I was betrayed.

I don't know who I'm speaking to, of course. Someone, I hope. I hope you are someone who wants to listen. There is value in being heard. I never appreciated that when I was younger.

It is one of the universe's deepest and cruelest jokes that it takes a lifetime to learn the lessons you need in order to live.

# *Thirteen*

IT SEEMS STRANGE TO ME NOW, RIDICULOUS EVEN, TO LOOK back on this time. To consider it as a series of steps taken, you understand, when now we consider the state of the world as fixed. The way we live now has been the way we live for long enough that it feels permanent. Unimaginable that it should change. That it should ever have felt different.

Astonishing how quickly that happens. Tradition, custom, the ways of the world—they really are little more than everything we have taken for granted since our own childhood. Everything can change within one or two generations.

"We've always done this!" someone will cry when they feel their habits threatened. But in reality, no. We've done this for, what, fifty years? For no time at all.

And still, I don't know how it happened. I don't know how we went from understanding how to mentally separate people from their early memories to making it illegal for people to remain tethered to them at all, or even to remember their families. But somewhere along the line, we did.[1] And that decision was made consciously and deliberately.

Secretary Marshall continued to write columns on state-run childhood centers,[2] but her stance against them had changed. Ev~tually she developed her own arguments for freeing ourselves from the bondage of parenthood. Rosemary assured me that the Secretary had moved on from criticizing my work. I was relieved, but I did not feel moved to read her work myself.

The idea itself was not the Secretary's, though. It was a policy suggested by the Societal Council. I do not know if Nora wrote the policy.[3] Perhaps Ekaterina. Separating children from their birth families did not fit within the ethos of the Arboretum, but the goals of the Arboretum were never dogmatic and fixed. They were dogmatic and ever-evolving.

According to Rosemary, Secretary Marshall continued to cite my work, though she no longer named me specifically and had begun advocating for my practice rather than against it. No one seemed concerned about her inconsistency. I don't know if my ideas had spread so far that I was no longer iden-

---

1 The Age Ten Laws were passed in 1948 after a lengthy and controversial legislative process. The author suggests that this was a simple affair, thus implying that it was misguided and ill thought through. By her own admission, she paid little attention to politics, so even if we were to accept the veracity of her account—which we by no means do—we can assume that her understanding of the legal process behind the Society's edicts is not comprehensive.

2 To reiterate: we have found no evidence of the Secretary writing political features.

3 The initial proposed law was drafted in 1947 by Gustav Morgan. It was heavily debated by the council before being voted into law in 1948. Both Nora Bostwick and Ekaterina Yelchin voted in support.

tified as their creator, or if the Secretary did not want to publicly admit she was wrong for faulting me in the first place.

It was not important to me. I had work to do.

The Watercolor Quiet had evolved considerably over my years at Gateway—both my own application of it and the further iterations created by other practitioners.

It worked better on younger subjects. While they're still learning so much and so quickly that their neural pathways can be interrupted and rerouted with ease. It becomes just one of the myriad ways their brain has been altered on any given day.

This is not to say it does not work in adults as well, but it's different. Less clean, less efficient. It requires more work on their part.

And so, catching children when they are at the right developmental stage for the process to go smoothly is a fine balance. They must be young enough that their consciousness is still sufficiently malleable that the process is smooth but old enough to be deemed emotionally self-sufficient. I can only assume that testing was done and that the New Society, in all their academic wisdom, felt that age ten was the best and final point at which a child could be fully separated from their natural family.

I was not part of this process. I would not have cared to be part of it.[4]

---

4 It's interesting that Dr. Gregory does not mention Dr. Haverstock here. While the author is correct to say that she was not involved in the establishment of the Age Ten Laws, Dr. Haverstock was instrumental in crafting language for standardized processes within that defined the protocols. She was consulted from the earliest stages of testing and approved the final wording of the laws. We have not the faintest idea why Dr. Gregory

Perhaps I could have argued that family separation and state-run child cultivation would be effective for many children, but that to mandate such eradication of natural families would harm us as a species and perhaps create undreamt-of traumas in individuals. But this argument would have been a moral one, without basis in science and philosophy. How to prove righteousness in a field that has no previous study? Impossible. And without evidence for my concerns, my arguments would have been debated into oblivion, wrought into the shape that the Council wanted. So I did not. I cannot regret refraining from an action that never would have worked. And if I'm honest with you, if I'm honest with myself, it would not have occurred to me to get involved, even if I had been paying more attention to what was being proposed. It was not my role. Nora had been right about that.

Anyway.

Irrelevant.

All that matters now is that the Age Ten Laws were passed and rolled out around the globe. The process I had originated—helping children separate from traumatic events in their past—became mandated. And became harsher.

Along with designated therapists at every childhood center and orphanage in the world, I was now tasked by the government with ensuring that children were made to forget, entirely, everything that happened to them before they were ten.

---

would not mention Dr. Haverstock's involvement—it seems unlikely that she wouldn't have known of it. Indeed, given her close relationship with Nora Bostwick, it's possible that it was Dr. Gregory who suggested Dr. Haverstock as a consultant to the Societal Council in the first place.

From this point on, children would be raised from birth in childhood centers. There would be efforts made to ensure that siblings were sent to the same place, the reasoning being that some genetic bond would be valuable during their early years. And then all would go through the Age Ten treatments, forgetting their siblings and friends, before being sent to a different facility to continue their education.

There would be no more parents. There would be no more families. All that was to be severed. It was not until 1960 that all children were required to be state-raised.[5] But in my final, tarnished years at Gateway, we were charged with removing all knowledge of parents, siblings, and secondary family from the orphans.

I don't know why this still seems barbaric to me. After all, I had been severed from my family before I was ten. I got through it. I was fine. Plus, many of the children we served at Gateway had no knowledge of their families in any case, or were keen to forget them.

Irrelevant.

Anyway.

This new work—or new application of the work—wasn't particularly hard on the children. The children went through the program and emerged on the other side without knowing

---

5 The Age Ten Laws stipulated a twelve-year grace period for children born into traditional families, ending in 1960. During this time, financial incentives were made available for parents willing to offer their children to Society-run centers such as Gateway.

This was part of the wider Repopulation Initiative that started in 1948 and still continues today. The early years of the Initiative were marked by aggressive campaigns encouraging civic-minded people to offer themselves as surrogates.

what they'd lost. The parents were another story. They were compensated for their sacrifice. Given money, counseling. Given no other option.[6]

There were those who protested,[7] of course, but plenty supported the law. Gave themselves and their children over to it with regret but willingly. It was the civic-minded thing to do: to support the New Society because it was repairing and rebuilding our shattered world, and no one expects the cost of such a thing to be cheap. The Global Council and its laws were raising our quality of life, keeping streets safe, and providing work and food for those in need. Most important of all, the New Society promised to prevent another war. We would have eternal peace if we would only succumb.

I did understand. Everyone but the very youngest remembered the Reckoning, knew how close we came to the end of everything. "Great Courage for Great Change" was the Society's early rallying cry, and many acolytes jumped to sacrifice all for the hope of a better, more stable life ahead. But a stable life for whom, if not your own children?

You know, it didn't occur to me at the time, but it seems strange to me now that the laws were so inconsistent. Par-

---

6 Untrue. Until 1960, parents were urged but not required to turn their children over to be raised by the Society. Starting in 1960, adults who gave birth to children were immediately free from the burden of raising them.

7 After the Age Ten Laws were first proposed, there were protests in several major cities around the world, but they ultimately proved counterproductive for those opposed to the laws. Violence broke out at several of the protests, including days-long riots in Sydney, Bangkok, and Johannesburg. The casualties were high and served as evidence for the plan. Familial attachments led to conflict. They had to be eradicated.

ents and children were outlawed. Husbands, wives, romantic partners were never questioned.[8] Maybe those relationships weren't considered as dangerous, but this seems unlikely to me. Do people not fight for their lovers?

Of course, the people who drafted the laws had their own lives to think about. Nora once told me how strange things felt with Ekaterina at times. Before the Reckoning, their relationship would have been impossible. At least, impossible to make public. They would have been seen as friends. As spinsters sharing a home.

The world ended, and because it did, Nora could get married. Seems like this should have been simpler. It's probably unfair of me to suggest that Nora was willing to sacrifice the children of strangers, but not to give up her own wife. She was not so small-minded. But still. It makes me wonder.

Anyway, the new protocols soon became rote. It doesn't take long for routines to develop, even when those routines involve tears and regret. I did what was asked of me. I removed memories from children. Then they were taken to academies for higher learning and job placement. The

---

8 By her own admission, Dr. Gregory was not in the habit of keeping a close watch on political matters, so perhaps we should not be surprised that she is mistaken here. There are publicly accessible records of the debates that led to the drafting and passage of laws governing such relationships, as there are for all of the Society's laws. The matter of spouses was brought up, discussed, and voted on. Ultimately, it was decided that almost any interpersonal relationship has the potential to lead to conflict. We fight for our friends as well as our lovers. However, the Council's consensus was that relationships between peers do not have the same inherited prejudices and fears as those between connected generations. Given the psychological dangers of prohibiting any affectionate relationships at all, the idea of separating spouses was dismissed. The wisdom of this is debatable, of course, but it is unfair to suggest that it was never debated in the first place.

Watercolor Quiet was a smoothly efficient machine, when it came to young children. The parents were not my department.

Until they were.


IN 1950, EDGAR HARTLEY WAS brought to me. He was not like the other children. He was older, around fourteen, though he had the body and demeanor of a child of nine or ten. He and his parents had been found living in isolation in the middle of the woods, fifty miles outside Memphis. His parents—whose names I don't remember or, more likely, never knew—had fled there when they were just teenagers themselves.[9] They had built a small shack and lived off the land, hoping the place was remote enough that the tendrils of the war couldn't grab them.

And they were right, in the sense that the violence didn't find them. But no one comes through a war untouched, no matter how far removed from it they are.

The Hartleys and their boy Edgar had ventured out one afternoon from their home in the farthest corner of the forest and discovered neighborhoods they had never seen. Rows of houses, many still in the final stages of construction. It was the first sign they had that the Reckoning was over. The first sign they had that we'd already started to rebuild.

They didn't know that if they came back to us, their

---

9 It was not uncommon, during the Great Reckoning, for people to flee to remote areas and try to ride out the war. But not many of those who did were found alive afterward. There were natural as well as man-made perils, and not everyone who tried to live off the land was an accomplished outdoors-person.

fourteen-year-old son would be taken from them.[10] They were spotted and approached by Peace Officers, who offered them money and housing and counseling. The officers told them there would be education for their son.

What do you choose, in this situation? To rejoin the world, to establish a life in society, to agree to rules put in place during your absence? Or do you stay isolated on your own terms? I don't know how Edgar's parents arrived at the choice they did. I don't know whether much of a choice was given them. But Edgar ended up my patient, and, oh—for that I am grateful.

Sorry too. Achingly sorry. If I had known . . . But I did not and could not have, I don't think.

No, I really don't know how I could have foreseen Edgar's fate. So I am left to be grateful for the time I had with him.

And I had a lot.

Edgar was special. I don't know exactly how. He was clever, but many of the children were clever. He was funny but far from the only one who was. He and I, I think, were simply cut from the same bolt of cloth. Kin, in a way that exists beyond blood.

And something about him suggested to me that, however his parents felt, he was ready—eager even—for a life away from them. He was headed out of the woods and into a world where he could control his own destiny.

I took some time with him before starting him on the

---

10 As stated earlier, the Age Ten Protocols were voluntary until 1960. The Hartleys would have been given the option to continue to raise their son within the New Society, or to give him over to a childhood center in exchange for compensation.

full program. I met with him in his parents' home—the one they had been given just a few weeks earlier. I addressed the events of his life that might make adjusting difficult for him. After all, he had grown up knowing no one but his parents. But eventually I had to start the real work.

He would come to live at Gateway to go through the new, mandated version of the Watercolor Quiet. He would forget his previous life, and once he had he would be moved to an academy for an education. To be prepared for the world.

On his last night with his parents, they had a special party, just for themselves. Burgers, he told me, and cake with ice cream.

I watched his parents drop him off. They'd dressed him in his best clothes. Given him a big red suitcase that made him look so small. Everything was new, of course.

He looked like a child ready to start life anew. He left his parents behind and moved into the childhood center, and it was my job to make him feel as if he'd always been there.

By this time, I could run the Watercolor Quiet without thinking. Whoever you are, you've been through it or something like it. Something built on its bones. It likely would have been called the Protocols when you went through it,[11] and if it was truly effective, you won't remember how it goes. There are breaths. Then there are mantras. Then there are physical exercises that isolate each organ, each limb, each

_____

11 The Formational Protocols was the internal name used for the treatment of children in Childhood Development Centers. They are also commonly called the "Age Ten Protocols." It would not have been called that by the children or by their educators and counselors. It would have simply been called *school*.

joint, each muscle group. They're not for fitness but to re-map the brain's connections to the body. Then there is the Watercolor—figuratively painting blotches of light and shapes on the mind. I describe it as redecorating, but honestly it's more like painting over marks on the walls.

I took Edgar through the program, and it appeared to go without a hitch, so he was placed into the standard develop-mental schedule. I saw each of the children who were living in the center weekly, to both monitor their general well-being and keep track of any unusual responses to the treatments. These meetings consisted of a meditation exercise and an in-formal chat.

A few weeks into his stay at Gateway, Edgar came in a little upset.

"The teacher told the story wrong," he said. "The story of the girl and the damselfly. They said she killed it. She ripped its wings off and left it, and it died. That's not how the story goes."

"Oh?" I replied. "How does it go?"

"She looks at it. She looks at it very hard and very well, and then she says goodbye to it and lets it go. And then she sees it again and says hello, and they become friends, and that is how the story goes."

Edgar's version of this story was incorrect. I knew the old folktale well and had even incorporated it into a meditation exercise as part of the Watercolor Quiet.

There is a girl alone in the woods, and she envisions her-self the ruler of all the world, because she is alone and no one is there to tell her otherwise. She pretends that twigs are magic wands and puddles are lakes and that she is hundreds of feet tall. Then she sees a damselfly, and she captures it in her hand. The girl examines the insect closely, noticing its wings like stained-glass windows, its purple-green iridescent body, and its eyes like amethysts.

The girl tears the wings from the damselfly, and sets the damaged bug on a rock. She is about to kill it when she sees a rabbit. She forgets the damselfly and runs away. A raven arrives on the rock and eats the dying insect. The story is macabre on its surface, but it is a meditation on scientific discovery, on empathy, on learning, on the power of learning alone. It is neither good nor bad that the damselfly dies, because damselflies are eaten all the time. It is neither moral nor immoral that the girl disregards its insignificant life, because humanity disregards insignificant life every second of every day. It is only in context that the listener can make these ethical decisions for themselves.

The story of the girl and the damselfly provides an artistic façade for the scientific regimen of the Quiet. It's accessible and memorable, a touchstone for children to learn how to learn for themselves. But this was not Edgar's experience.

"Who told you your version of the story?" I asked Edgar.

"My mom told me. She told it to me lots, and now the teachers say she was wrong. They told me she lied, but she didn't. My mother never lies."

And so we had a complication.

# *Fourteen*

I REALLY DO NOT KNOW HOW PARENTS ARE SUPPOSED TO BEHAVE.

*Were* supposed to behave is more accurate, of course, because now there are no parents. There have been no parents for decades. I wonder if there is anyone alive who understands what parenting entailed. What it looked like. What counted as bad parenting and what counted as good.

There cannot be many people much older than myself, and I of course have no memories of life before the Great Reckoning. And while I'm sure they tried, I don't think anyone during that period could be called a model, or normal, parent. Parenting is a luxury—all we had was survival.

I suppose that in the years after the end of the Reckoning and before the implementation of the Age Ten Laws, there were normal parents. Something approaching normal parents. Maybe I'm showing my ignorance here. Maybe I'm just admitting that I never really thought about parents, despite spending years treating children. Those I had known—my own, the Jacobs—had faded into the past. They didn't seem relevant, now that the world was so different from how it had been in my own childhood.

I had then, and have now, no metric by which to measure Edgar's parents. I had not thought that I would need to measure them. I'd had little to do with the parents of other children at the center, and never imagined that I should. My job was to separate the children from their connection to their parents. There was no reason for me to step outside the bounds of my responsibilities. I assigned interviews and paperwork to other staff.

Perhaps I—

No. We don't need to come to this quite yet.

So the boy had failed the treatment. He misremembered the damselfly story. And he remembered his parents—at least, he remembered his mother—so I had more work to do with him.

I ran Edgar through the program again, making adjustments, skipping over some of the more basic steps we'd already taken and pushing through to more advanced techniques. I extended the process to four weeks instead of the usual two, I took more time over each stage, hitting more firmly on the crucial moments. I was more careful, more thorough—I thought that perhaps I'd been taking my skills and knowledge too much for granted, that I had missed something simple the first time around.

I would not make that mistake a second time.

As before, after the Watercolor Quiet was finished, we went back to standard weekly sessions. At our first few of these, I asked probing questions about Edgar's parents to test whether the treatment had worked this time.

"What is your mother's middle name?" I would ask, or "Does your father like bluegrass music?" and closely monitor his reactions. He never responded to such questions, though they tended to make him pause for a moment with a look of confusion. But who wouldn't be confused if someone kept asking them about parents they didn't know existed? So perhaps we were safe.

And then:

Once again, it was a complaint about life at the center. As we chatted during one session, I asked him about his day. How he was getting on with his friends, if he'd enjoyed his lunch.

"It was okay," he replied.

"Only okay?" I asked.

"Yeah," he said. "We had salmon. My dad makes it better."

I took a beat. Another failure. Then I continued.

"Tell me how your dad cooks salmon."

"He used to put something on it."

"A sauce?"

He thought for a moment. "Not a sauce. He made it sticky? I think he made something with berries, and when he made salmon, he would spread it on, and it made it sticky."

"Ah," I said. "I think you mean a glaze."

"Maybe."

"And you liked it better? Your father's glaze?"

"Yeah. I liked it."

I paused for a moment, then:

"Do you miss him?"

"What?"

"Do you miss your dad?"

He didn't answer. He wouldn't look at me. I sighed.

"Okay," I said. "That's fine. I think that's enough for today. You go back to your lessons."

The Watercolor Quiet doesn't erase the mind so much as it reorganizes it, packs unnecessary information and feelings into boxes. Edgar was older than most of the children I worked with, so it was not surprising that things were a little bit more complicated, his memories a little more stubborn. But I would have expected to see a specific item like salmon glaze confined to a place where his brain could not so easily access it.

I began to worry that our entrance interviews were failing us. Each child brought into the center went through several detailed interviews, as did their parents and other caregivers. The purpose was to build as accurate as possible a picture of the child's life so far—from important life moments to the details of ordinary, daily existence. We relied heavily on these interviews in the treatment—they gave us crucial insights about how to adapt it to each child's experiences.

If a child remembered a special salmon glaze his father prepared, for example, we would alter that to a barbecued brisket in his mind, or a blackened catfish. And we could place the child in the dining area of the facility. It's not possible to remap every single memory. Just as memories can be deliberately hidden, so can memories hide without our knowledge, out of sight of the most prying of eyes. But if you change enough of them, there's a tipping point over which the others topple.

It only takes a few weeks to see marked change in most children. But something in Edgar was different. It's unsurprising now. Looking back, it seems like something I should have expected. Nothing is one hundred percent successful for one hundred percent of people. But I was naive. I thought I was jaded. Burned out by the experiences of my life so far.

And I was. But being jaded—having experienced the world at its most brutal—doesn't prevent naivete. It robs you of innocence but can leave you credulous.

I told Rosemary about the incongruities in Edgar's progress. I urged her to revisit our interview protocols.

"I'll review our procedures for enrollment," she said, "but I don't think the problem is in our information-gathering. I think it's in Edgar."

"He's not adapting well to the program," I conceded.

"Miri, how many children have you served?"

"Me? Hundreds, maybe five, six hundred?"

"Six hundred!" she cried. "And that's just you. Think of the thousand or more children whose lives have been improved by your work. And the lapse rate is?"

"Zero."

"You've not had a single child return for reprogramming."

"Counseling," I corrected.

"Counseling. But even you must have been expecting a failure at some point. Someone who didn't adapt to it so readily."

Edgar had only been with us for eight months at that point. He was certainly showing progress, but it was mild, and he often regressed within days. Rosemary had a good point. Nothing is truly universal.

"If it makes you feel better," Rosemary continued, "his parents aren't faring much better in their treatments."

"You think there's something genetic that prevents them from internalizing the counseling?"

"That's what I'm trying to find out."

I decided to audit a session with Edgar's parents.

The Hartleys were undergoing their treatment at a nearby facility that catered to adults.

The focus of the adult centers was slightly different, designed more to help them adapt to everyday life after the turmoil of the Reckoning. Participants were assessed for education level, for natural abilities, for passions and interests. They received career counseling that would lead either to a new job within the Society or to a training program. And for those who, like the Hartleys, were undergoing separation protocols from their children, there was additional treatment to ease the pain of goodbye.

There was a different version of the Protocols, the Watercolor Quiet for adults. They were not required to lose their memories, but they were helped to detach from them. While going through this scaled-back version of the treatment, adults were offered the chance to stay at the facility. Given the daily sessions required, this eased the burden of participation.

The Hartleys had been staying there for five weeks, having failed to show progress after one round of treatment.

They were funny and charming. They were flippant about their regression. Like tourists on sacred ground, they were there for the experience but unable to truly accept the spirit of the treatment.

After their session, I asked to speak with them and was granted permission. I began my discussion as if just gathering feedback: "How has your stay been?" "Are you comfortable?" "Do you have questions about the Watercolor Quiet?"

So we chatted about that for a while before I asked them about their son.

Mrs. Hartley was silent for a moment. Her mouth trembled, and she swallowed hard before replying.

"It was horrible," she said eventually. "Giving birth—I didn't know, I hadn't—"

She broke off for a moment before:

"When we ran, we didn't think of what could happen. We were stupid, I suppose, but we just didn't account for it."

Mr. Hartley broke in to back her up. "We'd planned how we would survive, of course," he said. "We stockpiled enough food to last us for however long until we'd found somewhere okay to camp out. Somewhere near a river, you know, for fish, and with space to grow vegetables and things. We had tools and equipment; we knew how to build a house. Well, a shack, I guess. A cabin. We thought of everything we'd need to survive, we just—"

"We didn't think of what might happen if we did," she said. "I mean, we knew what we'd . . ."

"It didn't occur to us we might have a baby," Mr. Hartley said.

There was a pause. Mrs. Hartley shivered.

"It was horrible," she repeated.

"You were lucky you only had one, I suppose," I said.

Her face went white.

"No," she said. "Not lucky. I wasn't lucky at all."

Mrs. Hartley was silent, and I didn't know how to ask what she meant. But after a moment her husband stepped in to clarify.

"It didn't go right. I had to—I didn't know how to help, but I had to do something. I did my best, but I ain't a doctor. So."

"I went to see someone when we first got back," she said. "They said it's a miracle I survived at all, and I have to have surgery to fix . . . what he did. But. No more babies."

"I'm sorry," I said.

"Oh, that's okay," she replied. "You're not wrong, really. About us being lucky. It was horrible. I wish it hadn't happened. But it was hard enough with just him. With Edgar. Sometimes I wished we hadn't—"

She fell silent.

After a moment, Mr. Hartley asked, "How long do we have to keep coming up here for these sessions?"

"Completion of the contract requires completion of the program," I said.

"They told us three weeks," Mrs. Hartley said. "We've been doing these for longer than that."

"Three weeks is standard, but the program is not completed until you pass all tests and interviews."

"So how long will that take?" Mrs. Hartley asked.

"It's impossible to know for sure. It could take a couple of months. Maybe more."

"And when will we get the rest of the compensation?"

"On completion. When you're both signed off as having successfully received the treatment."

"And that could take months."

"It's unusual for it to take that long, but yes, theoretically."

"Well, we misunderstood," Mr. Hartley said, looking at his wife.

"Yes," I said, trying to appear sympathetic. "The Society has to be sure everyone who agrees to the protocols has been successfully treated. And it's better for you. If you were to leave without completing the program, you would miss your son. It would make you sad and angry. No amount of money can heal that kind of grief."

"Of course," Mrs. Hartley said to the floor, lost in thought.

"The counseling is to help you live your life freely and comfortably," I reassured her. "Do you feel you have not been able to make progress despite your best efforts?"

"No, no," Mr. Hartley said. "No, I think we were just enjoying ourselves too much."

"That's right." Mrs. Hartley brightened. "It's a nice center. The beds are so comfortable. There's a cinema."

"And the food," Mr. Hartley said. "It's nice to not have to worry about food for a change."

"Everyone here's just so nice, too," Mrs. Hartley added.

"Well, that's great to hear," I said. "But if you can give the program your all, you'll find even greater comfort in your new home. This part of your lives is temporary—once it's completed, you'll be able to build a real future. A real life."

"Yes," he said.

"Absolutely," she said. "We're sorry to have been fooling around so much. Wasting your time."

"I just want the best results for everyone," I said.

"We promise." Mr. Hartley gave me a toothy grin. His smile was contagious. "Cross our hearts."

"And we'll tell Edgar to get in shape too," she said.

"Well." I hesitated. "It's not possible for you to see Edgar. But I promise he's doing fine."

Mrs. Hartley did not look at all reassured, but she and her husband were still grinning.

# Fifteen

THE HARTLEYS DID IMPROVE. AFTER ANOTHER COUPLE OF WEEKS, they completed the program and passed their assessment. They returned to the home they'd been provided, and both started on new career paths. Mrs. Hartley, I believe, was studying economics, while her husband was working as a baker.

Protocol at that time dictated weekly visits from counselors, and Edgar's parents continued to pass cleanly. They seemed to have successfully detached from their memories of their time in the forest, and of Edgar. The contract had been fulfilled. They could live happily and comfortably ever after, and Edgar was a ward of the New Society.

Edgar improved as well, for a time. He began to demonstrate measurable progress in his treatment.

"Do you like salmon, Edgar?"

"I've never had salmon."

"Tell me about the girl and the damselfly."

"I like the raven, because the raven is nature, and nature is community."

But eventually he began to backslide. It was not the same regression as before. Instead of failing to internalize his therapy, this time he grew despondent. These bouts of despair were not frequent, but they were intense. He could not concentrate. He would cry and wail.[1]

It was natural for children in our care to struggle with depression, sadness, and separation anxiety, but those issues were always sorted out early in the process. Of course, new anxieties would crop up as the children aged. Feelings of insecurity are innate in humans. However, I had never experienced a child whose memory had lapsed but whose emotions had not.

Edgar's problems were now more difficult to solve, because I had no tangible memories or experiences to connect to his emotional outbursts. I was certain his sadness was related to his family, but he could no longer remember his family. I did not know how to help him.

"Why are you sad, Edgar?"

"I don't know?"

"Did anything unusual happen today in class?"

"No."

I considered restarting the entire Watercolor Quiet treatment with Edgar, but I could not reintroduce him to his family. We had already reorganized the library of his mind. It would be a dangerous shock to his system to jumble it again. It could destabilize his sense of trust in the world, and we might not get him back.

Rosemary took great interest in Edgar's case. Outliers are

---

1 Edited for clarity. The preceding several pages were faintly printed, suggesting that Dr. Gregory had to replace her typewriter ribbon. The last few paragraphs were nearly unreadable until we held the original pages against a backlight to read the shadows of the keystroke indentations.

vital to scientific research. They are maddening, of course, but theories can only be proved through a thorough and consistent lack of disproof.

Rosemary had been right, of course, when she suggested that encountering someone resistant to the Watercolor Quiet was inevitable—but however natural a flaw may be, it's still a flaw. Eventually the head of our institution got involved in Edgar's case. I began to lose control of my subject. And my work was questioned.

I had to provide comprehensive case notes and reports. Two different psychiatrists were hired to study Edgar Hartley, and I could see it wearing away his patience and his confidence. Everyone had a different opinion on what to do. Someone suggested medication. Someone else suggested music therapy. Someone else suggested increasing his workload. Someone else suggested reducing his workload.

My patience and confidence were wearing away too. Rosemary told me I needed to take a break.

"I have too many charges to oversee," I rebutted. "If I took time off work, they would fall behind in their development. I can only handle one struggling child at a time."

"I mean, take a break from Edgar," she said. "Let me take his case. You could be helping dozens of children instead of just one. And you'd do a great job."

"I'm doing a great job now." I was defensive. Edgar's success was my success.

"Of course you are. I can't imagine what a wreck he would be if anyone but you had worked with him. But maybe the best choice now is to switch up the treatment."

I looked at Rosemary. She wanted this. She had never shown an interest in working with the children. She was focused on research, but here she was with pleading eyes, like a dog in a kitchen begging for a piece of ham.

"No," I said. This clearly surprised Rosemary. "It's my methodology that's in question here. It will work, or it will not work. Either way, I'm responsible for it."

I offered Rosemary the chance to work with any number of other, much more typical children, if she was interested in developing her skills as a therapist or mastering the Watercolor Quiet, but she declined. And I declined to give up control of Edgar's case.

I chose to expand Edgar's schedule while decreasing his time in the Watercolor Quiet. He was put on the basketball team, and he began learning to play drums in the band. I had spent so much time one-on-one with the boy; I theorized that I was holding him too tightly, not allowing him to forge new relationships with other kids.

This plan was acceptable to our director and could buy me some time. Which is to say: it got her and everyone else off my back.

In the evenings, after dinner, I would work with Edgar privately. We did breathing and visualization exercises, but we also talked about his friends, about the food, about the games he played. None of what I asked him was pointed toward the Watercolor Quiet. It was not an attempt to solidify his new memories. It was simply a way to engage him, make him feel connected, make him feel loved.

To my surprise, these moments worked. Over the next several weeks, Edgar stopped crying and retreating into himself. He was retaining his new memories. He was demonstrating that he could pass his examinations. He was not only forgetting his parents but showing that he was emotionally unaffected by the separation.

Again, it didn't last.

At seven in the evening, children were returned to their rooms for private reflection—a half-hour session in which they listened to music alone with their eyes closed. In the final ten minutes, they were to journal their thoughts. These journals were reviewed weekly by our staff.

At 7:30 one evening, I met Edgar in the music room for one of our off-the-record chats. He told me about learning to dribble a basketball between his legs, even though that was against the rules during a game. He was anxious to show me. We didn't have a ball in the music room, and he offered to run to the gymnasium to get one. I said he could show me later.

Edgar told me a joke that Stacy Wenell told him at lunch. He said he laughed so hard that milk came out of his nose. The joke involved a hippopotamus trying to drive a car but then accidentally swallowing the steering wheel. The hippo had to turn its head back and forth to steer the vehicle. Edgar demonstrated, as Stacy had demonstrated to him, and his re-telling made him laugh again. I smiled, glad to see he was feeling so happy, so communicative.

I told Edgar that I was proud of him. I told him he had done great work. I explained that he had earned a break from these demanding evening meetings with me. Starting tomorrow, he would have his evenings free to watch television or read or play games with his friends. He and I would have some time away from each other.

His friendly smile, a faint echo of his laughter from moments before, sagged into a frown. His eyes watered. His despair had returned, and swiftly. Clearly I had said something that triggered a regression. This was terrible, but I was momentarily delighted. I could analyze this conversation, run tests to pinpoint which elements set off his emotional response. His crying was a setback, yes, but it could lead to new data.

Then he lunged at me. For a moment I thought he was about to attack me, and I stood up from my chair, but he did not attack. He hugged me. He held tightly to my waist and sobbed.

"Please don't," he wailed. "I like talking to you."

I held my arms up like wings, trying to understand what was happening. Embracing children in the program was not conducive to their progress. It was a form of parental love. In certain sessions, we deconstructed forms of touch, such as hugs and kisses on the cheek or forehead. But these took place in a controlled, heavily monitored environment, and they were meant to reprogram memories of nurture into an understanding of platonic contact.

"I love you," he wheezed into my hip. "Don't leave me."

"I won't," I said. I lowered my hands to his back and reciprocated the hug. It felt nice. I loved him too. And I was failing him because of this. "But for tonight we are done. I'll see you tomorrow night. Okay?"

"Okay." He wiped his face.

At that moment, the door to the music room opened.

"Oh, sorry!" came a voice. "Didn't realize anyone was in here. Was just going to turn off the light."

It was Rosemary.

"It's fine," I said. "We're just finishing up." I looked at

Edgar—he had wiped the tears from his cheeks, but his eyes were still puffy and red.

"Working late," Rosemary said.

There was judgment in her voice. I had not included these informal chats in my plan to the director, and I had not told Rosemary about them either. She had caught me working extra hours with Edgar, after having made clear that she disapproved of my excessive attention to his case.

"Hello, Edgar," she said.

"Hello, ma'am."

The three of us entered the hallway, and I told Edgar to return to his room. He said goodnight and turned to walk away. I was thankful he did not try to hug me again in front of Rosemary.

"He looked like he was crying. Did he regress again?" she asked.

"No, not at all," I lied. "He told a joke and made himself laugh till he cried."

"I'd like to hear that joke."

"I promise it will not have the same effect." I smiled. Rosemary smiled too.

We said our goodnights, and as I started to leave, Rosemary said, "Miri."

"Yes?"

"The head of the DCD came in today.[2] They want to take over Edgar's case."

---

2 The Department of Childhood Development, established in 1944 to oversee the consolidation of childhood centers and to set up and see through the repopulation program.

"Immediately?"

"Immediately," she said. And then: "I'm sorry, Miri. You really have made great progress. It's just that Edgar . . . well, his situation has merited a lot of attention."

I had nothing else to say, and I left.

I wonder if I would have behaved differently, had I known? That's a stupid question. Of course I would have. I would have taken him and run.

If I'd known that farewell was our final farewell, I would have done anything to prevent it.

# *Sixteen*

By 10:00 THE NEXT MORNING, THE ENTIRE STAFF CONCLUDED that Edgar was no longer on the premises. A search of the area began.

I supposed I should have been worried about the program as a whole. Clearly the DCD was. The system was still young, still establishing itself. It wasn't yet strong enough to withstand doubt, and there were those who would see this chink in the structure of the Watercolor Quiet as evidence that the whole endeavor was flawed. I should have been concerned about that, really. But I confess that all my mind was on Edgar. Had I lost him? Lost all our progress together?[1]

I had a hunch. My hunch would prove tragically wrong, but how could I have known?

I left the center and drove to the home of Edgar's parents.

When I arrived, they invited me in, and we sat in their living room. They were surprised to get a visit from me, or from anyone involved in the learning center, reminding me

---

1 Edited for clarity. Handwritten note in the margin of the original manuscript.

they had completed the program and only had to do weekly check-ins. My visit, of course, was not only unscheduled but completely against protocol. If Edgar was here, I wanted to find him before anyone else did.

"I'm sorry," I said. "I just had a few questions. Won't take but a few minutes."

They had their television set on; a morning news program was reporting on the reopening of the George Washington Bridge in New York City.[2] Mrs. Hartley turned the volume to low, but the flickering images remained, pulsing cold light into the otherwise poorly lit living room.

It was a nice enough house, but it had not been well maintained. There were newspapers and dishes strewn across end tables and countertops. They did not have many lamps or a fan, and with the windows and drapes closed, the room was stuffy and dark save for the television.

I clipped a heart rate monitor to an index finger on each of them and read from a list of standard questions about their current life. Name, age, what they had for breakfast, etc. These were to verify their retention of necessary short- and long-term memories. Then I ad-libbed. Typically the questionnaires use simple prompts, asking the subjects to describe animals or places or smells or foods. They're designed to see if the descriptors trigger unnecessary memories or emotions. If there's no noticeable change in heart rate or facial expression, and if no unsatisfactory answers are given, then the interview is a success.

---

2 The George Washington Bridge had been partially destroyed in 1932. The rebuild was completed in 1951.

The questions I asked though were not standard or typical.

"Has anyone visited your home in the past twenty-four hours?"

"Just you," said Mr. Hartley with a deep chuckle.

No change in heart rate.

"Do you receive guests in your home?"

"Only if you count the mice." He laughed again.

No change in heart rate or facial expression.

He laughed a lot. It was his attempt to ingratiate himself. He did this all the time, and what feels charming in short bursts of casual conversation was, in this moment, annoying me.

"Yes or no, Mr. Hartley," I said.

"I answered your question," he said. "Lighten up."

"Mrs. Hartley," I said, hoping she'd be more helpful than her husband, "do you receive guests in your home?"

"We already answered that question." Mr. Hartley's jolly veneer was chipping away, revealing a rough tone underneath.

"I think Mrs. Hartley can answer the question," I said, looking straight at her. She did not look me in the eye.

"Mrs. Hartley."

"No," she blurted, and the light on the heart monitor flashed.

"Has anyone in your family been—"

Mr. Hartley cut me off. "You're making her nervous," he shouted.

The heart monitor light continued to flash. It was not a highly accurate indicator of a lie. But my hunch was strong enough that I trusted it wasn't a false positive.

"Your son, Edgar, has been sneaking out of the center to spend time here. Is that true?" I asked. I hadn't pieced it together until the night before, when Edgar hugged me. His depression came from his lack of complete detachment.

"Son? That's ludicrous—we don't have a son!" Mr. Hartley exclaimed, taking the heart monitor from his finger. He reached over and did the same for his wife. He was smiling again, but this belied the anger in his voice.

"After I visited with you at the center, you vowed to do better. You vowed that Edgar would do better." I laid out my accusation. "And you did. The whole Hartley family pulled together and completed their exams with great speed. But really you didn't. You beat the system, and you coached Edgar to do so too."

"We didn't . . ." Mrs. Hartley tried to interject, but I continued.

"You knew it would be just four more years till Edgar turned eighteen, and he would be turned loose into the world as an adult. But you knew that if you could keep visiting with him . . . what? Once? Twice a week? You could keep your child."

"That's quite a story," Mr. Hartley said, grinning.

"So what will you do?" Mrs. Hartley said, still not looking up from her lap. "Will you write up your report? Have us removed from our home? Sent back to the woods? Or will you imprison us, like you have our son?"

"I have a job to do," I said. "I have obligations to the Society. To the Council."

Mr. Hartley had walked to the window. He was peeking outside to see if I had come alone. I began to question my judgment in coming here at all.

"You ain't writing down nothing," he commanded, stepping toward me. I wondered if he planned to assault me or just intimidate me with his large frame. "Because none of this is true."

"It is true, though. Isn't it, Mrs. Hartley," I said, and she dropped her head. "But you're right. I'm not writing any of this down."

He halted.

"I didn't tell anyone that I was coming here today," I continued. "And I've told no one of my suspicion. I just wanted to know if Edgar had come here last night or this morning."

"No!" Mr. Hartley snapped.

"No?" I was dubious.

"No," Mrs. Hartley said, looking concerned.

Her response stunned me. I had been so confident that my hunch was right. I'd known everything that was going to happen: that they would pretend ignorance, that Mr. Hartley would be so boisterous as to override the heart monitors, that I would catch them in a lie by appealing to Mrs. Hartley's emotions. I trusted Mrs. Hartley, and her answer about Edgar's whereabouts was believable—and disheartening.

"Oh," I said, my face slack, my mind blank.

Mrs. Hartley seized on my stumble. "You look surprised," she said, standing up. I remained seated below her. "Why do you look surprised? Do you not know where our son is?"

"Well, it's . . ." I began speaking before knowing exactly what I was going to say. I couldn't tell them he was missing, but I couldn't very well deny it either. I had given myself away. I thought of saying that children sometimes run away from the center, which was true, even if it had been years since anyone had.

But any runaway undermined our authority and competence. Plus, this was a couple that had clearly skirted completing their therapy. We could take action against them—at the very least they could be fined—but if we had lost their boy, they could destroy the public's trust in the Protocols. The fact that their memories were unchanged could be reframed as our incompetence rather than their deception.

I could not decide quickly enough, but it didn't matter. Mrs. Hartley continued, "You don't know. I see it on your face. A mother sees these things. A mother knows these things."

Her voice crescendoed to a shout. "Tell me what happened to my boy!"

She was leaning over me. Mr. Hartley was without words or smile, a rarity for him.

"I'm looking for him," I promised her. "That's why I came here. I saw him last night shortly after eight, walking to his dorm room. But none of the other children saw him return to his room. And this morning he was not on campus."

This information did not calm Mrs. Hartley, but she stayed quiet.

"We're all looking for him now. He may have very well already been found," I continued. "I came here first because I knew he missed you. I realized it last night, during my session with him. He had grown so sad, so lonely. I thought it was a byproduct of his therapy, but last night he hugged me, told me not to leave, and I knew. I knew he still wanted his mother. He wanted you, Mrs. Hartley."

Mrs. Hartley was looking into my eyes, and I did not stop looking into hers.

"It was then," I said, "that I understood he'd been seeing

you both, regularly. His sadness was from separation, from being forced to live the rest of his life away from you. He was trying so hard not to lose any of his memories—and succeeding. But he was also keeping all of this a secret. It hurts to keep secrets. It hurts to know something about yourself, about your life, that you cannot tell anyone for fear of reprisal."

Mrs. Hartley sat back down opposite me. I placed my hand on hers as I leaned forward.

"I'm sorry, Mrs. Hartley. I am. And I will find Edgar."

She pulled her hand away. "Yes," she said. "You will."

# Seventeen

WHEN I GOT BACK TO THE CENTER, I WAS GREETED AT THE front entrance by a man in a dark suit and sunglasses. He told me to follow him.

"I need to go to my office first," I said. He was already walking down the corridor.

"That's where I'm taking you," he said.

"I know where my office is, so why am I following you?"

"Because I told you to," he said. "It will be better if you don't talk so much."

"Did they find the boy?" I asked.

"Yes," he said.

"Is he okay?" I asked.

He stopped. We were in front of my office. He gestured for me to enter, as if I were a guest and this were his office. "Have a seat," he said.

"I asked if he was okay," I said.

"And I told you to have a seat."

I stepped into the room and sat at my desk. He pulled up a chair across from me.

"Tell me about your relationship to Edgar Hartley," he said, taking out a pad and pen.

"Are you with the police?" I asked.

"Tony Muñoz, Internal Investigations Division, St. Louis office," he said. He pulled an identification card from his wallet and held it up to me: his face and the IID logo. I was unaware that there was any such department.[1] To you, I suppose, it's beyond questioning. For you, I suppose, whoever you are, they've always existed.

"I don't know the Internal Investigations Division, St. Louis office," I said. "Is this new?"

He pulled his badge away and slid it back into his coat. He was still wearing his sunglasses. Outside, the clouds were gathering.

"Tell me about your relationship to Edgar Hartley," he said.

"He's one of my wards," I replied. He didn't look up or say anything. His pen stopped while writing the word *ward* and then hovered over the page, so I continued.

"We treat children who have suffered trauma, or who have been orphaned. We take them through the Age Ten Protocols and prepare them for higher education."

"You're an orphanage," he said. "Yeah, I already know that. Who are you? How do you know the boy?"

"He's one of dozens of children I work with in therapy, to help them with their emotions, their memories. I just explained this . . ."

---

1 The Internal Investigations Division was established in 1949 to serve as an international force tasked with looking into situations or persons who could prove dangerous to the New Society and its citizens.

"You took a special interest in Edgar, though," Muñoz said. He wasn't asking questions. He was dictating a misleading if not outright dangerous narrative.

"I take a special interest in all of the children here," I said. "Is Edgar all right?"

"You tell me," he said.

"You said someone found him," I said. "I haven't seen him since last night. I've been looking for him."

"That's where you were this morning," he said, "looking for the boy. And you were at . . ."

"I went to his parents' house."

Muñoz nodded. I had confirmed what he already knew. "And last night, you were the last person to see him, at . . ." He flipped through his notes. ". . . approximately eight fifteen P.M."

"Yes. Rosemary was with me. My assistant."

"Yep." He stood up to leave.

"I thought you'd ask me more questions," I said.

"Not just at the moment," he said. "Stay here, though. Don't leave."

"I have a session with another child at eleven forty-five," I protested.

"Stay here," he repeated. "Don't leave."

He shut me in my own office, and I sat dumbfounded. Where was Edgar? What had he done? Had he run away and then told a story about me? Had he told them I encouraged him to leave? Had he told someone I had acted inappropriately? Perhaps I had triggered something in him, and Edgar had left the building and done someone or something harm.

I decided I would give Officer Muñoz a few minutes, and

if he hadn't come back I would go find someone else who could answer my questions. But before I could get up, my door opened again. It was Rosemary.

"Miri," she said urgently, "where have you been?"

"Looking for Edgar," I said.

"You shouldn't have left. I've been looking for you all morning. They've been looking for you all morning."

"Well, if by 'they' you mean the IID, they found me."

"That's not good, Miri."

"I heard they found him. Is Edgar okay?" I asked.

Her face darkened. She looked sad, almost ashamed.

"Rosemary, what happened to Edgar?"

"I don't have much time, and neither do you. So just do what I tell you to."

"What happened to Edgar?"

"He's dead," she said.

The room spun, and I couldn't think straight. If I had been standing, I might have fainted. "What . . ." I couldn't think of the word. ". . . happened?" I finally spat out.

"They don't know," she said. She was impatient with my question. "But I have something more important to tell you in a very short amount of time. Listen to me."

But I couldn't. I could barely focus on her words at all. How could I focus on anything?

"Rosemary, no," I whispered. "It can't be true. He can't be dead."

I could still feel his arms around me, still see his pleading eyes, begging me not to leave him.

"We've spent so much time with him. He's made so much progress. He has a life ahead of him. He *has* to."

"Miriam," Rosemary said. "Look at me."

I gulped and took a breath and looked her in the eye, and I couldn't help but see the truth there.

"Tell me how he died," I said.

"They found him in an empty lot," she said. "It's marked for development, but it's been sitting unused for years. Completely overgrown. It's not far from here, about two miles."

"How did he die?" I tried to slow the pace of my speech, hoping that this would slow Rosemary's. It worked, a bit.

"They don't know."

"What do you mean, they don't know? Was he shot? Stabbed? Did he fall? There must be something that indicated how he died."

"They don't know, because his body was . . ." She paused, choosing her words carefully. ". . . not immediately recognizable. Miri, it was torn open."

I gasped. My face hurt. I wanted to cry—not for catharsis but for liquid relief for my burning eyes. It was horrible to hear, and must have been even more terrible to have seen. But I wanted to see him. I wanted to see him to know it was him. To know this wasn't a nightmare, or worse, a lie.

"Torn open," I repeated. "By animals? Coyotes or . . . ?"

"They don't know. I hope coyotes."

"What an awful way to die," I said. "Wait—why do you hope it was coyotes?"

"Do you want them to say it was murder?" she demanded. "Listen, Miri. It's terrible what happened to Edgar. I share your grief. I do. And we will know more soon. But I need you to listen to me, okay? Can you do that?"

I drew a deep breath and said, "Yes."

And then I listened. "You need to leave," she said. "Not just the center but this whole area. It doesn't matter where. Just go far away."

"What are you talking about?"

"I wish it were different. I want you to stay. You're too valuable to lose. I'm only telling you to leave because I want you safe. It is not safe here."

"Rosemary—"

"I think the IID believes Edgar was murdered. They haven't confirmed that yet, but they haven't ruled it out either, and they're asking a lot of very pointed questions if they think it was animals. I don't think they suspect you or me or anyone here. Not yet, anyway. But they're going to want answers."

"And I'll tell them everything I know," I said.

"Not necessary. Secretary Marshall is on her way here today. And she's going to smooth this over."

"Secretary Marshall? What does any of this have to do with her?"

"She can help us."

"Why would she help us? Her of all people?"

"I've told you. She's come around on this center. On you. She knows that what we do is important; she knows the Society can't afford for people to lose faith in the Age Ten Protocols."

I didn't say anything, but my face must have shown how I was feeling because Rosemary rolled her eyes and softened her tone.

"Miri, I know the Secretary well. We've met frequently since she first started championing our work. I gave her tours of our facility. I cultivated this relationship over many years. I've been able to make her understand things, and we've grown close."

"And you think she can help with this?"

"The Society cannot have children dying violently. Nor can they have children failing their therapies. And especially, the Society cannot have public scrutiny of a very grisly case, not in the infancy of the Age Ten Laws. The Hartley family is a danger not just to our center but to the Society's plan. It's cynical, yes, I know. But it's also the hard truth."

She continued: "Secretary Marshall has the Hartley family's paperwork, and she will see to it that the parents are treated with great care for their trauma. She will ensure they are well compensated. She will see to it that they do not speak further of Edgar's death, because they will not know of Edgar's death. But Edgar's death will be a story. A dead boy is always a story."

I was beginning to feel queasy. I still hadn't fully taken things in.

"He was a difficult child," Rosemary continued. "He did not deserve to die. No one here wanted him dead. It is a terrible, terrible tragedy. But he struggled to make friends, to adapt to his environment, and he did not want to be here. He was constantly running away. Isn't that what you discovered?

"And in the end he did run away, and he met with a terrible accident. A tragedy. But we have all learned so much from it. And many changes will be made. His death is not the fault of the Watercolor Quiet, nor of the Age Ten Protocols. His death was not the fault of this center, or of anyone who works here.

"But Miriam, your treatment of Edgar toward the end was unorthodox. You changed your methodology against your better judgment and without prior approval of senior staff. You hid it from everyone. And the results, while not your intention, were disastrous."

I was breathing hard by this point, desperate, but the tears wouldn't come. I was still struggling to take in what Rosemary was saying.

"This isn't coming from me. It's not my decision. I was just asked to talk to you about it. To tell you that you are being removed from your position. You won't be charged with anything, but you will take the fall for this. I will stay here to work with Secretary Marshall to protect what you have created. And to protect you.

"The Secretary has excellent connections, and I'm certain I can get the IID to drop the case, to write it up as an accident, and to have your name removed from any press we attract about this. But you have to leave. Today. Do you understand?"

I didn't fully understand. I knew that Edgar was dead. Whether by human or animal or his own doing, it didn't matter. What mattered is that he suffered, and I failed him. What mattered is that I was considered responsible for his death. What mattered is that I could not stay and fight against the IID—an opaque agency whose reach I could not even begin to imagine. I did not want to go to prison. I wanted even less to go through months or years of interrogations and trials.[2]

---

2 The official report on the death of Edgar Hartley is a matter of public record. The IID ruled that his death was a homicide but failed to name a suspect in the case.

Finally, I knew that my time here was done, that I had little choice but to leave.

I wanted to say all of this, but before I could, the door opened. It was Officer Muñoz.

"Marshall's here. She wants to see you," he said to Rosemary.

"Do you understand?" Rosemary pleaded once more with me.

"Yes," I said.

"We'll see each other again," she said. "But don't write or call. Not for a while, okay?"

She touched my shoulder briefly, then quickly turned and left. I felt certain it would be the last time I would see her. And in that moment, her departure filled me with sorrow. But now I wish I had been right.

# Interlude

At this point there is a further gap in Dr. Gregory's account, albeit a significantly smaller one. Employee records of the Gateway Childhood Center, while scattershot at the beginning of Miriam's tenure there, were scrupulous by the time she left, placing her exit in the autumn of 1951.

Miriam's account picks up again roughly two years later, in 1953.

Unlike the previous lapse in the narrative, however, for this one we have some awareness of what the doctor was doing because her work became a matter of public record. Her practices had already influenced public policy, of course, and we are entering the only period in her life when she discussed them directly with the public.

By all accounts, she moved to Baltimore fairly soon after departing Gateway. Whether or not it was her aim in moving there, she had access to much greater resources for research in Baltimore, as the libraries of both Johns Hopkins and Georgetown were made available to her. She gave occasional lectures at both institutions during her years in the area, though she did not seek full-time employment at either, claiming she preferred to work independently.

It was during this time that Miriam first began to write about her work for publication.

Her first book, *A Farewell to Trauma*, was published in February of 1953; she claimed to have worked on it full time for eighteen months. The book is a dry psychological text that seeks to explore how experiences during childhood can impact one's ability to manage adult life.

Dr. Gregory would concentrate on academia over the following years. Rather than returning to work with children herself, she chose to operate as a consultant to childhood centers that needed help, to work on further psychological publications (both in medical journals and books), and occasionally to teach psychology students.

After the rather shocking ending of the previous section, it behooves us to urge the reader to maintain some emotional distance from the text. As Miriam brings in more sensational (and unlikely) accounts, it is easy to lose perspective.

Such histrionic episodes are among the key reasons we questioned the wisdom of publishing the manuscript at all. There is no value in provoking outbreaks of feeling over events that may never have occurred, and forming an undue emotional connection to the subjects of the text only serves to further muddy its already silt-ridden waters.

The value of this manuscript lies chiefly in that it is a rare depiction of a life lived during the greatest social upheaval the world has ever known. It is also valuable for the insight it provides into the mental state of a person who had an undeniable impact on the world as it operates today.

*Part Three: Discovery*

# *Eighteen*

I KNEW I LOVED TERESA MOYO THE MOMENT I SAW HER, AND THE first thing I did was spit on her.

Of course, I can't really support that statement. Love at first sight is a fallacy, and I am a psychologist. It would be irresponsible for me to advocate for such a simplistic view of human affection. I suppose then I am as inconsistent as the next person. As flawed as anyone else. I suppose I just miss my wife. I haven't seen her in more than a decade. I do not even know if she is alive.

But one must be rational, and love at first sight is an impossibility. Love is based on knowing someone as fully as it's possible to know them, and cherishing all that you find in them. Initial attraction is just that—attraction—and when we perceive it to be more, it is only that we have projected someone we've imagined onto a real person. If that projection turns out to be close to the truth, that is mere coincidence.

So it is more accurate to say that my first impression of Teresa suggested that she had qualities I would love, and by the luckiest chance, I was not far wrong.

I am not sure it's relevant, this about Teresa and me, but

I'm going to write it all out anyway. I have spent so much of my life alone. It always felt natural to me. Right. Expected. I should have known that I would return here, to my solitude, I should be able to accept it by now. But when I think of Teresa, solitude feels like a curse. A punishment.[1]

But maybe that's not fair. Maybe all we ever get is that we are happy for a time. So here: let me tell you of how I was happy. For a time.

HAVE I JUMPED AHEAD TOO far? I can't remember where I left off. I stopped writing and bundled all my pages together and put them in a box under the bed, and for a while I decided to forget that they existed.

I spent my days walking. Sitting alone and looking at strangers. Walking some more. I think I passed a year this way without writing a word.

Maybe I should let another pass.

But that is risky. I'm here to die, after all, and what if I die without telling everything?

Anyway. Irrelevant.

Isn't it? Or is it the most relevant thing of all? I'm here to die, but I must finish my task before I do.

I'm not sure what made me feel like that, what made me push my past away. It's like a sudden injury. I don't want to touch it; I don't want to look at it because that would make it real. But now it is not real—and not being real, it is nothing, and I don't have to know about it.

---

1 Edited for clarity. Page shows signs of water damage.

I'm not going to read over what I've written. It's enough dredging all this up once. Isn't it enough?


I WAS SITTING ALONE IN a diner outside Baltimore when Teresa walked in.

The wind announced her entrance—a grand *whoosh* followed by the clamoring of tiny bronze bells strung to the door. Teresa looked more amused than flustered as the blustery wind pushed her inside. She righted herself quickly, grabbing hold of the Please Wait to Be Seated sign she'd almost knocked over, and looking around the restaurant. Her cheeks were flushed from the cold, and her eyes sparkled. She looked like she was searching for someone to share the joke of her entrance with.

She caught someone's eye, or other, and her smile broadened and opened into a generous laugh, and I was jealous. Jealous that she had found someone other than me to laugh with. I wanted that charm for myself.

I wanted to bask in that radiance every day. I pictured myself spending my mornings being warmed by her golden glow, my nights with my body curled against her, in a crescent curve that matched her smile.

I watched Teresa for a few moments, feeling her charm catalyze in a chemical reaction with my loneliness and stress. The resulting concoction was infatuation, adoration. Puppy love—the kind that makes you say things like "golden glow."

But I was in the diner to work. I was partway through

reviewing the edits for my second psychology textbook.[2] The deadline weighed heavily on me, like a hand upon my head, turning my focus downward, back to the manuscript, and soon I was so engrossed I forgot Teresa was even there.

I sat for what was probably an hour, maybe two, reading my editor's notes, making new notes of my own. My sandwich lay cold and mostly uneaten; my coffee had been refilled three or four times.

This was how I often worked, and most of the staff knew me well by then. I had a tacit agreement with my regular waiter, Donny, that if he saw my cup was empty, he would fill it silently and immediately, and I would repay him by never acknowledging his presence. We had a deep and abiding relationship.

But on this occasion, I had lingered past his shift, and eventually I realized that my mug had sat empty for at least ten pages.

I finally looked up, glanced around the diner, and flagged down a waitress I didn't recognize. She offered to bring me a clean mug, which was overkill, but I wanted more coffee, so I didn't complain. Two minutes later she had brought me exactly what she promised, and I, in my attempt to win her friendship as I had with Donny, gave her complete indifference. I grabbed the mug as soon as she set it down and put it to my lips. There was betrayal in the very first sip.

I don't know if she had brought me a coffee meant for someone else or had simply made an assumption about how

---

2 *Watercolor Memories*, published in 1954–another very dry psychology text.

I took mine—either way, the result was the same. She had filled my coffee with milk and sugar. I understand that some may enjoy coffee this way, but I've always felt that the additions give coffee a rotten, almost fermented, taste.

Normally I would have swallowed this abomination with a grimace, or gently pushed it back through my lips into the mug. But I was so preoccupied with my work, so wound up on the caffeine I had already consumed, so rushed in that first sip, and so unprepared for the unexpected taste that I reacted regretfully. I spat the mouthful out.

I had turned my head just enough that the spray launched straight into the aisle next to my booth, splattering in a nearly perfect beige circle onto the pristine, stylish white dress of Teresa Moyo. She stopped, her face full of shock, near terror. But in a moment her body relaxed, and she looked directly at me.

My eyes must have been huge and horrified, because she softened her expression with a slight smile and said: "Well, that's hardly fair. The coffee isn't that bad."

It took me a moment to regain my composure, for several reasons, but eventually I managed to gulp out an apology.

"Please . . . you must let me make this up to you. I'll pay for your lunch," I said, "and the dry cleaning bill, of course."

Teresa cocked an eyebrow at me. "I've already paid for my lunch," she said, "and all my dry cleaning is done through my work." She narrowed her eyes, appraising me with a slight smile. "There's only one option," she said. "You'll have to take me to dinner."

I blinked.

"Tomorrow night okay?" she said.

o   o   o

AND THAT IS HOW I ended up a day behind on my edits.

At least, I assume I did. It's been forty years. I cannot recall precisely how the writing process went. But I cannot imagine I spent the next day steadily working, when I had dinner with Teresa to anticipate.

I believe I thought too hard about where I should take her—one place was too casual, the next too formal—and what I should wear, what would impress someone as stylish as she was. I don't even remember what I wore in the end, but I remember where I took her, because we went back every year for the next decade or so.

It was a small, quiet Turkish restaurant called Idyll—a play on the name of its owner, Idil. I remember I got there early, overeager and afraid of being late, and sat alone for a while, a glass of wine untouched on the table in front of me.

The weather was milder that day, and she managed to walk in of her own accord rather than being blown in. Again she was dressed intimidatingly well: a blouse in a warm mustard yellow that brought out the deep, dark shine of her skin. Again I marveled at her, how her close-cropped hair brought out her cheekbones, how her black eyes sparkled.

The hostess led her to our table, and Teresa smiled at me as she sat down.

"A little less dramatic an entrance than yesterday," she said.

"I wouldn't say that," I replied, and immediately blushed. Teresa gave her delighted, open laugh.

I was only embarrassed for a moment. It is—it was—very hard to be embarrassed around Teresa. She was so curious, so vivid that she made embarrassment seem like a waste of energy. Soon we were talking as if we'd both been storing up talk for years, waiting for each other.

Her experience of the Great Reckoning had been less transient than mine, I learned.

"My parents moved over here before I was born," she said. "They were refugees from an earlier war,[3] one they had nothing to do with. They were farmers, and their farm was destroyed, so they came here to build a new one."

She told me of their home in a small town in Wyoming, where she was born and lived throughout the Reckoning.

"The fighting never came near us physically," she said, "although the army showed up now and again to recruit people. It felt foolish to leave and risk coming into greater danger somewhere else."

"Greater danger?" I asked. Teresa paused for a moment.

"At the beginning, it seemed like things would be good there. The military needed food, and we were growing food. They promised us—the whole community—yearly payments, regardless of how much food we had to sell, so we didn't have to worry too much about the ash clouds.

"But after a while they stopped coming. Stopped picking up food, stopped paying."

"Why?" I asked. "What happened?"

She shrugged. "Maybe they found a cheaper way to feed

---

3 The Boer War, also known as the South African War, was fought between the British Empire and the Boer states of South Africa, from 1899 to 1902. Although it was solely a colonialist conflict that did not involve the African population as combatants, many African residents lost their homes and livelihoods and were forced to flee.

their soldiers," she said. "Maybe the person in charge of arranging it all died, and no one knew about us. Whatever the reason, we watched that year's crop rot in the fields and had no money to set in the next year's."

She took a sip of her wine.

"Of course, we really should still have been fine. We could grow enough food for ourselves, we could look after each other. You would think we could've looked after each other. But instead . . . I don't know. People were afraid."

"Of what?"

She laughed again but quietly this time. Sadly. "Ghosts," she said.

"What about your parents?" I asked.

"My father enlisted early on—I was eight, I think—and his letters home stopped a few years later, although no one ever told us what happened to him. And my mother . . . She died when I was fifteen. I think it was a heart attack in the end, but really it was just time. Exhaustion. Frustration. Things hadn't been easy for her—for either of them—even before the Reckoning. They tried really hard to be part of the community, but the community didn't try back.

"And once the war broke out, there was suspicion. I don't think it was focused on us, necessarily, but when you feel threatened, it's easy to fear the faces that don't look like yours."

She took another sip of wine.

"It was a bit easier for me," she said. "I had the right accent, at least. I didn't need to be taught new customs. But that wasn't enough when things got bad."

"They blamed you? The other people in the town?"

"They blamed everyone. Me. Each other. Everyone retreated behind their own fences, peering out at each other trying to see who had it in for them. I looked the least like them, so. Still, I had nowhere else to go, so I stayed."

"What did you do?"

"I fed myself and clothed myself. And I suppose it's a good thing I did, because that's what really gave me a life after the Reckoning."

"What do you mean?"

"I started by mending my clothes as they tore, but eventually I had to start making new ones. At first I hated it—it took such a long time, and I stabbed myself with needles a lot. But I guess I got good, and eventually I found I loved it. I began experimenting with whatever I could find, which wasn't a lot—it was hard enough to get exciting new fabrics in rural Wyoming even before the war."

"And now?"

"Now people all over the world wear my clothes."

Sooner or later, I noticed that the other tables had chairs stacked on top of them, and the waitstaff were quietly standing in the corner.

"I suppose we should call it a night," I said.

"We should," she said. "Or we could find a bar."

So that's how I fell in love.

# Nineteen

IT ALL FELT SO NATURAL. THE WAY WE SLOTTED INTO EACH OTHER's lives. We didn't make solid plans to meet again after that dinner because we didn't feel like we needed to.

Later that week, when I was working in the diner, Teresa came in and, without a word, sat down at my table. She took out a sketchbook and began working on designs for a new line she was planning.

After a while, the ideas stage of her work was done, and we shifted from the diner to her studio, the hum of her sewing machine serving as white noise for me. By this time, I'd completed the edits and rewrites for my second book, sent it off to my publisher, and turned my attention to the third.

I was under contract to write it, but the subject had not been specified. The delivery date had, though, and now I was tasked with deciding what to write about.

"Is it weird that you're not doing any more work with children?" Teresa asked one of those days, as I sat cross-legged on the floor of her studio, considering and rejecting ideas, papers and notebooks splayed out around me.

"I would've thought," she continued, "that between books

you'd spend time working with people again, and then write about that. It seems a bit of a stretch to expect you to write a whole book out of nothing, without any time for research."

I didn't reply.

"I'm sorry, Miri," Teresa said. "Was that rude? I don't know how any of it works."

"No, it's okay," I said, though I wasn't sure it was. "I just spent so long doing that before, you know. I spent years working with people, researching, developing techniques. There's a lot I haven't written up yet. I have plenty to work from."

"Oh," she said. "Okay. Sorry, I misunderstood—I thought you were struggling to come up with something."

"It's more that I don't know what makes the most sense to write about now. After the last one."

"But wouldn't it be good for everyone if you were developing your work further? You've made such a difference to things."

I was silent for a while after that, running my pen across paper in some semblance of a person jotting down thoughts and ideas. But it was moving independently while my mind spun off in other directions.

It had been a few years since I'd worked directly with other people, either adults or children. This was something I didn't think about. This was something I tried not to think about.

The memory of my dismissal from Gateway floated somewhere in the ocean of my mind, and I left it there. I thought about Gateway only insofar as it served my current work. I mined my past for its expertise, for its store of knowledge, and I set those down in books hardly anyone would ever read.

It was better that way. It was a life I could handle.

I didn't have to think about Edgar.

I wouldn't think about Edgar.

But because I would not think about the work I'd done with people in my past, I stopped thinking about work I might do with people in my future.

I could have sought out a position with another childhood center, after I had left Gateway. I did not. I could have looked into training practitioners in the Watercolor Quiet. I could have reached out to Nora for an advisory role within the Council, though I knew little of political affairs and didn't particularly wish to know more.

I didn't do any of those things.

Instead I wrote. I sat and wrote down what I knew, what I'd learned, what I'd developed—and each word I wrote was a brick in the wall between me and where I'd come from.

I left that wall up for a long time. It's amazing how easily it's coming down now.

IT WAS WHEN I WAS moving a few boxes of my things into Teresa's that I saw the first news story. In those days, it could be tough to find a decent place to live if you weren't connected to a center of some kind.[1] I'd been living in a small,

---

1 Early rebuilding priorities focused on establishments that could serve the needs of multiple people, such as childhood centers, academies, and hospitals. In those cities that had seen widespread destruction of residential properties, many such buildings were designed to have temporary living quarters for staff included. Baltimore, in particular, had struggled to recover economically after the Inner Harbor Fire of 1935, which spread throughout the city. It took two months to fully extinguish the blazes and smoldering

damp apartment in what would have been a basement, if the building above was still standing.

Teresa had overcome this problem at the same time as setting herself up with a workplace. She'd restored a small warehouse that had survived largely unscathed, though the street around it was nothing but empty lots where rubble had been cleared away. She'd converted the warehouse, given it a front-facing display room and shop, with the bulk of the space used as a design room and sewing hub. And up on the top floor she'd put in a large, airy apartment for herself.

It made sense for me to move in to her larger, healthier apartment; by the time I did, I hadn't been home to my own place in two or three weeks, and I'd lost some clothing and notes to mold.

"Oh, I'm a terrible knight in shining armor," said Teresa, when she saw the damage. "I should have dragged you back to my castle sooner. The moment I clapped eyes on you."

So we packed up my things, wrapping breakables in old newspapers and piling boxes into a rented van. There was a spare bedroom that I was converting to use as an office, and as I was setting it up, in the paper crumpled around my desk lamp, I saw that first story.

At the time, I don't think I gave it too much attention—I just paused for a moment to scan it before going back to work—but looking back, that moment feels weighted. Loaded with dark portent.

A lot of things feel that way when you look back as you're

---

debris, and a year to rebuild crucial facilities. It was another ten years before sufficient housing was built for the city's population.

edging closer to death, it seems. Or maybe that's just me. Maybe that's just loneliness and regret.

Anyway.

It was short, unimportant. A back-page, "local man" kind of story, not real news. It was about a young man called Horatio Reyes—a chef who was opening a new gourmet sandwich shop in town. I suppose you could call it a "revitalization profile." Certain parts of the town were being rebuilt faster than others, little localized clusters of community and industry. This piece was one of many that were in the back pages of the papers around that time, and this one was pinned to a redemption arc.

Horatio Reyes was a convicted felon, the article said, rehabilitated and ready to start over with a new business, a new home, a new respect for the Society's laws. (That last was my addition, you understand.)

Two years earlier, the story claimed, Reyes had been a newly released convict with no clear ambitions and no real plan. And now look at him go, opening a small lunch spot. His crime, for which he'd been detained for some eighteen months, had been persistent contact with his daughter. The article did not specify what form this had taken.

"That seems unfair," I said to Teresa after showing her the paper. "There ought to be a little more understanding of this kind of thing. People can't help their attachments, on their own—he should have been given help, not imprisoned."

"I suppose they're being a bit overcautious," she replied, "but it's not like there's no reason for that. When you think of one individual case, of course it seems harsh, but there has to be consistency. We're just starting to rebuild—we can't risk violence breaking out again."

"I just don't think criminalizing it is the answer."

"But we don't even know what he did. Maybe it was serious; maybe he was interfering with the girl's safety."

"And maybe he was just sending her birthday cards."[2]

"Well, Miri, you've hit upon the crux of the issue. We just don't know enough about the situation to know if what he did was right or wrong. Now, stop working, I've opened a bottle of wine."

It was easy to put it out of my mind in the moment. After all, Teresa was right—we didn't really know anything about the situation. But I remembered it. Years later I remembered it.


I THINK IT WAS AROUND this time that Nora came to visit. We had kept up a correspondence over the years—her letters had been a chief comfort in the months after I left Gateway—but had only seen each other face-to-face once since the Arboretum, and that had been brief. She had so many demands on her time.

The apartment at the top of the warehouse had a roof terrace that Teresa had decked out with potted trees and strings

---

2 Horatio Reyes had been sending birthday cards, as well as letters and old photographs, to his daughter, Tina Reyes. Ms. Reyes had already graduated from an educational academy and was studying trademark law at Georgetown. Mr. Reyes's contact with her caused a regression in her memories, which resulted in her having to retake the Formational Protocols. Her degree was delayed by two years.

The chain that connects familial relations to tribalism to nationalism is an important, big-picture point. It was the primary motivation behind the Age Ten Laws. Arguments against these laws were concluded in 1948. Absence of families is the status quo, and to violate the basic tenets of the Society (as Horatio Reyes did) is not merely a theoretical transgression but a form of abuse against his unwitting daughter.

of lights, and I think it was there that Nora and I sat one evening. So it must have been around that time. Or maybe after we were married. But definitely while we were still living there.

Nora was powerful by this point, of course, she had just won an election or some such,[3] but she wore her power lightly. Gracefully. As always. She was passing through the area on Society business and came to see me. After we ate we sat outside for some hours drinking wine and talking.

Mostly it was just chitchat: catching each other up on where we'd been. She told me about the house she and Ekaterina had built on a lakeside near Vienna. Rohaan came to stay whenever he could, she said, though he was often busy with his work. He was instrumental in establishing a new agency to help support the Council—the IID.[4] It had been running for six or seven years, but its role was still changing.

"Is it not all a bit controlling?" I asked at some point. "All these laws and agencies? I confess, I don't often keep up with politics, but are you not concerned that, out of fear, we might lean too hard into oppression?"

I had not told Nora how much the IID had had to do with

---

3 Ms. Bostwick won a third term on the Societal High Council in 1955. That would place this scene several months after Miriam and Teresa's wedding, which took place on the 23rd of November the previous year. You may find it strange that Dr. Gregory refused to follow the news or politics, given the rapidly changing world in which she lived—and indeed her personal relationships with key figures in government. It seems to show a dedication to willful ignorance that is difficult to defend.

4 Rohaan Youssuf was aide to Anand Balakrishnan during Balakrishnan's first years as the New Society's first Council Chief (1943-1949). Youssuf and a dozen others were tasked with the formation of the Internal Investigations Division, a project that began in 1946.

my departure from Gateway. I hoped that word of it hadn't gotten back to Rohaan.

"Oh, Miri, you've grown up," said Nora. "And yes. Of course I am concerned that we could go too far in our efforts to prevent another Reckoning. Being concerned about that is the only way to ensure that you see it early—that you catch the embers of autocracy before they go too far—and smother them out."

"Everything's changed so much and so fast. Sometimes it feels like some shadowy figure is making all our decisions for us."

Nora laughed. "Ah, but isn't that what people elect us for? The decision-making part, of course—I don't think we're particularly shadowy. Every law, every decision, every council debate is made public through open forums and in newspapers."

"I tend to avoid newspapers," I said.[5]

"Well, then we're definitely shadowy figures."

The idea of Nora, whose smile could light a whole power grid, being shadowy made me laugh as well.

"And what of your work?" Nora asked. "I'm surprised to find you not practicing."

"Yes, well," I said. "Everything changes so much so fast."

"Did you want that to change?"

"I had a lot that I needed to note down properly. There were years of work I hadn't documented."

"Is that all?"

"Practicing is complicated," I said. "I think there was something uneven going on. A kink in the treatment."

---

5 Dr. Gregory certainly has a lot of opinions about Societal Council laws and policies for someone who did not read the news.

"You're not going to flatten that out sitting up here writing books."

"I have to be better prepared if I'm going to try, though. I need time."

Nora looked at me for a while but didn't say anything more. Eventually Teresa joined us with a newly opened bottle. Talk turned to the new developments in the city—what we were excited about, what we dreaded.

There was a new theater going up, and an art gallery that Teresa was eager to visit.

"Oh yes," said Nora, "theater has been one of the things I've missed most. I'm glad we're finally recovered enough that it can become part of daily life again. Of course, we've been working on it for some time—my bill for arts funding passed four years ago—but the planning process for new builds or even refurbishing and repairing old theaters is . . . well. Involved."

"I've never been to the theater," I said. "I can't even imagine it."

"At its best, it's electric," said Nora. "I was eleven the first time I went—my parents took me to New York for my birthday, and we saw *The Pirates of Penzance*. I never quite got over it."

"I've always dreamed of going," said Teresa.

"Really?" I said. "You've never talked about that."

She laughed. "Did you want me to lay out all my qualities the day we met? No, my love, I'm unfurling myself like a peony. Something new to discover every day, for the rest of time."

"I did always love peonies," I said.

Nora looked at me with a small smile on her face. "I have to say, Miri," she said, "I'm surprised to find you so mellow."

"Mellow?"

"You were always such a tense wee thing. Hyperaware, your eyes darting around, trying to observe everything at once. Now look at you—limpid eyes, flowing limbs—why, you're almost slouching!"

"Oh," I said, "I see you've come here to tease me."

"Never," said Nora. "I'm honestly quite emotional at the sight of you. You kids never had a childhood, never lived in a world where you knew everything would be taken care of. I kind of assumed you'd never be able to relax in adulthood either."

"Nora, it's like you don't know my work at all."

Nora threw her head back and laughed for a while at that. "Oh god, Miri, you're making jokes! I could weep! That serious stoic child all grown up and thriving—it's a tonic."

"Well. I suppose you can take credit," I said, a bit embarrassed. "You helped me reach adulthood, after all. And you're making the world into a place that's easy to relax in."

"That's the goal," she said, throwing back her last sip of wine. "And now I think it's time for me to head back to my hotel. Or I'll drink too much and embarrass the Council."

Teresa went to bed shortly after Nora left. She kissed me on the head as she went inside, and looked at me with a furrowed brow. "I'm glad you learned to relax," she said. "I'm glad you learned to relax with me."

I sat outside alone for a while, looking out over the city. It didn't look much like a city at that point. There were patches of light and stretches of darkness.

Patches of clarity and stretches of obscurity.

# *Twenty*

I THINK IF I COULD PROPOSE TO TERESA AGAIN, I WOULD DO IT differently.

I don't know how, exactly, but differently. Perhaps I would take her on a tour of our brief life together so far. The diner where we met. The restaurant where we went on our first date. My horrible, moldy apartment that she refused to stay over in. The street we were walking down when someone on a bicycle knocked us down, and Teresa broke her arm. The shop where we had a fight over pickles—the kind of fight that is both real and hilarious at the same time, anger and laughter driving each other ever upward. Ending up back at home, out on our roof terrace, roses everywhere—no, peonies everywhere—the city before us.

Or maybe I would have kept everything in one place. A picnic in one of the many green spaces that dominated the city. Empty blocks, cleared of the rubble that once covered them, left alone to the wildflowers for so long that they became urban meadows.

Perhaps I would build her a fairy tale. Hire a horse-drawn carriage to pick her up and carry her away to a ball held in her honor, and as she walked in have a choir break out in praise of her. Sweep her across the dance floor in a perfect waltz before proposing a toast to her perfect nose and clever eyes. Kneel before her in front of everyone and proclaim myself hers forever.

Well. I'd have had to learn to waltz.

I didn't do any of those things. I didn't think to. I didn't think to do anything at all, because in reality I didn't even think to propose to her. It happened absent of my will but true to everything in me.

We were doing the dishes after dinner. Not a special dinner, not a carefully planned meal. I think it may have been leftovers. I was washing and she was drying, and she kept handing plates and silverware back to me because, she claimed, I hadn't cleaned them properly, and each time I called her neurotic and she called me a slob. During one handover, the plate slipped out of our hands. The shock of it made Teresa cry, and I just said it.

"You have to marry me."

Not "will you marry me," not "we should get married," not "would you like," or "how do you feel," or anything at all that allowed for a decision to be made.

"You have to."

"You must."

"I need you to."

It's obvious what that says about me.

Anyway.

Teresa looked at me for a moment, her eyes wide and still full of tears, her breath ragged.

"Miri, I—"

I gulped. We stood there for a moment, for a lifetime, staring at each other. Breathing.

In.

Out.

And then:

"Okay."

I'M SORRY. I HAD TO stop there for a while. For a few weeks. This isn't—none of this is relevant, not really, but it is to me. It's the only relevant thing. To me.

So we got married.

We got married on a cold, gray, damp day, and everything was beautiful. I didn't need sunbeams because I had her. I didn't need blue skies or sweet summer breezes, because the depths of winter felt like spring.

I'm getting carried away. Lost in sentiment.

The point is, we were married.

And things kept on.

Teresa liked to make fun of my reading habits. I would be quietly sitting in a cozy armchair on a Saturday evening with a cup of tea and book.

"What are you reading, my Miri?" she'd ask, and when I told her, she'd lean forward, her chin resting on her fist, gazing at me intently.

"You don't say," she'd say. "That sounds just fascinating. *Interpersonal Behaviors: A Guide to Abnormal Psychology*? Interesting plot, is it? Compelling characters?"

"I don't understand what's so hilarious about my reading this," I would reply.

"I know!" she would cry. "That just makes it funnier!"

"Why? What are you reading?"

"*Rebecca*," she'd say primly.

Oh! Do you know, I think I remember this one perfectly. Sometimes I'm not sure how particular conversations went, I do my best but I can't be certain. But this memory . . . somehow this stupid memory still feels sharp. Immediate. This is how it went:

"Sounds like something bucolic and smug," I said. "Full of maiden aunts and an abundance of children."

"I believe, my Miri, that you are thinking of *Rebecca of Sunnybrook Farm*. This is just *Rebecca*. An entirely different situation."

I paused for a moment. "Oh my god," I said. "I think you're right. I read that other *Rebecca* when I was a kid. There was a copy in the prison library. Doesn't it end with everyone's problems being solved by someone dying and leaving her all their money?"[1]

"I believe it does," said Teresa.

"But that's not the one you're reading."

"It categorically is not. The one I'm reading has a lot more intrigue and suspicions and ultimately murder."

"And that's a more appropriate thing to be reading than *Interpersonal Behaviors*?"

"It's adorable that you're reading that right now. On a Saturday."

---

1 Before the Age Ten Laws and the formal dissolution of family ties, it was customary for people to prepare a legal document known as a will before their death. It was traditional for them to leave their money and possessions, including property and other assets, to their children or to other relatives.

Disagreements over inheritances were frequently a source of conflict before the Great Reckoning.

"Why?"

"Miri, you're using your leisure time to read work material, and you don't even know why that's weird and that is just the sweetest thing."

"You think I should be reading a novel?"

"When was the last time you did?"

I thought for a moment and then said nothing.

"Miri!" Teresa cried. "You haven't read one since you were in prison, have you?"

"It hasn't occurred to me," I said. "I read everything they had in that library. It was the first time I had access to a big collection of books, you know. When I was moving around, sometimes I'd find a house that had books in it but not always, and sometimes they'd be in a language I couldn't read, and they were too heavy to take with me when I did find them."

"But there were books at the Arboretum, right?"

"Oh, yes, of course, and I read a lot of them. Philosophy, psychology, chemistry—"

"You read chemistry books rather than novels?"

"We were trying to figure out a problem in the soil; it was too acidic or something."

"You are hopeless."

"Well, what do you want me to read then?"

"Why don't you read this!"

"Teresa, you're reading that."

"That's what I'm saying—we can read it together and then talk about it! It'll be fun! We can go out and get you a copy tomorrow."

From then on, whenever Teresa found a novel she wanted to read, she would get two copies so we could read it at the same time. It quickly became a habit—my opinions infuriated her, and that delighted me.

"The problem is, the second Mrs. de Winter has a pathological fear of confrontation. If she could overcome that, she could just have a conversation with him."

"Miri, come on."

"Although Maxim would need to deal with his control issues."

"Miri! You're not supposed to diagnose them!"

I would keep my face as passive as possible: "Why not?"

"Because! It's fiction! They're characters in a story!"

"Does that mean they can't have psychological conditions?"

"That's not the point!"

"Then what is?"

Teresa would peer at me for a moment. "You're doing this on purpose, aren't you?"

"Doing what?"

"I can tell! You're laughing at me?"

"I'm not laughing."

"Yes, you are! You're laughing in there, inside your clever, wry head, while I'm all out here with my feelings."

So you see.

Happiness, for a time. Comfort.

For a time.

WE HAD BEEN MARRIED FOR five years before things started to change. I think it was around five years. And I don't mean to suggest that things started to go wrong—not all change is troubling. But if I were to pick a time to keep forever, if I were to have a life of stasis, those are the years I would pick.

But life is not stasis. All things change, and so these things changed.

I was in my office going over line edits on my latest book[2] when Teresa first suggested it. At the time, I think I welcomed the interruption. The book was my fifth or sixth, and I was beginning to feel like I was running out of things to say. I'd started to wonder why I was writing them in the first place—they were destined to be read only by psychologists and psychology students, and I wasn't sure how much help they'd really be to them. But aside from the occasional lecture or consultation, writing them was my full-time career at this point.

Anyway.

Teresa came in with a cup of tea for me. She set it down on my desk and walked over to sit in the armchair by the window, curling up her feet underneath her.

"Miri," she said, "I've been thinking." She sat for a moment without saying anything, looking out the window instead of at me.

"I saw this woman a couple of weeks ago," she said eventually. "I was buying coffee, and she was in the line ahead of me. She was pregnant."

She took a deep breath. "Miri, what if I got pregnant?"

I took a breath. Took a moment. "Pregnant?"

"Yeah," she said. "I looked at her, this woman—she must

---

2 *The Contradictions of the Self*, published in 1960.

have been almost due, eight months or so along, I think, and she looked so hot and uncomfortable. It was the middle of that heat wave the other week, you remember? And I looked at her, and god, Miri, I was so jealous. I wanted to be pregnant. I really wanted to be pregnant."

"But you'd have to give up the baby."

"I know, of course, but I wasn't even thinking about having a baby. It just . . . I don't know, I looked at her and it felt like that should be me. Like that is a thing I should be doing."

"Being pregnant?"

"Being pregnant."

We both sat silently for a moment.

"It's a huge sacrifice to make."

"I know."

"I know they've been calling for volunteers[3] for years. I know it's a worthy thing to offer, but are you sure you can really give all that?"

"It's not about giving. I want this."

"Okay, but are you sure you want all of it? The impact it will have on your body will be immense, and that could last long after the pregnancy is over. And you say you just want to be pregnant now, but when you are, you'll form an attachment

---

3 The Repopulation Initiative was purely voluntary for the first sixteen years of its existence. This was less a deliberate choice and more a result of ongoing debate about the level of compensation participants should be entitled to. A small but vocal contingent argued that it was unfair to offer less to those donating sperm than to those donating their bodies. While this argument was never in danger of succeeding, its proponents did manage to block successive votes on the issue—which was resolved only when two of the men concerned were discovered to have been embezzling funds from the committee. Their dismissal left the group with too small a minority to have any sway.

to the baby. But it won't be your baby. You'll have to let it be taken to a center. You'll never see it."

"Miri, I know all this. You know I know all this. I don't need you to explain pregnancy to me. And it's not a whim. I've been thinking about it for two weeks. I've been thinking about it all the time."

I hesitated for a moment before replying.

"Okay, Teresa. But will you do me a favor?"

"What?"

"Will you give it another few weeks? Give it two months, say, and if you're still sure, then that's that."

"I don't need another two months."

"I just don't want you to have any regrets."

And two months later we were sitting in a doctor's office.

TERESA'S FIRST PREGNANCY DIDN'T GO smoothly. Her morning sickness was debilitating, and lasted throughout.

She had to stop working in her fourth month, and by her sixth she needed so much help from me that I stopped working too. Not that I minded—I was singularly uninspired at that point in time.

For a while, all she could eat was porridge, and then she had a two-week span of craving incredibly spicy curries. Her water broke three weeks early, and the one bright spot of the whole debacle made itself apparent—her labor only lasted ninety minutes.

I slept on a chair next to her bed that night, after the baby—a girl—had been taken to the nursery. Teresa slept for fourteen hours.

I was leaning on her bed doing a crossword when she woke up. She was tired. Wan. But there was a blazing light in her eyes I'd never seen before.

"Wasn't she beautiful?" she said to me, when she saw me looking at her.

"Of course she was," I said. "You made her."

A few tears seeped out from her eyes.

"Are you okay?" I asked.

"Yeah. Yeah, of course I am."

"Are you sure?"

"I'm sure. I'm glad, Miri. I'm glad I did it. I'm glad she exists. I'm going to miss her, but I think I would have missed her anyway. But that would be worse. It would be worse to miss her because she never existed at all."

"Then I'm glad too. I'm glad you did this."

And I was. And part of me still is. The world only gets better if it's rebuilding itself out of the DNA of people like Teresa Moyo.

But I do wonder sometimes. This was the first step. Or perhaps that's not fair—maybe there are so many steps in so many directions that it's impossible to determine if any one of them had more meaning than the others. Or perhaps it was all going to happen anyway.

Well.

There is a woman out there who exists because Teresa decided that she should, and how lucky everyone who knows her must be.

# Twenty-One

ALTHOUGH THE PREGNANCY HAD BEEN HARD, TERESA'S RECOVERY was quick. She was eager to get back to work—she claimed that while she'd been so ill, her mind had been busy. She had a raft of ideas for a whole new range of formalwear, and her eyes shone with inspiration and industry.

I would watch her as she worked sometimes, her hands flying over sketch paper drawing out her plans, or gently guiding delicate fabrics under her racing needle. From time to time she would pause, letting her pencil sag to the side or her foot drift from the pedal of her machine, her eyes dropping.

"Teresa?" I'd say, when I saw her like this. "Are you okay?"

She would look over at me, an eyebrow cocked, her familiar playful smile on her lips. "Of course, Miri. I was just thinking I might try this design in silk."

And she did try the design in silk, and it became one of her most popular looks. Shelley Winters wore it on some red carpet or other.[1]

---

1 Shelley Winters wore a Moyo dress to the third annual Golden Globe Awards in 1962. The Awards were introduced as part of the Societal Council's efforts to revitalize the arts industry.

And she kept working, her eyes overbright, her hands always moving. For a while she was exhaustively productive, but she never tired. I found it grating sometimes, if I'm honest. And why not be honest at this point? I was struggling in my own work. Ideas never seemed to come. Making plans seemed beyond me. I had lost any ambition, and I wasn't sure what to do without it. I felt like there must be a next step for me to take, but I couldn't see it in front of me.

I was restless, directionless. Looking back from this distance, it seems likely that I was depressed, but at the time I just felt like a failure. Teresa's enthusiasm and output stood in stark contrast to my own blank daze.

We lived like that for, I think, five years. Is that right? I don't think I was paying much attention then to the passage of time, but I think it was around five years. Five years of dizzying output for Teresa. Five years of gray dissatisfaction for me.

So this time, when she said she wanted to contribute again to the repopulation efforts, my reaction was different. It would be something to focus on. It would make Teresa my focus again. Instead of trying to hide my stagnant work life from her, I could put it aside entirely. I could take care of her just like I had the first time. Although of course I was concerned for her well-being.

"Remember how hard it was on you," I said, cautiously. "You were so sick."

"I know, Miri. It was hard, I haven't forgotten, but I think it's worth it."

"I know they're paying people now,[2] but that doesn't—"

---

2 Legislation to compensate those who contributed to the repopulation ef-

"Miri, you know it's not about money."

"You've been so productive and happy with your work. If you're sick again like you were the last time, you'll interrupt all that for months."

"That's okay. I'll have time to get prototypes of the next range done at least, and then it won't matter if I get interrupted. My only worry is that your work might be interrupted as well."

I laughed, a little bitterly, but I was glad my tentative questions hadn't put her off.

"Honestly, looking after you would be a welcome break from dragging myself around trying to find what I should be doing."

"Well then," she said, "okay."

"Okay."

BUT OUR WORRIES WERE UNFOUNDED. Unlike her first pregnancy, Teresa's second proceeded without a hitch. Without a medical hitch, at least.

But while she wasn't physically sick, as she had been the last time, I noticed a change in her. This pregnancy seemed to be taking a deeper emotional toll.

Her golden glow seemed faded, her blazing eyes dimmed. Her normally early bedtimes got later and later, and her concentration frequently wavered.

"You know," I said to her one day around her fourth or fifth month, after having observed her growing listlessness

---

forts was finally passed in May of 1961.

for a few weeks, "they're offering healthcare to people who participate in the repopulation efforts. Counseling, you know, that kind of thing."

"I know," she said. "I haven't signed up for it."

"But it could be helpful."

"No," she said. "I'm fine."

I changed tactics a little. "Okay. But I meant that you could be helpful to them. There's a research element to the programs, you know—there's still a lot we don't understand about the surrogacy process. The emotional toll it takes, how long it takes to recover. You'd be helping people—people like me—learn more."

"Hmm," she said. "I hadn't thought about it like that. Maybe I'll look into that."

After a couple of weeks and a few gentle prompts, she signed up for one of the programs. Biweekly therapy sessions during pregnancy and an intensive two-month inpatient program after delivery.

It was strange to be without her in those weeks after her second birth, but I was able to visit her daily.

And I continued to see the toll her pregnancies had taken. Her skin, teeth, and hair looked as healthy as ever, but her glow continued to fade. She smiled less, talked less. Her humor had grown dry—as faint and weightless as talcum powder.

I had supported Teresa. I had been proud of her for participating in the repopulation program, but I was beginning to worry that it had taken too much from her.

As the New Society was protecting the lives and minds of children, was it dismissing the needs of adults? The Society was raising competent, confident youth, who would give back to this world in extraordinary ways. They would be raised without the burden of families, without the cultural conservatism and selfish sheltering of parents. Without the privilege of generational wealth and connections, without the struggles of inherited poverty. These children would be the first truly equal generation.

And in turn, those of us born during the Great Reckoning—I have heard some people, derisively though not without some truth, refer to us as the Meager Generation—would be freed from the burden of parenthood.

We would lose the innate joy of raising a child, seeing them grow and develop, replicating our gestures and habits, improving upon our failings. It is a powerful loss, and the treatment program Teresa had enlisted in was supposed to help ease that.

This program was idealistic but not yet ideal, and I was unhappy with how little effect the counseling seemed to have on Teresa. During my visits to the postdelivery treatment center, I would grill nurses and doctors alike about her condition. I know I was obnoxious. I understand what an exasperated stare is, but other people's feelings weren't important to me. I was relentless in my pursuit of proper treatment for my wife.

By the end of the program, there seemed to be some improvement, and I began to feel a little guilty about my rants at the various medical staff. But only a little.

Teresa returned home, once again with her golden glow, and I was delighted. But I couldn't tell if the system would've worked correctly on its own, or if its success was due to my persistence with the medical staff. I had watched my wife go through a system that I knew could be improved. One that I knew I could improve.

My mind began ticking in a way it hadn't for years. I needed more data. A cross section of participants from various facilities. I would need to compile their responses over at least the first five years after they'd completed the treatment program. Would quarterly debriefs be enough, or would I need more regular contact with the women?

Thoughts kept whirring. I had forgotten that I could feel this energized, this optimistic.

THAT WAS MY BRAIN, THOUGH, and Teresa was my heart. I was glad to feel her beating within my chest once again. And to have her across the breakfast table from me each morning, and in my arms each night.

And that golden glow—to see that natural luminescence once again—was a relief. I found myself staring at her. Soaking it in. Making sure it was still there. And most of the time it was.

Occasionally Teresa would slip, just a little. There would be a sudden slight shadow across her eyes, like an actor who can't find their light. It didn't look like sadness or angst or depression. Just . . . just darkness.

It looked a little like deep thought, an all-consuming daydream, and I recognized it well. It was the kind of expression Rohaan frequently had, back on the farm during our Watercolor Quiet sessions. In fact, if I had not known Teresa personally, had seen her for the first time during one of these moments, I would have assumed a woman lost in thought.[3]

But this was not Teresa. Before her pregnancies, only sleep could prevent her from noticing everything and everyone in a room. In her waking hours, I could not walk past her without her saying, at minimum, a "hello," but more often than not starting a full conversation, even if about nothing at all.

But now she would wander, seeing things far beyond the rooms of our house. Or perhaps things far within herself.

And it was not the Watercolor Quiet. The Watercolor Quiet must be undertaken with intention. It demands energy and focus, and Teresa had neither of those.

When Teresa entered these states—these borderline trances—I would leave her be. I didn't want to disturb her rest, to shock her awake from this liminal space.

In the first couple of years after she bore the second child—a boy, by the way—these moments happened once every few weeks. I mentioned them to her a couple of times early on, but Teresa was unconcerned. She said she didn't think anything of them.

"They're just little empty-headed wanderings," she said. "Dreams of nothing."

I WAS EAGER TO START working on my theories of the post-partum program, but I didn't want to barge ahead with my own research and end up trampling on existing studies. From

---

3 Edited for clarity.

what I could tell there was extensive research being done on participants during pregnancy and in the weeks immediately following delivery, but there didn't seem to be anyone looking into the long-term effects.

I pulled out of my existing publishing contracts and began to focus my energies solely on this avenue of discovery. I don't think my publishers were too sad to see me go—my last couple of books had been insipid at best.

I applied for some grants and managed to get support from the Societal Council quite quickly. This was due in part to Nora. She had retired by this point and was not very well. Still, she had a lot of influence, and she believed in me.

I think I was offering something the Council already wanted. They were still trying to increase participation, and for them, being able to confirm that the health of volunteers would be monitored long-term was a good selling point. I began approaching treatment facilities to help me find participants, and the data started coming in fast.

I pored over it. I hadn't been so focused in a long time. Every day I woke with more energy than the day before, eager to get to my work, eager to discover everything I could. I was eager to start looking into how I could adapt the Watercolor Quiet to help this specific problem, but I held myself back for a while. I had a more organized mind than when I was younger; I understood the importance of a solid scientific process. The first months must be solely about gathering data.

But it was sometimes difficult to wait. And I was working without staff. I rented an office in the center of town to hold interviews so I wouldn't have to work around Teresa.

About three months into my research, I had a session

with a woman named Christine. She was a regular contributor to the repopulation program, and had been through four pregnancies.

She was chatty and comfortable, with a bright smile that didn't quite reach her placid blue eyes.

It was my first session with her, so I began with some basic questions about her experience with the program, starting with why she'd gone through it so many times.

"I wanted to help," she said. "We all need to help, don't we, in whatever way we can? We have to rebuild together."

"Is that the only reason?" I asked. "Altruism?"

"Well . . ." She hesitated for a moment. "We all help in different ways, don't we? Whatever we're good at, whatever we feel able to do?"

"And you felt able to do this?"

"I love doing this," Christine said, and she rested a hand across her belly.

"Sorry, are you going through the program again? I was under the impression you were finished?"

At this her eyes filled with tears.

"No," she said. "I can't do it again. They had to—"

She broke off and took some gulping breaths.

"It's okay," I said. "Take your time."

She took one more deep breath, and then:

"They gave me a hysterectomy. My last pregnancy had complications, we almost lost the baby, there was damage to . . ."

She trailed off, tears still falling from her eyes.

"And how did you react to that?"

"I was devastated," she said. "I really love it."

"Loved it?"

"I really loved being pregnant."

"What did you love about it?"

She looked down for a moment, shook her head slightly. "I don't think I can explain it. It's just—it's something bigger than words, you know? Bigger than ordinary life."

She paused again for a while. "At first it's just the sense of anticipation. Potential, you know? Then slowly it becomes about how it's changing you. Your own body adapting and readying itself. It's intoxicating. Like there's something more running through your veins than just blood.

"And eventually you can feel this new person, this new life. It moves and kicks and sleeps, and you can feel it. I can't describe it."

"I think you've described it better than you think," I said. "How did you feel after the deliveries?"

The change in Christine's face was remarkable. All life, all energy fled from it, as if I'd flipped a power switch. After a moment she cleared her throat.

"It was fine," she said. "I was fine."

"How long did you wait before signing up again?"

"Six months," she said. "They wouldn't let you sign up until at least six months had passed."

I WALKED HOME THAT DAY instead of taking a cab. I wanted the time, I wanted the fresh air. Christine's session had been a lot to take, and I wanted to let it settle in my mind before I started going over it from a scientific perspective.

I wanted to steady my own heart.

When I walked into the house, it was dark, and I assumed

Teresa was out. I hung up my coat and bag and headed to the kitchen to start cooking dinner. I bustled about for a couple of moments, before I turned and saw Teresa, sitting completely still at the dining room table.

"Teresa?" I said. She didn't move.

I walked over to her and placed a hand on her back. She still didn't move. I sat beside her, keeping one hand on her back and placing the other on her chest, over her heart.

"Teresa," I murmured, over and over, gently massaging my warmth into her.

As her muscles slowly loosened, I saw her hands upon the table, her fists finally unclenching. In her left hand she was holding something. It was yellow, a piece of paper, shiny, laminated. It looked familiar, but it wasn't until her fingers opened a bit more that I could see the name of the hospital where she had given birth and spent two months in rehab. And next to the name was a five-digit number. Her patient ID tag.

Why had she kept that old thing? But Teresa's patient tag had been green, I remembered, and much larger, with a clip that attached to the gown. This was smaller, with a white string hanging from it. I leaned closer and saw handwriting on a printed line: *17:02/M/5-Oct/8lb9oz.*

It was the baby's ID tag, not Teresa's.

In my surprise, I must have stopped rubbing Teresa's shoulders. She straightened up and looked at me. She saw what I was seeing and said, "I named him Moses."

"But that's not how it works," I said, dumbfounded that two months of inpatient therapy hadn't remedied this very simple issue.

"I know how it works, Miriam. I just liked the name. In

my mind, he's Moses. In his mind, wherever he is, he can be whatever they call him. I don't care. He's always going to be my Moses."

She got up and left the room and took her golden glow with her. She left the shadows with me.

# Twenty-Two

I STARTED KEEPING A CLOSER EYE ON TERESA AFTER THAT. I'D been carefully monitoring her emotional state already, of course, but I asked her if I could help more directly. We started having meditation sessions together a couple of times a week.

I'd decided to keep track of her movements as well. We no longer lived above her workshop—in fact, her workshop wasn't her workshop anymore. A few years earlier, she'd expanded her business, bringing in new designers to develop their own work within her company, and outfitted a new space that could accommodate them all. We'd moved into a small house a short walk away from the new warehouse.

Keeping an eye on her when she no longer worked just below our home required a bit of maneuvering on my part, especially since I didn't want to cause her any more concern or upset.

This may sound extreme to you, but I had good reasons to go to these kinds of lengths. I had been collecting accounts, over the years, of people being prosecuted and even imprisoned for contacting family members. Ever since reading that first story, it had been a little ticking obsession, never intruding into the light but always running in the background.

There were many like Horatio Reyes, and I collected all their stories.[1]

Siblings finding each other long after passing through the Age Ten Protocols, parents contacting children they weren't supposed to know, even a grandfather who'd written a letter to his daughter's son.

It was hard to be sure of the details or outcomes—the court system at this time was not a matter of public record—but there were enough whisperings to make it clear that there was real risk. I was terrified that Teresa might do something that would get her arrested. Imprisoned. I didn't know any way of holding that risk at bay, other than to keep as close an eye on my wife as I could.

She would not be the next case.

My fears for Teresa's safety, my concerns over these inappropriate punishments—all of it added up to something solvable, I was sure.

My research with people who had been through the repopulation program was ready for its second stage: I was ready to begin putting participants through the Watercolor Quiet—restructured and targeted to their specific needs—to help them let go of the children they had carried but could not raise. I began to put together a proposal for a new lab that would serve my existing research needs, as well as actively helping people recover more fully from the surrogacy program.

---

1 It transpires that Dr. Gregory did read the newspapers after all. Selectively, it would seem.

I was even starting to think that this could be applied further, that I could use it to address the Society's need to detain those adults who were found to have illegally contacted family members—any family members.

I put together a proposal for a unique facility with a broad mandate—custom designed to treat adults who had either resisted the treatment they'd received as children or who had gone through experiences as adults that required new treatment.

It put me on edge to send it off. I knew it would take a while to be approved, and I was impatient. Eager to get started, desperate to know Teresa wasn't in any danger.[2]

I waited for months, my entire being pulled taut like a clothesline in a gale. My mind went in several directions at once, and each felt like they demanded my whole self:

All my energy devoted to the piles of paperwork, the case studies, the theories, the costings, now making their way through the bureaucracy of government. All my focus trained on the subjects of my study as they progressed through the Watercolor Quiet, proving my theories every day. All my attention lavished on Teresa and her broken heart.

I wasn't getting a lot of sleep.

IT TOOK EIGHT MONTHS FOR them to turn me down.

The response was supportive, excited even. There was an eagerness to hear more of my promising research, a hint that in the future the Council might find a place for me to operate more closely with them. But at this moment, there

---

2 Edited for clarity, pages appeared to be out of order.

wasn't funding available. Everything was tied up in more pressing concerns.

I wrote back with an appeal, of course, but the message always came back the same. Not now. Not yet. Someday, maybe. No one understood my sense of urgency.

Nora had died a few months after I began the initial research, and her voice of support uplifting my work was gone too. I was bereft, of course, on a personal level—I had lost a friend. But her death also left me unmoored. I didn't know who else to turn to for help.

It was then that I ran into Rosemary.

I was getting coffee, going over my proposal again in my head, wondering if there was something I hadn't included, some way to make it clear how important it was, and I wasn't paying much attention to what was around me.

I was walking out of the café, clutching my cardboard cup, when I heard her.

"Miri?" she said. "Miriam? Dr. Gregory?"

I turned, and for a moment I didn't recognize her. I didn't really see her. It took a moment for her to come into focus—when she did, there was a bemused smile on her face. I wondered how many times she'd said my name before I'd heard her.

"Rosemary," I said. "What are you doing here?"

I hadn't seen her since I'd left Gateway.

Since Edgar.

She laughed at my question, at my rudeness, and I wondered what she thought was funny. She seemed somehow brighter than she had when I'd known her last. Shinier. Harder.

"I'm looking for work, actually. I'd love to catch up with

you, though—why don't you bring your coffee back inside, and we can chat?"

It's funny that turning points in our lives often feel so banal. Or, I suppose it isn't funny. Sometimes it's not funny at all.

Anyway. Irrelevant. I said yes and everything changed. Not right away of course; I wouldn't notice how they were changing for years.

Rosemary was sympathetic about my efforts to open a new facility. She'd worked within the prison system,[3] it turned out, and my funding rejections didn't surprise her.

"There's no drive for innovation there," she said. "I think most people see prisons as a place to put people they don't want to think about. Shove everything under the rug and leave it at that. No one likes to take the time to think through what the real goals are."

"But surely preventing people from committing crimes in the first place is to everyone's benefit," I said. "And categorizing this as crime anyway is wrong, in my opinion. These people need help, not punishment."

"Miri, you may just be too logical for this world," said Rosemary.

"That doesn't make any sense."

"When has anything ever made sense? But, you know, it's a lucky break running into me like that."

"What do you mean?"

---

3 Between 1956 and 1963, Dr. Haverstock served as a consultant with the Department of Corrections, Manitoba branch, in Former Canada. She advised on issues related to prisoner well-being during her time there; many of her suggestions were adopted across the continent, and later across the globe.

"I mean, let's join forces. I've spent a lot of time observing people over these last few years, and I've developed a few pet theories of my own I'd like to test out. I think my research could run alongside yours. We can build your facility, and each of us can get back to what we do best."

"Your research?" I said. "Tell me about your research."

"I will, of course, Miri, it's very exciting—but not now. I've gone off in a bit of a different direction from the work you and I used to do together, and it'll take me a while to catch you up on things."

This seemed like an odd thing to say to me, her former teacher, but I let it go. After all, Rosemary was a professional now. She hadn't been my student or assistant for years.

"And you think the Council will give us the funding, if it's both of us."

"Perhaps," she said. "But if you're with me on this, I think it's likely that we won't need Council funding at all."

"What do you mean?"

"Oh, I've got a little something up my sleeve," she said. "You leave it all with me."

And so I did. God help me, I did.

ROSEMARY TOLD ME TO SIT tight for the time being. She had some things she would have to arrange, some people she had to see. She'd have to go out of town for a while. We'd talk soon.

It all seemed a bit strange to me, but with each day that passed I was more desperate to get started. The work I was doing with my patients was promising, but there wasn't enough yet to take it as evidence to the Societal Council—to ask them to reconsider the current penalties for Age Ten breaches.

Teresa noticed that I was distracted and suggested I take some time for myself.

"Let's go away for a few days," she said. "Take some time to relax. Let's go to the beach."

"The beach?" I said. "It's winter; it'll be freezing."

"It'll be bracing," she said. "Come away with me—let's let the winter ocean dwarf all our problems. Let's sit by the fire with scotch while the roar of the waves drowns out all other sounds."

"Anything you want," I said. "Always, anything you want."

It was easy to book a beach house for the week—there was no demand. There were also few stores open in the area, but we didn't mind. We walked along the freezing beach, staring out at the slate-colored waves, and the world felt empty but for the two of us.

In the evenings we read beside the fire. We lay in bed arguing about what we'd read. Teresa glowed softly. Our mornings were spent in the Watercolor Quiet. Gently. I started to breathe again.

On our last morning, I made pancakes for breakfast and gazed at my wife as we ate. Her smile was wide, her eyes were bright.

"It feels a shame to go back," I said. "Everything's so perfect here."

"Ah, but Miri, it's only perfect because it's temporary. An idyllic break from reality. If it became reality itself, the charm would be broken."

"I think I'm a little afraid," I said. "Reality seems risky. What will happen to us there?"

She laughed. "So portentous," she said. "But remember, reality is magical too. We have our lovely little life in our lovely little house. You're treating patients, and it's made you alive again. Don't think I haven't noticed."

"And you?" I said. "What about your reality?"

"Ah, well. My reality is color and flow. I have a summer line to completely redo when we get back, I've been thinking about it all week. It will be all flame, all movement."

"We didn't have to stay this long," I said, "if you were so eager to be home. If you have work to get to."

"No," she said. "This was perfect. The perfect place, the perfect length, the perfect company."

We took one more walk along the beach. We hadn't seen many people around during the week, but there was someone in the distance now. Throwing a ball for a dog.

"We should get a dog," Teresa said.

"You want a dog?"

"Don't you? A sleepy greyhound curled up at our feet? Trotting after us whenever we get up, in case we're about to give him a treat?"

"I've never thought of having a dog," I said. "Or any pets."

"We should get one," she said again. "I can see him now. I'll call him Moses."

"Moses?" I said slowly.

"What, don't you like that name?" she asked. "I do. I always loved that story, you know."

"The story?"

"Yes. The baby in the basket? In the river."

"Yeah," I said. "I know it."

"It just always felt like safety to me."

"Safety? The baby in the river?"

"Yes. He's so small, and he's in this basket on the wide, wide river, and the world around him is so full of violence and anger. And the river holds him and takes him to exactly the right place, exactly the right person. And he's saved, and he's loved, and everything's okay. The river makes everything okay."

I was silent for a while. I didn't want to push things too far. I didn't want to knock her off this even keel she'd discovered. But I had to know.

"Have you never used the name Moses for anything else?" I asked. "For a doll or something, when you were a kid?"

"No," she said, "never. I've only ever wanted the name Moses for a dog. For our dog."

"For our greyhound who'll curl up by the fire. And follow us wherever we go."

"Oh yes, Miri, can't you just see him?"

"I can. Yes, I can see him."

"So we can? We can get a dog?"

"I suppose, yes, we can get a dog."

"Well, now I really can't wait to get home," said Teresa.

I waited till we got back to our house. Till Teresa had unpacked her bags, had a shower, made herself a cup of tea. Till she'd read a few chapters of her book and gone to bed. Till I could see her sleeping soundly, turned on her side with her hand resting by her check.

And then I let myself go. I sat at the table and cried, until I felt like I'd brought the whole sea back with me.

# *Twenty-Three*

WHEN I WAS YOUNGER, I WENT ON A ROLLER COASTER. I SAY younger, but I don't mean young, not really—not as young as you're supposed to be the first time you go on a roller coaster. I suppose I was around thirty-five? Maybe a bit older? As you can understand, I'm sure, there wasn't a lot of opportunity for roller coasters in my childhood.

So when I was in my mid-thirties, maybe my late thirties, I went on a roller coaster for the first time. For the first time, I felt that dark pit of anticipation in my stomach as the car crawled up the rising track, the mechanism clunking underneath me. For the first time, I felt that strange weightlessness as the hill peaked, the feeling of rising as you are about to fall. And for the first time, I felt that intoxicating mix of fear and exhilaration as the car plummeted back down toward the earth.

I never went on another roller coaster. It wasn't that I didn't enjoy the experience, just that it never presented itself organically again, and it didn't occur to me to seek it out. I wonder if there's one near here? I wonder if they would let me on it? It seems unwise, somehow. Surely people of my age are a danger on roller coasters. Higher risk of heart attacks. Higher risk of all the other riders having to watch someone die on their day at the fair.

Anyway.

I keep thinking of that memory now, as I contemplate what I have to tell you next. This moment, what I'm about to relate, in retrospect it feels a lot like that moment at the top of the track. Weightless. Powerless. We had the inexorable climb upward. We're about to plummet to earth. But now, just now? We're held in the eternal half second between.

It's a lie, of course, viewing it like that. It makes what happened seem like fate. Like I was strapped into a car that was locked on a track that was always going to climb to the heights and plunge to the depths. That I was just a passenger.

But in reality, I made choices. I was presented with options, and I made decisions, and sometimes I asked questions in order to make better decisions but sometimes I did not, and that was a choice too.

So here we are. The last moment. The last time I could have prevented everything. The last time I could have given myself a different legacy.

But how do you prevent something you can't predict? Or maybe I should have predicted it. Maybe that's my real crime.

I didn't see the future—I chose not to ask the questions that would have allowed me to see the future, and I have to live with the consequences.

Not for much longer, but still. I have to live with that legacy.

○  ○  ○

IT WAS SOME MONTHS BEFORE Rosemary returned from wherever she had gone. She called me and suggested we meet.

"I could come to your home," she said. "I'd love to meet your wife. Why don't I come for dinner sometime next week, and afterwards you and I can talk shop."

Did I feel reluctant at the time? Did I feel the bile rising? Or is that just hindsight? I think it's more likely that I was excited. Rosemary seemed to be the only avenue to what I wanted—or at least the speediest avenue. I think I had been impatient for her to return; I'd been waiting for exactly this moment. It's only now, only with the knowledge of everything that came after, that I recoil from her invitation like it was a rotting corpse.

So. Rosemary came to dinner. She charmed Teresa immediately. It was easy for her to charm Teresa—all she had to do was talk about me.

"Oh, I was so in awe of her," Rosemary gushed. "She worked magic, it seemed to me at the time. It was palpable, the impact she had, a growing circle of calm that spread out until it touched everyone. And it touched the world, in the end."

"Oh Miri, I wish I could have known you then."

"I can't imagine I was so very different," I said. "I don't feel like I've changed that much."

"You know, I think that's the wonder of it," said Rosemary. "You were already so assured. So young but so confident in what you did. So sure of your ability—you knew exactly how to help people, and you knew you knew."

"Is that so remarkable?" I asked.

Rosemary and Teresa both laughed.

"Oh god," said Teresa. "I can't believe I'm married to someone who's never known self-doubt. Miri, you have no idea. I'm so envious."

I wish I could go back now and tell her not to be. People should doubt, I think. Maybe doubt would have saved us.

Anyway.

We had dinner, and it was, I believe, nice. It feels laden, now, with doom, but we've been over that. At the time it was pleasant. The food was good, the wine was plentiful, and we were full of hope.

After a while, Teresa stood to clear the dinner things away.

"Let me deal with this," she said, "while you two talk. I know Miri's been excited to hear from you, Rosemary."

So Rosemary and I moved through to my study to talk. I could feel the blood moving through my veins, I was so on edge. Or maybe it was the wine. We sat down and I waited for her to start, but she just looked at me. Her eyes were bright, her mouth pressed closed as if to contain something within.

"So?" I said eventually.

"We can do it," she said. "We can build a facility. Custom designed to meet our needs. An intensive inpatient clinic to deal with resurgent memories in adults, to prevent breaches of the Age Ten Laws, to help people who've contributed to the repopulation efforts, to help any adult who needs it. Anyone, for whatever reason."

"Okay," I said slowly.

"I've already approached people to design the buildings," she said. "I found an incredible architect who'll work at a cut rate. I've got a line on the scientific equipment we'll need. I have a security consultant lined up. Everything we need."

I blinked.

"But how will we pay for all that? A cut rate is still a rate, and we'll have to buy the building materials and equipment—this will go into the millions."

"Don't worry about that—I have all the funding we'll need covered."

"How? From where?"

"A few different places. I told you I would. I'm good at getting money out of people. And this is a worthy cause."

"Yeah, but I still want to know where it's coming from."

"Of course, that's fine. That's sensible. I can give you a full list of contributors."

"Okay." I felt breathless and uncertain. Like there was more I needed to know, but I wasn't sure what it was or how to find out.

"So, what's next," I said slowly. "What do we do? I suppose we would have to find a place to build it."

"I hope this isn't presumptuous of me," said Rosemary, "but I've already scouted a location."

"You have? Where is it?"

"Not too far from here," she said. "Not close enough to be a reasonable commute, though. I thought it would be better to keep things a bit remote. We don't want people wandering past the campus and asking questions."

"We don't?"

"I've already put in an application to the Department of Development for the property, but we can pull out if you're not sure. It's a beautiful area, though, surrounded by trees."

"This is all happening so fast."

Rosemary laughed. "It won't feel like that for long. We still have to go through the building permit process, and then construction itself will take a while. It'll be at least a couple of years before we can actually open the place."

I sat in silence for a few moments.

"Miri?" Rosemary said. "Everything okay?"

"Yes," I said. "Yes, of course. Thank you for doing all this work—it's very impressive. I just—I think I need to take some time over this, if that's okay. I need to think things through."

"Miri, this is what you wanted. It was all your idea."

"I know, of course, I know. I just feel a little winded. I'm not processing it properly. Can you give me a couple of weeks?"

"Sure, of course. These things move slowly anyway; a couple of weeks is nothing. But is there any way I can put your mind at ease? Any way I can help?"

"Just give me time," I said. "I only need time."


I KNEW I WAS COMMITTED to this new venture with Rosemary, really. Practically committed, because the first stages were already in place, people were starting work—designers were drawing up blueprints, clerks were processing applications. But more importantly I was emotionally committed. This was exactly what I had wanted. A place where I could help people manage life in the world without the burden of troublesome memories. A way to deal with those who broke Age Ten Laws that didn't involve undue incarceration. Somewhere I could continue my research, learn ever more about how we operate.

Perhaps, I reasoned, my shock and reluctance were merely

surprise. Disbelief. A world I'd dreamed of had opened before me, and I couldn't wrap my mind around it existing in reality.

Whatever the reason for the feeling, it was strong enough to make me hesitate. I went for long walks—weighing pros and cons, lowering and raising my expectations, just generally feeling torn and confused. I talked myself in and out of it a thousand times.

I'd almost completely decided to pull out of the arrangement when I came home after a late-night walk to find the house cold and dark.

"Teresa?" I called.

I walked through to the kitchen to see if she was there again, sitting like stone at the table, but the room was empty. I walked through each room in the house, calling her name, but the house was empty. It's not the sort of thing that normally makes someone worry, this. It was not quite ten o'clock at night, and Teresa was a grown woman with friends and a social life. She could easily have gone for a drink with someone and forgotten to let me know.[1]

I called her assistant, Kiera, to see if she knew of any plans Teresa had for the evening.

"I don't think so," she said. "But it's not my job to keep her social calendar. She left the workroom at lunchtime today, though. Said she had a meeting or an errand or something."

I thanked Kiera, hung up, and made a mental note not to grill Teresa on her staffing choices.

By then I was worried, though, and furious with myself.

---

1 Edited for clarity.

I'd grown distracted after Rosemary had come back, and I'd spent so little time with Teresa.

I'd been worrying less about her since our trip to the beach, but I had been foolish. She'd seemed steadier, and so I thought she was safer. But safer is not safe. There is always risk, and I had taken my eye off it.

I set out in search of her. I went past the childhood centers in our area, in case she was trying to get into one of them. She hadn't been told where the children she'd borne had been sent, but even if she knew, it would be no use by this point. Her second child—the one she'd called Moses—would be almost three by now; he'd have long since been moved from the nursery center to an early childhood center. He would probably be with his sister now, although not for much longer.[2]

But still, Teresa was operating from a place of emotion, not logic. She would not have taken the time to rationalize where the children she had borne were likely to be, she would go to the first place she thought of.

But she wasn't at any of the centers within easy traveling distance. I didn't know where to look next and began to drive around in a panic. I was operating from a place of emotion too.

I almost missed her. It was dark, and I almost missed her. It was, I think, my fourth trip down that street, so I already had missed her really.

She was sitting cross-legged on the footpath outside the

---

2 Since the first implementation of the Age Ten Laws, efforts have been made to house biological siblings at the same childhood center, to allow for some form of familial support in their earliest years. Of course, on turning ten, each child passes through the Protocols, forgetting their early attachments, and is moved to an educational academy.

hospital she'd given birth in. She was very still. I pulled over, got out of the car, and sat beside her.

"Teresa?" I said.

She turned to look at me, her face blank.

"I wanted to remember. I wanted to remember them," she said. "Do you think if I could touch them, I would remember what they look like?"

"You have to come home, Teresa," I said. "Please. Let me take you home."

She didn't resist as I helped her stand up and guided her to the car. She said nothing on the drive home.

I took her through a calming meditation session when we got home, and she fell asleep quickly.

The next morning, I called Rosemary.

"So you're sure?" Rosemary asked on the phone the next day. "You want to proceed?"

"Yes, I'm sure," I said. "I'm very sure."

"I knew you would be."

"We should draw up all the paperwork as soon as possible," I said.

"It's done," she said. "I'll bring it to you later this week to sign."

"Good. Thank you. That sounds good."

"Before you sign," she said, "there's something we need to talk about. If we're going ahead with this, we need to be open with each other. We need to be honest."

"Of course we do," I said. "I agree."

"So, then," Rosemary said, "we need to talk about the boy."

I was silent.

"Edgar," she said.

"What do you mean?"

"I think you know what I mean. I think you know what happened to him."

Again I was silent.

"Miri? Miriam? You know what happened to him, don't you?"

"Yes," I said quietly. "Yes, I know what happened to Edgar."

"And?" she said. "Aren't you curious? Wouldn't you like to see my notes?"

I swallowed hard. My heart fluttered in my throat, in revulsion, in fascination.

"Yes," I said. "Yes, Rosemary. I'd like to see your notes."

# Interlude

We have earlier suggested that the woman the author refers to as Rosemary is, in fact, Dr. Rose Haverstock. We expect readers will know of her many years of service as a government advisor, as well as her many philanthropic endeavors. Dr. Haverstock advised on the writing of several of our foundational laws—notably the Age Ten Laws, the Career Placement Act, and the Equalities Act.

She also founded the Seattle Addiction Intervention Home in 1956 as well as the Trauma Recovery Institution, which now has outposts in New York, Chicago, and Dallas. In addition, she founded the Global Aid Organization, which provides emergency support to communities suffering the effects of natural disasters, such as earthquakes, floods, and wildfires.

We want to stress at this juncture that we cannot be in any way certain that we are correct in this assumption. Based on the timeline of the events and the situations the author outlines earlier in this manuscript, Dr. Haverstock seems the most likely candidate, but it seems wildly unlikely that she had any part in what is related here. Dr. Haverstock died before the manuscript was discovered, so we cannot ask her. Even if we could, we would be loath to suggest that she committed the crimes Dr. Gregory accuses her of.

To accuse anyone, let alone a person of such standing, of the murder of a child is in itself a shocking claim, absent concrete evidence. And the accusations made in the final section of this manuscript go even further in painting a highly unlikely picture of active, deliberate villainy.

Indeed, the slanders the author casts at Dr. Haverstock, more than any of the other inaccuracies and mistruths, call into question the veracity of the work as a whole. In our discussions about whether it was prudent to publish this text at all, it was this that came closest to convincing us to refrain.

It is possible that the author is talking about someone else entirely—she certainly did not trouble herself to be specific in general. It appears that it was unimportant to her that she be perfectly understood.

If Dr. Gregory intended us to recognize this Rosemary as Dr. Rose Haverstock, then I believe we have no choice but to dismiss her claims regarding her as a complete and utter fabrication. An attempt to give herself a greater and more heroic role in the history of the Society, perhaps. This seems the most likely explanation, by virtue of the fact that the institute she describes does not exist. We have made every possible effort to verify its existence and whereabouts and there is simply no evidence of it at all.

At worst, this part of the manuscript is a deliberate attempt to smear Dr. Haverstock's real medical clinics, which have provided crucial aid and succor to those who need it, for decades now. This suggests a spiteful pettiness that beggars belief. We can see no reason for trying to discredit such a prominent pillar of the community other than jealousy.

*Part Four: Carpentry*

# Twenty-Four

YOU ARE POSSIBLY HORRIFIED THAT I CONTINUED TO WORK WITH Rosemary after this revelation. After learning what she had done. You are possibly horrified that I'd been speaking with her at all, for all those months, if I knew—if I even suspected—that she had been behind Edgar's death. And you are right. You should be horrified. I am horrified. But it's too late to do anything about that now.

Maybe I'm lying. Maybe I'm not horrified. I don't feel horrified. I don't feel much of anything. Just tired. I'm so tired. It's taking everything I have to keep going. But stay with me. We're nearly there.

Horrified or not, there's no reason to burden myself with regret. I can't change it. I can't reverse it. I did what I did, and if that makes me morally indefensible, then it's probably no more than I deserve.

We must move forward, and, oh! things are going to get much worse.

Perhaps I should have known better. Perhaps you think I ought to have known better. Perhaps I did know better, some-where underneath it all, but chose to ignore my knowledge because ignorance was more appealing. Perhaps ignorance suited my immediate needs more than knowledge did.

Perhaps some people are inherently self-interested. Like cancerous cells, they take and they devour and they spread. It does not matter if they know they will destroy their host, their entire ecosystem. It only matters that they feed themselves.

Or perhaps these considerations are irrelevant. I did not act on the knowledge I had. I ignored it or I did not. What happened happened, and it happened because of me, and in all the years since, I have done nothing to stop it.

So.

Rosemary told me she could take care of everything, and I did not try to persuade myself not to let her. She had always been so good at taking care of everything. I knew how to run the Watercolor Quiet. I knew how to tinker with its processes, how to transcribe its methodology. I did not know how to build an institution, how to delegate, how to fund, how to manage schedules and projects beyond my own. Rosemary was committed to her own research—she always had been—but that was not the only thing she was good at.

She always had a knack for authority. So we would run the facility together—we had not yet given it a name, nor would we during my time there—but she would have her hand on the details. And I would continue to study and improve the Watercolor Quiet.

It was for the best, Rosemary said. People were suffering, and we could help stop that. We could help them. And we could learn so much.

And I did think—I let myself think—that her past was just her past. That she'd learned what she needed to learn from that regrettable incident and moved on. I didn't ask her explicitly, and I admit now (because what is the point of pretending?) that I didn't ask because I was afraid to. I hedged. I fluttered around the fringes and avoided getting too close.

I didn't want to ask what she thought and felt about Edgar's death, and if she were here now I still would not ask her.

What I did ask was "How will it work, your research? What will you be doing?"

"Well, Miri, you know I respect your work more than anyone's, but I think you have the psychology avenue covered. And you know as well as I do that I never had your patience for exploring the mind. I'm much more interested in what makes it work. Physiology. The brain itself and the body around it."

"But you're not going to do anything . . ." I trailed off.

"Anything . . . ?" Rosemary said. "Anything bad? Of course not, Miri. I want to do brain scans, test heart rates, see what influences them, how they correlate to behavior, that kind of thing."

"Right. Of course."

"There might be overlap between our research, of course. If you have clients you're struggling with, I might be able to help you with them. Or vice versa. Naturally."

I believed her. I persuaded myself to believe her. She was giving me everything I wanted.

And I have to admit that it was good to have her back. We fell back into something like the rhythm we'd had all those years ago at Gateway. We made a habit of catching up over scotch in the evenings, talking through our ideas and plans, expanding on our wildest fantasies of what our little facility could be, what we could do there.

Or, I thought we were talking about our ideas. But maybe it was only ever mine. I've been trying to remember what those conversations were like. Did she ever talk about her own work at all? About her own goals and ambitions, her own theories? God. I'm eighty-odd years old, and I'm only now realizing how egocentric I am. I didn't notice, in those early days, that she was already keeping me out.

And buttering me up.

The Watercolor Quiet wasn't just about deconstructing genetic families, Rosemary would say. It wasn't just a political tool for growing our new world. It didn't just change memories, it healed psychological wounds. It cured trauma. It was the most significant medical development of this significant century.

I'm still not sure what specific laws people were breaking. Are breaking. I don't know how it's possible to legislate against memories.[1] But there were people in prison, and we could help them. There were people who might be sent to prison, and we could prevent that. At least, we could if we had access to them.

But Rosemary's ambitions went beyond the Age Ten Laws. She believed that with the proper research, we would one day be able to expand our practice even to violent criminals.[2]

---

1 The Societal Council does not legislate against the existence of memories, of course, as such a thing could hardly be policed. But the Age Ten Laws specifically prohibit people from contacting their genetic children. An amendment drafted by Donatella Griffin in 1961 added genetic siblings to the prohibited contacts, as well as grandparents and other close relatives.

2 Dr. Gregory seems to be implying here that she could provide a better, more productive and nurturing solution to crime than the New Society's existing prison system. Her claims suggest that she did not take the time to investigate how the existing system functions. The New Society has never had an appetite for punitive imprisonment—indeed, it would be a luxury

The Society had not seen fit to support our theory that adults serving time for breaking the Age Ten Laws could be rehabilitated. They did not forbid us, though, from trying to prove it. We would be breaking no laws, exactly, if we continued our studies. As long as we did not treat people from the same family at the same time on the same premises, there was nothing to legally prevent us.

But there was also no legal way we could procure our patients. Any known violators of the Age Ten Laws would be serving one-to-five-year sentences. And who knows about more dangerous offenders?

But Rosemary had told me she could take care of everything.

I didn't question her at the time, but I'll tell you now what I only knew later: Rosemary had spent time working in the prison system, and naturally she had kept in touch with her colleagues there. And while she herself could not arrange to have prisoners serve out their sentences at our new facility, some of her friends could arrange for them to be granted early release. Conditional early release.

The inmates themselves were told that their release from prison was based on their willingness to undergo a form of

---

they could not have afforded in the early years of recovery. Every bit of available manpower was needed to rebuild. When people were accused of crimes against the Society, the goal was always to provide counsel and aid so they could return to their lives and contribute to their community. There will always be individuals who are a danger to others, and the wake of the Reckoning left many with violent tendencies. But this has always been treated as a health concern rather than a criminal one. Modern prisons are designed to prevent people from leaving, yes—but the time prisoners spend there is designed to improve their health and equip them to return to society better than they left it.

behavioral rehab, and for many that seemed preferable. I have never seen inside a modern prison, so I cannot say what conditions incarcerated people are kept in. I imagine they're somewhat different from the prison I was kept in during the Reckoning. I would hope modern penitentiaries are both more comfortable and more secure. I cannot say. Whatever they are like, to some people our institute promised an improvement, or at least one step closer to a normal life.

As we received our clients (as Rosemary called them; I called them participants), I repeatedly chose not to question Rosemary. I didn't want to know how she was procuring them. I have no defense for this, other than that I was happy to be working again with people, to be studying live lab participants. I was happy to be doing research that could help Teresa's mental state—or if not hers, that of innumerable surrogates to follow.

And Teresa's mental state *was* improving. She and I had bought our own small patch of land halfway between the city and the facility and built a house there. We were surrounded by nature. Teresa could work out new designs in peace if she wanted to, or drive in to her workshop in the city.

I never brought her into the facility for treatment, but what I was learning there helped me improve the meditations I did with her at home. Rosemary noticed the change in her too—she would come for dinner every couple of weeks, nights when we'd all talk about anything but work. After a year or two, she said to me, "Teresa seems so much lighter, somehow. There was a weight to her before, but it's eased."

So why would I question anything?

I gave our participants all of my attention. I let the running of things happen around me. Rosemary took care of our finances. She made the security arrangements—which were comprehensive. There were cameras in all the corridors and rec rooms, and a robust staff of security nurses.

"You won't need to worry," Rosemary told me. "You can have anything you want. State-of-the-art laboratory. A dedicated and skilled research team." And she was right. I told her what I needed, and she got it for me. Why should I question her approach when it was not my job to question it? I won't be judged until after I'm gone, and why should I care about what people think about me then? Rosemary provided me what she promised: "clients," a staff, and a large facility with seemingly endless space.

It was fantastic. For the most part. Sometimes it was merely fine. There were thunderclouds coming over the horizon, but for now our sky was clear and blue and bright. With all the land to choose from, I did not think the storm would descend specifically upon us. Or me.

I did not truly begin to know how wrong I was until the computers arrived, maybe three years after we'd started. They weren't the computers you're familiar with now, of course, this was the 70s after all. They were not like the one my landlady has downstairs in her office now, with its brightly colored screen. You couldn't play card games on our computers. But the work you could do with them—that was incredible to me.

Computers were not around twenty years earlier when I worked at Gateway, and even if they were, we could not have afforded them. Before computers, statistical calculations took hours or even days. And if there were follow-up questions, that process was repeated. But computers allowed us to ask question after question after question about our data. And each iteration took only a few minutes.

I loved the computers, as I loved everything Rosemary was providing me, but they seemed to be too much. Out of our league. I could not keep the questions from rising in the back of my mind.

Eventually I had to ask her. And I did so one night, after a seemingly benign meal, while Teresa was in the kitchen.

"Rosemary, where is all the money coming from?"

"We're providing a service," she said. "People pay for services."

"But who? The Society turned us down. The participants aren't paying."

"Do you like the computers?" she asked.

I tried to cut her off before she could distract me, but she continued: "It's amazing what they can do. I saw your reports from last week. I've never seen so many numbers: 17.8 percent, a 10:7 ratio, 789. I don't even remember what those numbers meant, just that there were so many of them. There was even a graph. It was beautiful—it looked like stairs drawn by Picasso. I've never seen reports from you that nice, that detailed."

"Thank you," I said. "But—"

"I want you to be happy here, Miri. Are you happy?"

"Yes, of course."

"Good, then I'm happy. After all, we're partners, you and me. But our partnership is not a marriage, where your concerns are the same as my concerns and vice versa. We run a business together. And that only works if we focus on our work. I have mine and you have yours."

"I am one of the owners, and the money concerns me too," I interjected. "How can we afford all of this?"

She sighed: "It's the prisons, Miri. Okay? They're given a budget by the Societal Council. That budget goes toward the care of the inmates. And care of inmates is expensive. They have to pay for food, clothing, everything else. It adds up."

"But the prison itself isn't paying. The Society is paying."

"Yes, obviously. The Council funds the prisons based on number of inmates, and the prisons pay us for those we take off their hands. I charge a prison 60 percent of the total fee per inmate. They no longer have to bear the costs of that prisoner, but they get to keep 40 percent of the fee."

"What do they do with it?"

"I don't care, and neither do you."

I paused for a moment.

"It doesn't have to make perfect sense," she went on. "Not to you. It has to make perfect sense to me, and it does. I can work a budget to my advantage, I know how to get gold from pennies. And you don't have to worry about it."

"All the money is from prisons?" I asked.

"Most of it." She laid her napkin across her plate.

"Most? Where does the rest of the money come from?"

"Oh, Miriam, why is this so important all at once? The government isn't the only place with money." She looked at me for a moment, her lips pressed together. "We have a few private contributors."

I had been drinking my wine too fast and was feeling a bit tired. The combination made me slightly more argumentative.

"Who? Why hadn't you told me this before?" I asked.

"I want you to be happy. I do. Would you like to see a list?" she asked. "Of our contributors?"

At this point Teresa came back into the dining room, carrying a cheese board.

"Don't tell me you've started talking about work," she said. "I thought that was against the rules."

"We'll stop, I promise." Rosemary winked at Teresa and turned back to me. "I'll have a report printed for you. I got computers for my staff, too, you know."

"Thank you," I said.

"Don't thank me yet," she said. "I was saving this for later in the week, but we're already talking about funding, so here goes: I'm having builders out next week to look into developing your new lab."

"What new lab?"

"Miriam, you've been talking about this for months. The cassettes!" she said with an indulgent smirk.

She was right. I'd long believed that the Watercolor Quiet could be more effective for therapy-resistant patients if they could undertake it in complete isolation.

Part of the reason the therapy was less effective in adults was that adults find it much harder to divorce themselves from their surroundings. They are more easily embarrassed or made self-conscious, and so less likely to fully commit emotionally to the process in the presence of a therapist.

I had wondered whether, if we began to administer some of the therapy via a recording that they could follow on their own, wherever they were most comfortable, they would be more able to complete the program.

But this would be a massive undertaking. It would need at least double the time a normal, in-person treatment would take. Each patient would have to go through some standard therapy to start with, so that the recordings could be tailored to them. Then an operator would have to record a series of cassettes specifically for that patient—and I had no idea how long it would take to record each one. I assumed we'd have to allow for mistakes, for stumbles in speech, that kind of thing. And then some follow-up therapy, in person again, to ensure that the tapes had worked.

It was also important that the tapes be of excellent quality, with as little background noise or distortion as possible. Things like that would distract the patient and inhibit their participation in the program.

So the lab would need space for in-person therapy. It would need office space, to write up and plan each course of treatment. A carefully soundproofed recording studio to create the tapes, and technicians trained to record them. Those people should not be therapists, I thought. A voice participants wouldn't recognize would be preferable—not someone they knew from counseling sessions, or from walking past them in the corridors, or from anywhere else. Someone with a soothing, relaxing voice that could seep past any self-consciousness or resistance.

It was an expensive prospect. And it was just an experiment. It might not work at all.

"Thank you, Rosemary," I said, cautiously. "And we can afford that lab?"

"Of course we can," she said. "What you do is priceless—any cost is more than worth it. Our contributors understand that, and so do I. If you say this will help you do your work—

help make sure our clients can return to their lives with no danger of falling back into the trap of their memories—then we will spend whatever it takes to make it happen."

"It's never been attempted," I cautioned. "It might be no better than just going through treatments face-to-face. It might be worse."

"And where would science in general be without experimentation? Miriam! Where is your confidence? You are the greatest mind in your field. You created the Age Ten treatments out of nothing. I don't believe you've ever had a bad idea in your life. If you think there's a chance that this will help your work, then I think we should try it. And what is money when weighed against the health of the human mind?"

"That's it!" Teresa broke in. "No more work talk. Does anyone need more wine?"

There was no use in arguing the point further anyway. If Rosemary believed the new lab should be built, then it would be built. And I cannot pretend I wanted her to change her mind. I wanted the lab. I had no idea if my theory was correct, but the correctness of theories was not that interesting to me. I mean, the results were just the end of the journey. The point was the investigation. Because even if you find out a theory is wrong, you learn so much on the way to failure that it's worth the work.

And if I was right—if I could help people even more with this technique—then that was simply a nice, convenient result.

I was excited. The builders hadn't even started working, and already my mind had raced ahead. There was possibility ahead of me, and that was all I ever wanted.

# *Twenty-Five*

ROSEMARY DID SHOW ME A LIST OF FUNDERS, BUT IT DIDN'T ANswer my questions. It was a complex, cross-referenced chart of names and numbers, sprawling out across a dozen pages. It held no meaning for me, it looked more like a bank ledger than anything else. And in my confusion and exhaustion from trying to connect names, dates, and amounts, I gave up and threw it out. I felt at that moment I didn't need to concern myself with finances when I had a new lab to oversee. These funders would expand my studies. They had taken me out of the day-to-day of academia. They had given me luxurious facilities for my research. And they were building me an annex for my new cassette-driven therapy.

I don't want to make it seem like I had nothing to do with the construction of my institute.[1] I have said Rosemary was

---

1 Again, there is absolutely no evidence that this institute exists. Dr. Haverstock is known to have founded several clinics and treatment centers over the course of her storied career, but none of them match the description provided, either in nature or location. The abundance of unverifiable detail on this topic makes us question whether this entire manuscript is simply a

taking care of everything, and perhaps I've created a false impression by that.

I was very interested in the layout and design of the facility. A person's environment has a palpable impact on their state of mind and well-being, and it was always important to me that we made sure our participants were in the best possible state of mind. I wanted them to feel like they were guests, not prisoners—though of course we could not let them leave until we were sure the treatment had worked.

Our location alone helped make security a little easier. Rosemary had found a clearing in a forest in the central part of the Delmarva Peninsula, with a highway not too far away. I think there used to be a town or village of some kind, before the Reckoning, but very little remained. It was either bombed out or abandoned for so long that it crumbled. It was small, in any case. Perhaps *town* and *village* aren't the right words. Rest stop, maybe. Way station.

We were surrounded by pine forest. The smell of cedar. There were cliffs in the distance, with a waterfall flowing down them. I always meant to visit the waterfall, but it was so far, and there was no clear path. You couldn't take a car, and traveling by foot would take hours, perhaps even a full day.

The facility's buildings were set back from the road, which was long and usually quiet. A simple country highway leading to the ocean in one direction and Chesapeake Bay in the other. We were untroubled by attention from the outside world. We had complete peace. Our participants had com-

---

work of fiction (best-case scenario) or a disruptive attempt at political disinformation (worst case).

plete peace. The only noise we heard, apart from our own, was birdsong. It was idyllic, really.[2]

Rosemary insisted that we have some high-security rooms for potentially violent offenders or clients who required a more careful approach. I allowed her to have those, though I did not believe we would need them—at least not for the foreseeable future. We would need to conduct a lot more research before we were ready to try our treatments on high-security prisoners. Rosemary agreed but said, "You cannot grow unless you plan for growth."

They were ostensibly cells, but I didn't like to call them that. I don't know what I would have preferred calling them. Perhaps I didn't want to name them at all. They were in the south wing and my offices were in the north wing, so I didn't need to trouble myself with their existence.

The standard rooms were much more important to me. My rooms were as spacious and airy as I could get them, with wide windows and large bathrooms. I stopped short of making them full suites, but I wanted to make sure they were more than just a place to sleep, so each had a comfortable reading nook and a desk. The rooms were painted a soothing greenish gray, and the beds were made with soft linen sheets.

For a while I wasn't sure what to do about decorations. Art is so subjective that it's hard to find something most people will like without ending up with something generic and uninspiring. Eventually I decided to leave it up to each person. Instead of hanging artwork permanently, I set up a stall

---

2 Fictitious or not, calling an illegal medical prison "idyllic" is certainly a new one.

in the central hub with a wide selection of framed prints that patients could choose from as they wished.

We had to have security measures in place, of course, and Rosemary took charge of that, but I insisted on keeping active surveillance to a minimum. There were cameras in the corridors and covering the entrances and exits, but the patients' rooms were kept completely private.

The rooms in my part of the facility were kept completely private.

We made sure there were plenty of options for activities patients could make use of in their spare time. We built a tennis court and a small movie theater; we put in a swimming pool and a gym. We didn't want people to be uncomfortable or discontented while they were with us.

And I suppose it paid off.

Five years or so in, we were fairly well established, operating at around 70 percent capacity. Still, Rosemary kept trying to attract more participants. She spent a lot of her time giving tours to potential contributors and prison administrators. She put a lot of energy into showing off our amenities, drawing attention to the stylish interiors, showing off the library and the rose garden.

"As you can see," she would say, in a well-practiced spiel, "we've equipped the institute with everything we can think of to make our patients' time here pleasant and productive. They'll be receiving comprehensive psychological treatment, of course, but we want their experience to be something akin to a focused retreat. A time of reflection, a chance to rest but also to learn. An opportunity to read and think more deeply than day-to-day life affords.

"Our aim is to focus on our patients' well-being. We don't want this to feel like a prison."

She was also an expert at balancing the promise of comfort with the threat of discipline.

"This is not to say that we cannot accept people who have shown violent tendencies," she'd go on. "On the contrary, we are hopeful that eventually our treatments will be able to help reform and suppress the violence that propels them. We are fully prepared to deal with anyone who cannot suppress those instincts."

I asked her at one point what she meant by being "prepared to deal with" patients whose violence was not quelled by our treatment.

"It's a sales pitch, Miriam," she said.

"I'm not researching anything to do with violent offenders," I argued. "And I don't believe your research has progressed far enough for that either. We can't promise something I can't deliver."

"I wouldn't make too many assumptions about the state of my research, if I were you, Miri. It's a bit rude."

"Then why don't you tell me about it?"

"We both have our areas of interest, Miriam, and I think you know what mine are."

"Is that all you're going to tell me?"

"I don't think you really want to know any more than that. Besides, as I said, it's just a sales pitch. We want them to see every possible thing we could offer."[3]

She was right. I didn't want to know any more. And I must

---

3 Edited for clarity.

beg forgiveness here. Understanding, if you can manage it. I am complicit, I know I am complicit. But I was doing better and more important work than I had ever done before. I was creating something important, and where else would I get that opportunity? Who else would support me as Rosemary did?

But it was becoming difficult to focus on my work. I knew what I was doing was important, but unwanted questions kept crowding my mind. After all, I reasoned, wasn't it my institute as well as hers? Shouldn't I know as much about it as she did? If we were partners, then what reason had she to evade my questions with such deft determination?

She had access to all my research, all my work. If she knew about mine, should not I know about hers?

But I did not know anything about what she was doing. Besides collecting money and growing our institute, that is. And it was growing. In our fourth year, we added several new buildings and increased our staff to cope with the participants she was pulling in. But as the campus grew, so did the physical and emotional distance between Rosemary and me.

Our old catch-ups in her office or mine were a thing of the past. And though she still came for dinner from time to time, it was much less frequent, and she was as determined as Teresa to keep work talk off the table.

If distrust is a flower, secrets are its soil, and distance is its sunshine. The less I saw Rosemary, the more I fretted over her separate research projects. I was not opposed to working with more high-security participants at the institute, but I expected that I would have a say in the matter. I did not.

As the months passed, I tried other tactics to understand what Rosemary was doing. I tried to be gentler, more persuasive: "I'd love to have a look at your research, Rosemary. I could help you. I was your mentor, after all."

Her reply: "I will always value your feedback, Miriam, but I'm working outside your area of expertise now. You are still focused on the mind, while I am much more interested in the body."

Eventually I attempted a more forceful tack: "Rosemary, are we not partners in this place? I feel it's important that I understand everything we do here. I think I should be able to look at your files."

Her reply: "Oh Miriam, that would be so much extra work for you. And for me too, as I would have to explain so much of what I do to you. You're already so far behind me."

It was this comment, I think—a throwaway remark—that spurred me on to action. How dare she condescend to me, when she owed all she'd ever learned to my training? How dare she pretend the happenings of our institute were not my concern?

And so I went to the filing room. And I found nothing. Well, I found files, of course. Plenty of files on both my work and Rosemary's, but nothing that accounted for her evasiveness or for her elusiveness—half the time I didn't even know where she was. It seemed to me that she was storing files somewhere else, but I couldn't imagine where.

Not in her office, I could see that with my own eyes. I'd spent plenty of time in her office over the years, sharing a drink after a long day, checking in on things. Although there was plenty of room for filing cabinets in her office if she'd wanted them, she'd elected to use the space for bookshelves and anatomical models.

I began to grow even more concerned. Why was she working so hard to hide her work from me? What could she be doing that the records couldn't be kept in the filing room? It was completely secure—only she and I and our head of security had the key, and the door was unlabeled, blending into the blandness of the corridor. It didn't make sense unless she was covering something up.

But still, there was doubt. Was I looking for something to occupy my mind? Conspiracy theories are like micro–religious beliefs to help us find comfort in the unknown. Whether we're looking for the supernatural, or the organized, or the extraterrestrial, they're a way of avoiding more banal truths. I wanted to make sure I wasn't creating a deep malevolence out of something as innocuous as friends drifting apart.

But as I couldn't think of any other way to calm my fears, I went through every file I had access to. And this only bolstered my belief that Rosemary was deliberately hiding her work.

I'd stayed late one night when I knew Rosemary to be away on what she called a "donations blitz" in New York. I was looking through one of the older filing cabinets from our earliest days of operation.

There were files of building regulations, invoices for contractors, records of prisoner transfers—but nothing that pertained to her research or treatments.

After a few hours, tired and jaded, I almost gave up.

And then I found the blueprints.

I hadn't looked at them closely before. They were just blueprints. They had ceased to be relevant to me as soon as the actual buildings were finished. Why keep looking at plans once they've been accomplished?

But now I noticed something I hadn't before. I had known secure cells were being built, of course. We had to have some way to deal with problem patients, somewhere to isolate people who might be a danger to others—to let people cool down if they became volatile. But I hadn't looked too closely, as the design wasn't important to me. It was only now that I noticed there was more to the south wing than I realized.

I had thought it was a simple one-story building. Two rows of small cells facing each other. A security room with surveillance equipment. A small recreation area. But now I noticed there was more underneath. A basement that extended down to three additional floors, hidden underground. They were not labeled on the plans, just subdivided into rooms of various sizes.

I should have waited until the next morning. Waited until daylight. But I knew I'd lose momentum. I would be too afraid (or perhaps too complacent) in the morning. And so I went to investigate immediately.

I had a key to the building, of course, but not to the high-security cells. These were not my patients. I couldn't even tell if there was anyone in them. I walked down the corridor, past the security room, and turned left at the end. There, as the plans had shown, was an elevator door.

I pushed the button, but nothing happened. There was a keyhole above the button, which I assumed meant I wasn't going to be able to use the elevator. But I tried. I went through four or five keys on my key ring before I heard a noise behind me.

"What are you doing here?" said a voice. A strident voice.

I turned to look and saw one of our institution's security

nurses. She was tall, broad-shouldered. She stopped only inches from me and bent her head down to emphasize just how much taller and broader than me she was.

"I don't seem to have a key to this door," I said, "but I need to go downstairs. Can you let me through?"

"You don't need to go downstairs," the nurse responded. "You don't need to be here at all."

"Where I need to be is none of your concern," I replied. "I own this facility; it is my prerogative to go where I will."

"You will not go downstairs."

"Are you even listening? You work for me. Unlock the elevator."

And with that the nurse grabbed me by the shoulder and forcibly escorted me from the building. I stood outside for a moment, gathering my breath and my outrage.

I had no idea what to do next.

# *Twenty-Six*

TERESA WAS ANNOYED AT ME FOR BEING HOME LATE THAT NIGHT, and I didn't know how to explain myself.

It was bad luck, for the most part. Bad timing.

"Where were you?" she asked, as I dropped my keys on the table by the door. She was worked up, I could tell, but doing her best to hide it. "I tried calling."

"I'm sorry. I wasn't in my office. I was . . ." I hesitated. ". . . in the archive. I got caught up in research."

"Everything's ruined."

"What?" I said. "What's ruined?"

"Dinner," she said, with a wobble in her voice. I couldn't tell if she was angry or upset, which I knew would only upset her further. She often complained that her anger tended to come out as tears. But I was also confused—we were usually pretty casual about dinner.

"Oh, love, did we have plans? I must have forgotten."

"No," she kind of wailed, "it was a surprise!"

By then I had made it through to the dining room, where there was a lavish and now cold dinner laid out. Individual quails each on a bed of arugula and walnut salad. French onion soup with crusty sourdough bread. There was even a cheese board set to the side. There were candles lit—they were already burned halfway down—and there were roses at either end of the table. "Oh," I said. "Teresa."

She'd sat down and was cupping her chin in her hands.

"Look in the fridge," she said. Her voice wasn't wobbling anymore. It just sounded dull. Tired. I went through to the kitchen and opened the fridge. Two servings of crème brûlée sat on the top shelf, their sugared tops waiting to be torched. A little blowtorch was sitting ready on a bench.

"I didn't know we had one of those," I said, as I walked back into the dining room.

"We didn't." She took a shaky breath. "I bought it specially."

"This is all so incredible. I'm sorry. I just . . . I mean. I didn't know."

"I know, I know, and I'm not blaming you. I mean, I am, I'm really upset with you, but I know it's not your fault."

"I'm sorry," I said. "What was the surprise?"

"Just a surprise," she replied. "Just because. We haven't had a special dinner together in a while. I miss you."

She was right. While my work at the facility was taking off, so was Teresa's. As her focus moved away from her pregnancies, she had become more dedicated, more innovative in her work, and she was increasingly in demand.

She traveled a lot in those days, showing her clothes all over the world, making custom pieces for celebrities. She'd started planning her own design school and was talking to the Council about it.

Watching her grow gave me such joy. I was relieved that my work with her had been effective and delighted to see her blossom, her golden glow spreading ever further around her. But too often we didn't get to see each other much at all.

I missed her too.

"It all looks amazing," I said. I sat down in the empty chair beside her and took her hands in mine. "And I know I was supposed to be home when it was still hot, but I am really very hungry."

Teresa's mouth twitched, but she didn't say anything.

"Shall we eat?" I said. She hesitated for a moment, swallowed, and then nodded and picked up a fork.

"What were you researching?" she asked after a moment.

I sighed. I wanted to tell Teresa everything, to pour it out before her so she could cover me in understanding and comfort. But I didn't know how to talk about it without sounding paranoid.

"I was looking at some of our construction plans," I said.

"I didn't know you were adding on again. That's exciting," she said, without excitement.

"We're not, but we've grown so big. I realized there's an entire wing of the facility Rosemary had built that I didn't even know existed. I don't even know what goes on in there."

"Isn't that the point? Not that you don't know about it, but that you're each doing your own work? Does it matter if you don't know everything she's up to?"

"I just want to know what she's working on. I think it's strange that she would want to keep things hidden from me."

"Is that what's happening?"

"I think so. I think she's afraid I'll disapprove of whatever she's doing."

"But why would it matter whether you like it or not? Her

work is her work, and yours is yours. You're partners. Why don't you just ask her about it?"

I set my fork down a little forcefully. It clanged loudly on the side of the plate. The sound gave away anger, set loose by exhaustion, by worry.

"Teresa, I have. I have, over and over, and she keeps avoiding the question. She won't tell me what she's doing. Don't you think that's suspicious?"

"Rosemary? Surely she wouldn't be doing something actually wrong. She's a good person," Teresa said matter-of-factly. "I talked to her a few weeks ago, actually. She wanted to have dinner. She said she misses how all of us used to have dinner together."

I didn't reply. I'd never told Teresa what had happened to Edgar, and I'd watched her friendship with Rosemary bloom without making any attempt to restrict it. It was fair for Teresa to question my growing coldness toward my colleague. My old friend.

But I also did not want Rosemary in my house.

"It's my facility. I should know what goes on in it," I said.

She sighed. "Let yourself be happy, Miri. Please."

Well. I didn't.

It was clear that Rosemary wasn't keeping anything that would show clear malfeasance in the filing room or in her office—or anywhere else I might find it. But there might be something else.

She wasn't keeping secrets for no reason, and I needed to know what the reason was. I decided to dig through any files I could find. During business hours this time, but while Rosemary was still away.

Instead of looking for details of participants or research, I started looking for a money trail. I'd always been uneasy about how little I knew about where our money came from, but now there was a new question. If I was right, and Rosemary was doing unethical research—well, who would want to fund that? And why?

It wasn't as easy to find as I thought. There was no one central list of all the concerned parties, and the list I'd seen a couple of years earlier hadn't made much sense to me. I decided to do this search piecemeal, bit by bit, taking my time over every morsel of information I found. So I developed a habit of taking a file back with me every time I dropped off one of my own in the filing room. I would look through it in my spare time, note anything that didn't add up, and take it back when I was done. No one would notice me taking out financial records, I reasoned, if they were mixed in with my patient files. I wouldn't be doing anything unusual. Not visibly, at least. And over time I would assemble a comprehensive picture of just who cared enough about our work—about Rosemary's work—to give us so much money.

And slowly I confirmed to myself that I was right. Something was going on that shouldn't be. Here's what I knew after months of painstaking secret research:

Number one: Rosemary was working in some capacity with illegal militia groups. I found four or five different groups, all with innocuous-sounding names like Absolution Industries or Proteus Development. Each of them I looked into, only to follow a trail of misdirection and obfuscation. One group appeared to be involved in military training. Another had something to do with weapons.[1] I still don't know what some of them were doing, but I added them to my list because they were clearly hiding their activities. This information alone was enough to shut her down. These groups were engaging in deeply illegal behavior and more than that, it was terrifying. Who would be planning a war? Or expecting one? We'd had a globally functioning peaceful society for decades. All our efforts to ensure that war would never break out had been successful for a generation. Who would be planning insurrection? And how had they been evading notice for so long?

Number two: We had received some staggering gifts from corporations. There were large sums of money donated by companies identified only by acronyms, but there were also receipts for gifted technology and equipment. Including tools— electric saws and industrial-size drills, lots of them. This I could not understand at all. Why would we need any of it? Maybe when we were building the place, but what would we do with it now? And why would we need our own band saws and lathes and what-have-you, when the contractors we hired used their own?

It was clear that this stuff was kept in the basement levels below the cellblock, but what use could it possibly have? We were psychologists. We were doctors.

Number three: This last was the most surprising of all,

---

1 These allegations are, of course, baseless in the extreme. Armaments have been illegal across the world since the early days of the New Society, as has combat training, and the government has worked tirelessly to ensure that these prohibitions are upheld. To suggest that they have failed is incendiary enough on its own, but to implicate Dr. Haverstock (if we are to assume this is who the author means) is truly shocking.

but it wasn't really one piece of information. Rather, little bits here and there that, when gathered together, made a disturbing whole. One of the acronyms belonged to a company founded by Gareth Revere,[2] for example. There were personal donations amounting to tens of thousands from Bettina Chou.[3] A company that gave us dozens of industrial-scale tools had seven Societal Council members on its board of directors. I was disturbed to see Ekaterina Yelchin's name on that company's board. I was not surprised to see Secretary Marshall's name there too—though by this time she was no longer Secretary Marshall, she was Council Chief of Greater North America. Time and time again, the names of government officials showed up in our records—not officially, not directly, but always there. They gave us money, they gave us equipment, they gave us access to people with more money and equipment—but they refused to give us public support.

The Society could fund us through corporations with ties to political figures, but it always had plausible deniability.[4]

The Societal Council had turned down our applications to them. We had tried and tried to have our work recognized by the government and the Society at large and we had been denied and denied. We tried for years to work with them because we believed our work was important to everyone. And anything that would help the general populace should be done through the government. Private facilities simply cannot

2 The Minister for Fisheries in New Orleans from 1965 to 1980.

3 Education Secretary for North America from 1960 to 1972.

4 Dr. Gregory was right about one thing: "Conspiracy theories are micro-religious beliefs to help us find comfort in the unknown." (see pg. 298)

help everyone. We only opened on our own because it was the only way we could do anything at all.

So why, after all their insistence that they wouldn't openly support us, why were so many of them contributing to our operations in secret?[5]

The only explanation I could think of was that they were funding Rosemary's work, not mine. They had been very clear about not wanting to be involved in any of the work we'd included in our proposals—in any of the work that I knew about. So they must be funding us because of what she was doing.

But what kind of research could it possibly be? What kind of work would they throw so much money at, yet keep so secret?[6]

What were they hiding?

I spent hours poring over the files. Night after night, I came home from the facility only to shut myself in my study, staring hard at my notes, my eyes flickering from page to page, as if a pattern or shape would suddenly make itself known.

Sometimes Teresa would poke her head in. She always seemed tired.

"I'm going to bed," she would say. "You staying up again?"

"What time is it?" I would ask.

---

5 This really shouldn't need saying, but, to avoid any possible doubt, there is no evidence that the Societal Council secretly funds private medical prisons that it refuses to publicly support. To suggest that they do, or that they ever have, is obviously ludicrous. The Council members Dr. Gregory mentions by name have not secretly funneled cash or equipment to anyone. To repeat, there is no evidence that the facility here described ever existed, but if it did, there would be no reason to believe the government was involved in any kind of double-dealing surrounding it.

6 The foundation of the New Society is transparency. It is universally known that transparency is crucial in preventing conflict. Nothing is done in secret, not anymore.

She would tell me the time without looking at her wristwatch. Often it was after eleven.

"I love you," I would say.

"Love you too," she would say, before turning away and closing the door behind her.

# *Twenty-Seven*

ONE THING WAS CLEAR TO ME. I WOULD HAVE TO BE METHODI-cal. If I was right that Rosemary was up to something, and if I wanted to discover what it was—if I wanted to put a stop to it—I would have to be just as disciplined and efficient as she was. More so, if I could manage it.

I had learned patience years ago. I had perfected it. And so I would be patient. I would be a slow drip of water building to a stalagmite below.

I knew Rosemary must be keeping the most incriminating files in the cellar levels of the cellblock, and I knew that it would be difficult for me to get down there. There were ways, of course. There had to be. The right security nurse, perhaps. Or the right moment in their schedule. And I would have to find a key. But while I tried to find a way to get down there, I could do a closer review of the documents that Rose-mary considered less damaging, pulling out everything that seemed relevant and collecting it together.

To do what with? was the obvious question, but that too I could take time to consider. I couldn't keep my work at the institute, so I brought it home. I set aside file boxes for the purpose, clearing space for them in the cabinet in my study. I wasn't sure how to label them. How to think about what I was looking for. I suppose I had become a bit obsessed with all the tools Rosemary had been given, because that's the direction I took in the end.

Conspiracy theories are just theories. They are planks of wood built on pieces of plans. Each scrap of paper may or may not connect to each other, and the construction might turn out solid and clear. But if those tiny shreds of diagrams are not all part of the same idea, the wood is hammered haphazardly together into something absurd and unstable. Not knowing what I would find, or how the information would be nailed together, I labeled the boxes *carpentry*.


I COULD SEE THAT TERESA wasn't happy about what I was doing. Or what she assumed I was doing, because I didn't explain it to her. Our friendship with Rosemary went back six or seven years now, but Teresa didn't see the side of her that I saw. The Rosemary who was overtly secretive, who had security nurses remove me from the building, who hid records and avoided conversations about our business. My growing distance from Rosemary only made Teresa more sympathetic to her.

I didn't want Teresa to worry. And I didn't want her to criticize me. So I said as little as possible about what I was learning about Rosemary, and kept my stacks of files out of sight in our home.

I divided my research into three sections, each with its own file box.

The first was financial support. I listed every source of money we had and categorized them by how legitimate they appeared to be. Rosemary was right that we were being given a fee for each prisoner we took on, and there were clear records of each of these payments.[1] At first, I simply marked each of these with a green dot to show that they were legitimate payments, but then it occurred to me to check them more closely. I should have started this way, of course, but I was never as detail-oriented as Rosemary.

When I began to check the details of these payments, I noticed something striking. There were too many. They were all listed against patient IDs, in order to maintain anonymity to anyone without the proper clearance, and when I cross-checked the ID numbers, I found several that didn't correspond to any patient we'd ever had. These I began to mark with a red dot as illegitimate.

There were also the extensive donations we received. These could be sorted into three categories: those made by someone I could identify, and that seemed valid; those from someone I could identify but that did not seem valid—from

---

1 We have not addressed fully the claim that this "institute" was acquiring its patients by fraudulently having prisoners transferred to them. As an important tool of the state, the prison system is subject to dedicated scrutiny. All prison information is on the public record, available to be reviewed by anyone who takes an interest. The Society functions on trust of its subjects, and that trust can only be earned by complete transparency. Needless to say, we have checked the records of all prisons—not only on the North American continent, but throughout the whole Society—attempting to find any who were transferred in the manner described. We found no such activity. Dr. Gregory's claim that there is secret trading going on between state-run prisons and private facilities is a wild conspiracy theory to stake a claim in. We don't know where, of course, but then we also don't know that this place ever even existed, so do with that what you will.

someone whose professed views were inconsistent with our work, for example—and those made by someone I could not identify.

The very notion of contributors to the institute began to disturb me. If you can remove negative thoughts, you can remove trauma. And if you can remove trauma, you can remove memories. And if you can remove memories, you can do almost anything. If weapons manufacturers were backing our institution, then it wasn't crazy to believe that they saw what we were doing as a potential weapon.

The second file box was devoted to donations of equipment. Again, this could be subdivided according to who had given it and how valid their interest in our work was. I also categorized them by use—that is to say, the equipment whose use I knew, that which I could make some kind of guess at, and that which was a mystery to me.

I'm sure you can imagine the kind of intricate cross-referencing I had to do for this. It was incredibly difficult. Administration was never my forte.

The third file box was the most important, and by far the lightest. It was devoted to those documents that gave any kind of clue as to what was actually going on. After several weeks, it became clear that this box would remain mostly empty unless I could gain entry to the mysterious floors below the cells. I still didn't know how I would get there.

And now I had people waiting for me. When I say people were waiting for me I can't pretend they were on the edge of their seats. And I can't pretend there were many of them.

As I'd been accumulating my research, I had also been approaching people I thought might be able to help me. I'd decided against going directly to law enforcement.[2] There were too many prominent and powerful Society representatives on my growing list—it seemed likely that if I pursued this through the IID or the DCD, the inquiry would be swiftly shut down from above. I wanted to work with someone who would support me as I gathered evidence, who would be ready and able to reveal everything I found, and who could do so without running up the chain of the Society first.

I'd reached out to lawyers, to journalists, and even to some lower-level politicians and civil servants. It was a delicate task, of course. I still didn't know who else might be involved, so I had to carefully phrase my questions to each person. I didn't want to give away who I was or where I worked until I had more information.

Because I was vague about my dilemma and evasive about my identity, most of them brushed me off. I understand why. I must have sounded crazy.[3] But eventually I managed to convince a journalist, Lupe Alvarez,[4] that there was something worth looking into. She was skeptical, however, and impatient. It makes sense, I suppose. She understood it was a delicate situation and would take time, but she had no way of knowing if I was a source worth having.

Lupe grew impatient with my need for secrecy. I couldn't take phone calls from her at work. I had to call at set times

---

2  Not exactly the choice of the innocent.

3  Indeed.

4  Ms. Alvarez was a staff writer at the *Washington Post* from 1967 till 1978, widely respected in the industry. She passed away in 1987, and so we were unable to verify this claim—but as will become clear, it does not seem likely that this ever happened. Proof is not by assertion.

from pay phones. I wouldn't tell her where the facility was located, for fear that she would show up, tipping off Rosemary that I had leaked information. A story about a secret institute doing secret things with secret funding was intriguing to her. But I was unable to answer her most basic question: "What does this place do that is illegal or unethical?"

I did not know—all I knew was that Rosemary was hiding things from me, and that in itself is not a crime. Lupe told me to call her back when I had something worth her time.

I began to question my approach. Teresa had said to talk to Rosemary directly. That had become more and more difficult, but perhaps it was my best and safest option.

I knew that Rosemary was being secretive, and she knew that I was being nosy.

I called her office several times. Her assistant, Meg, kept telling me she was unavailable and would call me back. But Rosemary never called me back. I tried to schedule meetings with her, and they kept getting rescheduled.

Meg was always friendly and apologetic, and she seemed to have no real control.

"I'm not supposed to tell you this," she said on my seventh or eighth attempt, "but I don't think you're going to get hold of her."

"What do you mean?"

"She's taking other calls, you know. She's making time for other meetings. Just not any with you."

"Do you know why?"

"No, I haven't asked. I've only been here a few weeks, I don't want to get on anyone's bad side."

"Of course. Thank you, Meg. Thank you for telling me."

I didn't want to tell Meg that a good way to get on your boss's bad side is to reveal their secret biases.

So I skipped the formalities. I was the co-founder of the institute, I was above appointments and phone messages.

I walked directly to Rosemary's office. I opened the door and walked in, straight past Meg—who gulped at me, her eyes wide—and through to the inner office.

"Miriam," said Rosemary. "I wasn't expecting you. I'm quite busy, you know."

"Who is that security nurse who covers the cells?" I asked. "The tall one with the arm tattoo?"

"I didn't know you were acquainted with the nurses on the cellblock," she said.

"I'm not—that's the point. I ran into her and felt bad that I didn't know her name. It feels elitist, you know, to be running a facility and not know the names of the staff."

"And this is so urgent you had to barge into my office and ask me?"

"Of course not," I said. "But it's been a while since we've touched base, I thought I'd stop by, and might as well ask while I'm here."

"Her name's Anjelica," Rosemary said, looking at me steadily. "Where did you say you ran into her?"

"Oh, I didn't, but in the cellblock, of course."

"Hmm. You usually don't go down there. Or have any need to be down there."

"I don't," I said. "I don't. But sometimes I go for a walk to clear my mind. This campus has grown so enormous, and I always manage to walk by something I've never seen before."

"Well, the cellblocks aren't the most scenic of hikes," she

said. "You should let me know next time, before you go down there. I take it Anjelica didn't let you walk as far as you'd like?"

"No," I said. "It made me curious. I'd love to see more— are you free right now?"

"Well, I'm not giving tours, if that's what you're asking. And I have an important phone call in just a few minutes."

"Maybe you can just answer one quick question. There was an elevator in the south wing that seemed to lead to a basement. I didn't remember there being an elevator or a basement on the plans for that building. It's fine, of course, if there are cells. If you think we need more cells—I was always happy to leave that decision to you. I just wanted to know what's down there."

"It sounds like your walks don't clear your mind at all," Rosemary said. "It sounds like these walks flood your mind with worry. Miri, the basement of the south wing is storage. Cleaning supplies, uniforms, that kind of thing. It was an addendum to the original plans. Maybe you didn't get a copy of the addendum. I can have one sent over later today, if you like."

"That would be nice."

"Consider it done," she said. "By the way, are you planning some renovations to your home office?"

"No," I said. "Why would you think that?"

"Oh, well, Teresa said she wasn't entirely sure, so I assumed—new shelving units or something, you know."

"I don't know," I said slowly. "What are you talking about?"

"I was talking to her the other day. I'd wanted a new suit, and she recommended a tailor in Baltimore. She even made some suggestions for the color and pattern. I wanted to show her the finished product, so I popped by your home for lunch. It's been so long since I've seen Teresa."

I felt cold all over. I swallowed painfully.

"Anyway," Rosemary continued. "I peeked quickly in your office to see if you were there, but of course that was silly. It was a workday. You would have been here. Anyway, I saw a stack of boxes labeled *CARPENTRY*. Are you trying your hand at woodworking?"

My eyes began to hurt.

"The boxes in the top shelf of my cabinet?" I asked. "I must have left the door open. That's not like me."

I waited for a moment, but Rosemary gave nothing away.

"Anyway," I said, "those boxes are old. They've held all kinds of things: books, silverware, photo albums. Right now they're full of junk I have to throw out. Reorganizing, you know?"

Rosemary's assistant came in with coffee for Rosemary and said, "Secretary Ramadoss is on the line. She's early. Do you want to take the call?"

"Yes, thank you, Meg," Rosemary said. "It was great to see you again, Miri. We should catch up more often."

Rosemary held my gaze until I began to move away. I walked out of the office with Meg, who closed the door behind us.

"Dr. Gregory," she said. "I just wanted to say that it's an honor to meet you. To work here with you. I mean, I know I don't work with you, but in your facility. It's an honor."

"What?" I said, distracted and confused.

"You gave a guest lecture when I was an undergrad at Johns Hopkins," she said. "You were inspiring. It made me change my major. It's why I wanted to work here while I complete my doctorate."

"You're working here and studying at the same time?"

"No, well, it's the same thing. An internship, I guess, a chance to see some real-world research for my dissertation."

Suddenly what she was saying came into focus. Was there hope here?

"Has Rosemary shown you much research?"

Meg's face fell a bit. "No," she said. "I've only been here a few weeks. She says she doesn't have time."

"I see," I said. "Well, when she does, feel free to come and discuss it with me. I'm happy to help."

"Oh, Dr. Gregory, thank you! That means a lot to me."

I nodded at her and left. There was hope there, but it seemed slight. I couldn't imagine Rosemary letting Meg in on anything—not if she knew how the intern felt about me. But it was something. It was all I had.

That evening, I was distracted as I made my way home. I felt chilled all over.

I lay awake long into the night, thinking about Edgar Hartley and the dangerous secrets Rosemary could keep.

# Twenty-Eight

I KNEW I HAD TO STOP.

For a while I knew I would have to stop.

I did not think Rosemary would ever truly wish me harm, but it was clear that she didn't want me to know about the basement levels or what she did there. I wasn't sure what lengths she would go to in order to keep me from finding out, but I knew she'd be obdurate. Gentle, mocking, unyielding. Without any reasonable idea of getting into the lower floors, with the file room all but searched, and with Rosemary's smirking surveillance, I really had no choice but to drop the matter entirely.

And so I did. I appeared to drop the matter entirely.

For a while, this was the same in practice as it was in theory. I had come to a wall in my path, and all I could do was stop and sit in front of it. But while sitting in front of the wall, I was also contemplating it. Running my eyes over its bricks and its mortar, looking for cracks. Asking myself what tools I would need to carve out a gap wide enough to peer through.

While I carried on with my day-to-day responsibilities—

seeing my patients, mapping out their treatment plans, assessing their success—part of my mind was always sitting cross-legged, contemplating the wall.

IT WAS IN THIS STATE of contemplative readiness that I noticed Hilda Brownstead. Or noticed what she was doing.

Hilda was in her early thirties and had been arrested a couple of years earlier, after repeatedly showing up at her younger brother's house. She and her brother, Charlie, had been enrolled in the Age Ten Protocols voluntarily, during the grace period[1] before it became compulsory.

An investigation had shown that she'd been sending him letters for years, though he gave no sign of remembering who she was.

Hilda was sentenced to five years in prison, but this was reduced to probation pending her completion of therapy and reconditioning at our facility. It was her choice—prison or reeducation—and it was something of a gamble.

We would release prisoners to a parole board as soon as we could be confident that our treatments had worked. That could happen within months, or it could take—well, it could take longer. A prison sentence was a sentence. Defined. Certain. Of course our treatment also ensured that they would not find themselves arrested again in the future, as the memories

––––––––––––

1 Between 1948 and 1960, parents were encouraged and incentivized to participate in the Age Ten Protocols. After 1960, participation was mandatory.

and bonds that got them in trouble in the first place would be removed.

I'd been working with Hilda for around six months and she had not stood out to me that much. She had deep brown eyes and a cluster of red curls, cut close against her head. She was quiet and composed, one of those people who seem to take in what's around them more than they contribute to conversation.

Her first course of treatment had been done by another member of my staff, but she had failed the assessments at the end and wound up coming to me for a more intense program. Her progression with me had not been particularly noteworthy. I had given this treatment dozens of times and saw nothing out of the ordinary. And then I took her through her results.

Assessments were done with the participant in a focused, meditative state. A series of questions and suggestions were posed, each prompt sparking a long stream of thought and feeling. It was full of tangents; it was an exploration, a tentative mining of the subject's mind. It was designed to enable us to review the subject's subconscious—to ensure that, even in the depths of their psyche, no memories or connections lingered that could be a danger to them or to others. That there was no question of the treatment having failed.

I was partway through Hilda's assessment before I realized what she was doing. I was ashamed that it had taken me so long to notice—if I'm honest, the process had become a bit too routine. No, the process was not routine, should never have been routine; it was my work that was substandard. I was preoccupied. The success of the assessment process relied on my undivided attention, and my attention was very divided.

Anyway.

It wasn't what Hilda was saying that struck me. Nothing the patients said in these sessions was ever striking, exactly. They were unique. Each person had their own experience of the process, and that experience manifested in strange and unexpected ways. We were not looking for the unusual in these sessions; we were simply looking for evidence of superfluous or undesirable memories. Connections that had escaped the prescribed purging.

Hilda's verbal responses were more normal—if that's possible—than most people's. They would follow rote pathways and then spin off into poetry for a moment, before coming down to earth. There was nothing to suggest that any connection to her brother remained.

What struck me was her face. What she was doing with her face. The meditative state we induced to run the assessment was one that allowed for complete detachment from the scenes being described. It was serene, peaceful, emotionless. But something about Hilda didn't look serene.

There was a faint line between her eyebrows. A slight but persistent furrowing. I continued with the assessment and kept my eyes focused on her face. There were times when the line seemed to ease a bit and times when it grew stronger.

I glanced down at my notes and leaned forward.

"A door opens in front of you," I said. "It is green."

The line deepened a little. She intoned: "I open the door and walk through. There is a corridor. It is empty. It has no roof, and the rain beats down onto the floor. The water is rising, and a leaf floats on the surface. The leaf is being rowed by a queen bee and her . . ."

By this point the line had eased again. I picked another option.

I asked, "What happened to your purple cardigan?"

The line deepened a little. She intoned: "It got caught in a chain, and a thread pulled loose. The thread got caught on the gate, and it pulled and pulled until there was a giant hole. Big enough to wrap around the oak tree and make a tent for the squirrels. They put their nuts in the pockets and built a home for themselves, and . . ."

I tried the same thing a few times, choosing specific prompts and questions, and every time, Hilda would furrow her brow ever so slightly until her train of thought branched off somewhere else on its own. I clicked my fingers by her ears and shone lights into her eyes to check the strength of the meditation, and there was no response.

I finished up the assessment and ended the meditation session.

"How did I do?" Hilda asked.

I paused for a moment.

"I'd like you to come and see me this evening," I said. "In my office."

"In my last assessment, they gave me feedback right away."

I didn't acknowledge her statement. "I'll have a security nurse escort you when I'm ready for you."

Her eyes widened a little. She looked afraid. Or excited? Maybe both. I went to the door and called a nurse to take her to her room.

When I tell you that, at this moment, I saw Hilda more as a person of possible use to me than as a patient to be treated, I hope you will understand. I hope you will accept that I had been driven to extremes. That what was necessary stood in front of what was good. Neither necessary nor good are the same as right.

Maybe it doesn't matter. Am I writing this for absolution? I don't know. I don't know what atonement is worth at my age. Maybe it's enough to write it all down. No—I want action. I want someone to take action.

Anyway. Irrelevant. Your opinion of me is irrelevant. Read this or don't. Know it or not.

What matters is that I saw an opportunity with Hilda, and I took it.

I had been sitting and contemplating a wall for long enough to know that I couldn't see past it on my own. And now here was a crack in the mortar. Here was someone who could help me. Here was my opportunity. I spent the rest of the afternoon planning the details of how my idea could work, and making sure I had the equipment I would need.

I was nervous. I was hopeful. I was terrified.


I HAD HILDA BROUGHT TO my office around seven that evening, when I knew Rosemary had left. I telephoned Teresa, this time, to let her know I would be home late. She refrained from questioning what I was doing, but I could hear her concerns, her unspoken thoughts spiraling within the wires.

Hilda was quiet when she entered, but energy radiated from her in waves. I wondered briefly how she'd spent the afternoon—perhaps fretfully trying to understand what I had to say to her that had to wait till tonight? Her whole body was tense in her effort to contain the fear.

"Sit," I said, indicating an armchair by the fireplace. It wasn't lit—it was summer—but I figured it would be a more comforting situation than the wooden chair in front of my desk. I sat down across from her and took a moment to settle in.

"You look nervous," I said. "Do you feel nervous?"

"No," she said, nervously.

"Do you feel as if you are in trouble?"

"It feels that way," she said, "but I can't imagine why. Am I in trouble?"

She took a couple of deep breaths and seemed to grow a little calmer but remained wary. I understood. She had no real reason to trust me. I was deliberately keeping her off balance. Unlike my previous work, the treatments here were mandated. My patients weren't allowed to leave until I agreed they were ready. It changed the power dynamic dramatically. And I needed all the leverage I could get, because I needed Hilda to help me.

I decided to take some time to go over things before I was completely honest with her. "I wanted to talk to you about your assessment," I said.

She gulped. "Okay," she said.

"You weren't faking," I said. "You were really in a meditative state."

She nodded.

"But you were giving me false responses."

She bit her lip and said nothing.

"It's okay," I said again. "I just need to understand."

She took a deep breath. "Okay," she said.

"How did you do it?"

A faint smile suddenly drifted across her face. She was

still scared, still nervous, but there was something else happening too. She was proud of herself.

"You know neural pathways? Your brain builds paths
from one cell to another as you think, and the more you think
a certain thing, the easier it becomes to think it. Like walking the same route through an overgrown field over and over
again. Eventually the grass and weeds will flatten out and die
off, and you'll be left with a dirt path."

I nodded.

"I just built new pathways. I practiced thinking the same
thoughts over and over again. So that when I was assessed,
they'd be the ones that surfaced."

"But the treatment hasn't worked?"

"No," she said. "Thank god."

"Thank god?"

"Why would I want to forget? How can it be good to forget? Don't try to answer that—I know the reasons. I know
what the law is, and I know why it's there. But I love my
brother. I'm glad you can't erase him from me."

"Do you think he still remembers you?"

Her face fell for a moment. "No. No, I'm pretty sure he
doesn't."

"Why do you think you keep remembering? I don't want
to sound grandiose, but my programs don't often fail."

"I don't know exactly. Maybe because—" She thought
for a moment. "Charlie got really sick. When we were kids. I
was eight or so and he was just three. And he got really sick,
and I took care of him. I stayed by his side for, I don't know,
a couple of months? It was an intense experience—maybe
that's harder to scrub away. And it makes sense that it would

make me remember, but not him. He was so little, and he was mostly out of it."

"Hmm," I said. I was not so sure. Over the years, I had gathered a lot of information about people who were resistant to the treatment in varying degrees. I questioned all my patients about what they thought made them different, about what they remembered from before they were ten (of which they should remember nothing at all). I had never found any consistency. Some of them had had a traumatic experience in their early life, similar to Hilda's, but only a few.

We were silent for a few minutes. Then:

"So what happens next?" Hilda asked, deflating into her chair. "Do I do another course of treatment? Or do I get sent below?"

"Below? Below what?" I kept my eyes on my papers as I spoke. I didn't want to betray my emotions.

"I don't know. Everyone just calls it 'below.' I've heard that if you keep failing, you get taken below," she said.

"And what happens to the people who get sent below?"

"No one talks about it," she said. "One day they're asked to report to the south wing, bringing only their cassette player. When they come back, they're not really back."

"How do you mean?"

"They're normal, but not. They're happy, but they don't say much, and they definitely don't talk about what happened below. And usually they're discharged—or, I don't know, sent someplace else—a day or two after that."

"That's all very interesting," I said. "And you've seen these people? You know for a fact that something terrible has happened to them?"

"No. I mean, it's just rumors that get passed around. It seems silly, like some scary story made up by the staff to keep people in line, I guess."

I was silent for a moment.

"Hilda," I said. "If I let you leave this place, and you go back to your brother—which I think you will do—my job and this facility would be on the line."

"I promise I'll stay away," she said quickly.

"I'd rather have a passing assessment than a promise," I said. "But there is something else."

She took a deep breath. "Okay," she said. "What?"

"All our patients have some resistance to the Age Ten Protocols. That's why they're here. But most of them don't know why they're resistant. They don't control it. And our job is to figure out what even they don't know, so we can fix it. But you—you've done something I've never seen before. You planned your fake assessment, you carried it out perfectly. With a less experienced psychologist, you would have passed."

"What are you saying?"

Hilda was smart, cunning, and determined. She was the only person I knew who could help me. And I was the only person who could help her.

"Hilda," I said. "I can't trust you to authentically pass my assessments, or anyone else's. I can't keep you here, but I can't send you home either. Unless you can do one thing for me."

"What?"

I got up and walked to my desk. I opened a drawer and pulled out coil of black wire and held it out for Hilda to take.

"I need your help."

# Twenty-Nine

SO WE HAVE COME TO IT. THE POINT OF EVERYTHING. MY GRO-
tesque legacy.

I had helped Rosemary build something unspeakable,
and then I sent an innocent person right to its depths.

But I had to know what she was doing. What she was really doing, in every horrifying detail, and I couldn't think of
any other way. Does that make it worth it? A worthy sacrifice?
Not yet, not as I'm writing, but someday? If someone—you,
whoever you are, reading this—can do something about it?

I decided to send Hilda Brownstead below. If anything
should harm her, it would be Rosemary's doing, but mine also.

Let me remove the *if*: what Rosemary did to harm her
was my responsibility too.

My only solace, at the time, was that Hilda didn't really
believe the rumors. She was nervous, but in the way you
might be nervous about a haunted house. You stand in line
almost talking yourself out of it, but all the while you know
that the mystique is nothing more than lore and aura.

Hilda had participated in our cassette program—

autonomous relaxation and visualization exercises conducted by patients away from a therapist. The cassettes had performed well. They had increased our rates of success in the program, and become a mainstay of the facility. They helped treat trauma, reduce memory, even soothe aggressive and violent tendencies in some patients.

And now I would use my cassettes to gather data.

"The rumors you've heard . . . I think they might be true. There is a below," I told her, "but I don't know what's down there. And I need to."

"What?"

"My colleague Rosemary is doing something down there, but she won't tell me what. I call it carpentry."

"Carpentry?"

"It's not in this building," I said. "It's in the cellblock in the south wing."

"There's a cellblock?"

"We don't often use it," I said. "It's a precaution, really, in case someone gets violent and we need to protect the rest of you. There are ten cells, and that's supposed to be all there is. But it's not. There are more floors underneath. Below."

Hilda stared at me.

"More than that, I've found records indicating there's all kinds of strange equipment down there. Not the kind of equipment you'd expect in a medical facility. Saws and drills and all kinds."

"Carpentry," she said.

"Well. Yes. It's just a word. I made it up. I don't know what it really is."

"What do you want me to do?"

I took a breath. I was asking a lot of her.

"You're not wrong about your assessment results. If I report them as they are—if I suggest that you were able to work your way past not just our treatment but our testing—that will get flagged by Rosemary. It's exactly the kind of thing she would want to look into—to help with, she would say. To find a physiological response to a psychological issue.

"She would take over your case for a few weeks. It's my belief that she would take you below. Take you to carpentry."

"And you don't know what that is."

"I need to find out. I need you to help me find out."

"So what, you want me to wear a wire and go down to carpentry?"

"Not exactly. I can't imagine that Rosemary wouldn't discover it if you were wearing a wire. But I need you to be able to talk to me.

"I'll continue to send you tapes. But I want you to record over them. This microphone will plug in to your cassette player and should pick up your voice even if you have to whisper. Tell me everything you see and hear down there. Describe the rooms, the layout. As detailed a map as you can manage. And everything they . . . everything they do to you. The tapes are meant to be sent back to the cassette lab to be reused, but I'll be able to intercept them."

Hilda looked at the microphone I'd handed her and said nothing.

"I know it's a lot to ask."

"I don't know," she said. "It just all sounds so unreal. Like this place has developed its own hyperlocalized conspiracy theory."

"I hope that's true," I said. "But I can't explain what's going on in any other way."

"Oh, come on," she said. "There could be loads of explanations. There are plenty of more logical possibilities. Like she's just storing equipment down there. Or it's a lab for biochemical stuff, you know? Maybe she's working on new medications. Why have you leaped to the wildest one?"

"I thought you'd heard rumors. You said you were scared."

"Yeah, but that was just, I don't know, like the boogeyman. When it's all whispers and secrets, it seems like it could be real, but the moment someone starts acting like it is . . . I mean. It's all dragged into the light, and you can see what nonsense it is."

"That would be nice. But I don't think it's true. Please. Hilda, will you help me find out?"

She chewed her lip for a moment.

"If I do, you'll give me a passing assessment? Let me get out of this place?"

"I will," I promised.

"Oh, fine, what the hell. What do I do?"

"Nothing. Just keep going about your days, but keep the recorder with you. And if Rosemary comes for you, take it with you."

"Okay. Fine. I'll do it. I'll try to help you. Are you happy now?"

"No," I said. "Not remotely."


TWO DAYS LATER, AFTER I turned in Hilda's failed assessment, Rosemary called me.

"Miri, I'm sorry, I can't chat for long," she said. "I'm calling about one of your clients."

I took a deep breath and gritted my teeth. "Oh?" I said. "Which one?"

"A Ms. Brownstead. Hilda. Your report on her was flagged for me, and it was fascinating. I wondered if I could be of some help? I'd certainly love to do some of my own research."

"I was planning to start a new course of treatment with her on Monday," I said. "How long would you want to work with her?"

Rosemary laughed. "Oh Miri, you know the kind of work we do never runs to a schedule. And besides, I intend my treatment to be successful. If she passes, she'll be able to go home."

"What treatment do you have planned for her?"

"Oh, the usual," she said. "Why are you asking so many questions? We've traded clients before."

I closed my eyes. "Of course, Rosemary. Of course, if you think you can help her. Do you mind if I keep her on a cassette program?"

"Not at all, I love your little cassettes. They really do make people calmer. More pliable."

"Then I suppose, fine, you may take her."

"Fantastic," Rosemary said. "I'll have her transferred tonight."

So Hilda was taken to the south wing.

I STAYED LATE THAT FIRST night of Hilda's trip "below," waiting for that day's tapes to be delivered to the lab. As soon as they were, I found Hilda's, and took it back to my office.

"I just woke up," Hilda said on the recording. She was breathing hard. "I don't know what time it is. There are no windows. I guess that's not surprising. It's bright, though. There are fluorescent lights. I think they might leave them on all the time.

"I don't know what happened to me. I went to sleep last night in my room, my normal room. I've been sleeping in my sweats so I can keep the recorder in my pocket, just in case. But I thought I'd be awake. I thought they'd wake me up. I'm normally a pretty light sleeper. I would've thought that if anyone came in while I was asleep, I would have noticed. But I guess not.

"I don't know how much time has passed. It might just be later that night. It might be the next night. I don't know how to tell.

"I'm—I'm really sore though. Like, all over. I don't know what they did to me. There are some puncture marks in my elbows, so I guess they took some blood or something. Or injected something into me. Maybe that's it. They've injected me with something that makes your muscles ache and your bones throb. Can bones throb? I wouldn't've thought they could, but that's what it feels like.

"The room I'm in is small. Completely white. Painfully white. There's a small bed, like a cot really. A single chair. A single shelf. There's a camera above the door—I'm sitting directly below it so it can't see me. I hope it can't hear.

"That's—I mean, that's all I know. I know what my room looks like, and that's it. That's all. Not very helpful.

"I'm sorry."

There were more recordings from Hilda over the next three

days, detailing her mood, general health, and daily schedule. She described several physical exams, including blood being taken from her as well as hair and saliva samples. One of the exams was an endurance test: her heart rate was measured on a treadmill, the speed of which was increased to nearly unsustainable levels. Just before she fell off, it was stopped, and then she was immersed in an ice bath. Her voice was growing weary.

Sometimes there were just extended questioning sessions, lasting the better part of the day. Sometimes they resembled therapy sessions, except that they went on for hours—though she was never sure exactly how long. Sometimes they were more like interrogations, brutal and frightening. One or two were little more than chats—back and forth over irrelevant details of books and music.

She never seemed to be interviewed by the same person twice, and she didn't recognize any of them.

"Somehow the chitchat was even more terrifying than the interrogation," Hilda said on the tape. "What could they be getting out of that? What was the purpose? Where is it all leading?"

On the ninth day, I received just one of the two cassettes I had sent to Hilda. The tape was mostly silent. I almost turned it off, thinking she'd pressed the record button by accident, but then I heard breathing. It was distant and heaving. I listened closely—it sounded like sobbing. This went on for several minutes, but she did not speak.

Then the recording cut off with a sudden click. The voice of one of our audio technicians started in where Hilda had not recorded, going through a breathing exercise.

I received no cassette back from Hilda the next day, or the next, or ever again.

HILDA'S SILENCE BECAME MY SILENCE. I didn't know for sure if I should be worried about the tapes. The tapes were supposed to come back to the lab at the end of each day, but the staff could be a little careless about seeing they were returned. It could simply be that some security nurse or other was letting them pile up before bringing them back to my lab.

But I couldn't let go of the fear.

Dinners at home were quiet and strained. I couldn't eat. I had nothing to discuss. I wasn't reading books or watching television. Teresa and I did not play cards or go to movies together. She asked about inviting Rosemary over for dinner again, and I got up from the table without answering.

"You think you're making your own decisions," she said. "But we both have to live with them."

And I think that was the moment. That was the real moment. I ignored it at the time, I let it pass. I hadn't thought—I wasn't thinking—that the path I was on would mean leaving Teresa behind. But, really, I think this was when I left her.

I had made my decision, and we both had to live with it.

All I could think about was Rosemary and Hilda and *below*. The word was ringing in my ears. I existed slightly outside of myself. I went about my days, and all my limbs were numb.

I was desperate to find out what was happening, but I knew it was too dangerous to try. Rosemary had told me again and again that she couldn't explain her research to me, that it was too complicated, that it was not in my area of expertise and I had stopped pressing the issue. She had clearly demonstrated, through obfuscation and cryptic language and denying my questions, that I was to stay out of her business. If I brought up Hilda, it would only draw attention to her and we would be found out.

So I continued to send tapes to Hilda, but no more came back to me. I could only hope that they would return with her. Day followed day. I was not consciously marking the days as they passed, and yet I can tell you that there were thirty-seven.

I mentioned Hilda to Meg in case she had heard anything, but Rosemary was still keeping her assistant at arm's length. Meg knew what meetings were on the calendar, which phone calls were due, and how Rosemary took her coffee; and that was about it.

I cannot tell you what I did in those days. I was a step out of reality, I think. I was fractured. I know that I continued to come into work. I must have seen my patients. I must have overseen the recording of cassette programs. I must have planned treatments and run assessments. I can only apologize to the people I saw during this time. They did not get my best work.

Teresa started to remove herself from me. She was not around for dinner. She slept in a separate bed. She left rooms when I entered. I told her she was doing this, and she said I had it all backward. That it was me who was no longer there. Perhaps she was right. I don't remember who switched bedrooms. I don't remember who left rooms first. I don't remember any specific conversations. I don't remember many conversations at all. I remember being home sometimes, and I remember her being home sometimes. I can only apologize to her. She did not get my best self.

I did try. I think I did try to find a way to get to Hilda. I didn't want to make things worse for her, and everything was just so much harder. Like trying to do needlepoint when your fingers are numb. Like walking across a tightrope surrounded by thick fog.

I remember checking the filing room again. Looking for some kind of clue. Access codes or patient records or anything. It was fruitless. I knew it would be fruitless.

I tried to find the security nurses who covered the cells and the levels below, but I couldn't find staffing records for them. They never seemed to come into the main staff areas— I recognized everyone I saw there. I asked around if any of the other security nurses knew them, but no one did. Or no one would tell me they did. There appeared to be no cross-over at all.

I was alone and I was desperate and I was hopeless. It was at that lowest moment when Hilda came back. I was walking down a corridor—the corridor I had walked every day for almost ten years—and she was in front of me, and the world came roaring back into focus.

I expected her to react to the sight of me, but she did not. She walked straight past. I turned to look after her.

"Hilda," I said. "Hilda."

She didn't turn. It was as if she couldn't hear me at all.

I caught up to her and held her arm. I looked her in the eyes and said, "Hilda Brownstead." She looked into my eyes and said, "Yes?"

The last time I saw her, she had been a tight ball of energy. Now she was deflated. Her wide shoulders slumped.

Her eyes flicked up to me and then back down, like it was too much energy to keep them raised.

"What happened down there?"

She offered no response.

"What did they do to you?"

I waited longer this time, but still she was silent.

"Do you have the tapes?"

Nothing. I tried a different tactic.

"Hilda, tell me about your brother, Charlie."

Something, some feeling, some pain drifted across her face, and then it was gone.

"Do you remember the time he was sick?"

There was nothing.

"Do you remember staying by him all those weeks? Little Charlie, sick and alone, with his big sister looking after him?"

She winced. Then she said, "Why are you holding my arm so tight? It hurts."

"I'm sorry," I said and let go. "Do you remember my name, Hilda?"

"Yes," she said. "I have to go. My assessment is in five minutes. Then they'll let me go home."

Her eyes were wide and vacant. They were open windows on an abandoned house. She said she remembered my name, but did not say it. She had an assessment scheduled, her chance to finally go free, but showed no excitement. She moved as an automaton. Any knowledge in her head was devoid of emotion. The memories that remained were merely information.

I went to my office and tried to cry. I screamed silently.

I took desperate breaths. But I would not be given catharsis. I would have only guilt and shame, and that was all I deserved.

I had sent her to her doom, and I was no closer to having answers than I would have been without her. I gave myself over to helplessness.

For a while. But I knew I could not stay there in that misery. My guilt turned. It pivoted, redirecting itself into anger. Rosemary was harming people beyond recognition, and I had no choice anymore. I had to stop her. What she had done to Hilda could not be allowed to continue—and who was going to stop it, if not me?

It was my responsibility. She was mine to stop.

# *Thirty*

WITH INCREASING DETERMINATION AND INCREASING DESPERA-
tion there also came fear. I couldn't quell the suspicion that
Rosemary had sent Hilda back just for me. As a warning.

"*I could do this to you too*," she could be saying with this
gesture.

But what choice did I have? I had to find out more. I had to.

If Hilda wouldn't or couldn't speak to me, then I'd have
to find out what happened to her some other way. And I still
had hope. She may not be able to tell me whether she'd completed the task I'd given her, but that didn't mean she hadn't.

Many of the tapes had never come back to me, but that
didn't mean they didn't exist. If there was a chance Hilda had
recorded anything else that happened down there, I had to
find out. I had to get those tapes.

I stayed late that night, looking for all the world like I was
concentrating on a complicated treatment plan but again just
waiting until I could be sure Rosemary was gone. It struck
me now—and perhaps should have earlier—that Rosemary's
presence or lack thereof might be irrelevant. There were security nurses everywhere; there was our staff of therapists,

my new and growing roster of audio technicians. Could I trust them? Could I trust all of them? Could I trust any of them?

But there was nothing I could do about that now.

I didn't bother calling Teresa to let her know I'd be late. There didn't seem to be much point.

The hours passed, and the world around me grew quiet. There was no set bedtime for patients in the main complex, but apart from a couple of chronic insomniacs, most of them tended to be in their rooms by eleven. When it felt as still as it could be—it was never completely quiet or empty, as there was round-the-clock security—I ventured forth from my office.

I put on my jacket and slung my handbag over my shoulder. I nodded farewell to the staff I passed in the hallways, looking like I was heading out to my car. Or, depending on which direction I was walking when I was spotted, like I'd forgotten something and come back inside to retrieve it.

Eventually I made it to Hilda's room. I stood outside it for a moment, just breathing. In. And out. Then I raised my fist and knocked. Quietly. Cautiously.

I held my breath for a moment, but I heard no response. I checked the corridor around me, took a breath, opened the door, stepped in quickly, and closed it behind me.

I stood with my back to the door for a moment. The room was tidy. It barely felt lived in, except for a canvas bag that had been carelessly shoved under the desk. I could see a shape lying on the bed, but the lighting was dim.

I stepped toward the bed. "Hilda?" I said, keeping my voice low. "Are you awake?" I waited for a moment, but she gave no indication that she'd heard me.

I moved closer. I could hear her breathing faintly. "Hilda?"

I said again. It wasn't until I was right by the bed that I noticed the light glinting off her eyes. They were open, staring at the ceiling.

"Hilda," I said. "Are you okay?" I took hold of her hand gently, and she flinched. "Hilda?" I said, one more time. Nothing. She was asleep. Or dazed. Eyes open but inattentive. I noticed that one of her hands was lying across her belly, below her ribcage.

Guilt overwhelmed me for a moment. I didn't know if this was trauma—something serious but that she could heal from—or if it was damage. Permanent. Irrevocable.

Would she ever come back to herself? I hoped so. God, how I hoped so.

I turned away from her. Nothing in the room looked like it had been touched since she'd returned, except her duffel bag, so I went to the desk and pulled it out. I opened it and saw, mixed in with her clothes and toiletries, the tapes. All of them.

I zipped up the bag and carried it to the door. I listened for a moment to check whether I could hear anything on the other side, but everything was still. I took a breath and walked out into the empty hallway, walked quickly to the exit, and headed to my car.

The house was dark when I got home. Teresa either was already in bed or hadn't come home at all.

Anyway. Irrelevant.

Irrelevant to this part of the story. I'd made my decision.

I went straight to my office and dug out a tape deck I kept there. I splayed Hilda's tapes across my desk, attempting to put them in chronological order. I picked out the earliest cassette and slid it into the machine, slipped the headphones over my ears, and pressed *play*.

My heart was pounding. My mouth was dry. There was a moment of static, and then Hilda's voice cut through. The recording was slightly distorted: she sounded faint and a little out of breath. I turned up the volume as high as it would go and pressed the headphones hard against my ears.

But her recorded responses were nonsense. In one twenty-minute stretch, she described the bare lightbulb on the ceiling of her room. She couldn't reach the bulb, but she managed to stand on a chair she had put on her bed. She described the filaments, burning like dawn, like a forest fire, like a secret, like the eyes of a cat at night.

I got myself a glass of water before I listened to the next tape. I did not want to keep listening. After a few minutes I pulled myself together and pressed *play*.

For a while, all I heard was breathing.

"I . . . uh . . . ," said Hilda eventually, "I can't close my eyes. They're too dry. I don't know what to do. I need to close them to get them better, but they won't, they won't close."

She kept breathing in shallow, sobbing breaths. It was a while before she spoke again. "I think I'm nearly crying. If I cry it will be okay. Crying will help. Oh god.

"They, um—they held my eyes open . . . all day. They shone lights into them . . . and recorded . . . what they did. They asked me . . . loads of questions and recorded . . . what happened to my eyes . . . while I answered them. I don't even know . . . what I told them. I don't know what I said. They did it for hours.

"I don't know, I don't know how long . . . they did it for.

It's just always . . . so bright here. I don't know how time is passing . . . I don't know what day it is. I don't know how long I've been here.

"How long do I have to be here?"

Again there was a click, and the prerecorded audio technician's voice came out at me. "Breathe in," it said. "And out."

It was judging me.

The next tape was missing, so I tried another. The first side just played static. The second was the audio technician again.

I didn't know what to make of this. Were those tapes all I was going to get? Had she been so hurt so quickly that she hadn't made any more?

I scrabbled through the tapes to find the next one and shoved it into the recorder.

This time Hilda's voice came through the headphones, but for a while she didn't say anything. She was whimpering. Eventually she took a big, shaking breath.

"They cut me open," she said then. "They cut open my chest and pulled apart my ribs so they could look at my heart while I talked.

"Why? Why do they need to do that? What more can they do to me?"

I dry retched for a moment. Her voice continued.

"They went into my belly and behind my ribs. It was cold. They left something in there.

"I can feel it just below my ribs," said Hilda. "It's in there. It's long, like a centipede. It's holding onto me."

She kept breathing—shallow, sobbing breaths. It was a while before she spoke again.

"I can feel it just below my ribs."

She broke down sobbing. She sobbed for the rest of the tape.[1]

I pulled a large potted plant toward me and vomited into it. I let my head hang there for a moment. I still felt sick to my stomach. It was one in the morning, but I couldn't stop now.

The remaining tapes were even less consistent. There were more that had nothing recorded at all, and some with static. A few horrifying tapes were simply recordings of Hilda crying.

And then there was one that scared me more than anything I'd heard so far. Hilda started talking from the start—no, not talking. She was reciting, almost. In a strange, singsong voice.

"Crack it open," she said. "Crack it like a nut and look deep within.

"Poke at it, prod it, see its wires zap.

"See the thoughts zap along its wires from one side to the other.

"Crack it open.

"Crack it like a nut."

I gagged again but held the vomit back. My throat burned. I wondered if I should stop. What would I gain from keeping on? Clammy and shaking, I put the next tape in the deck.

For a while I wasn't sure what I was hearing. Atonal hum-

---

1 Obviously these descriptions are incredibly disturbing. If we had any indication that they were true, they would be extremely damaging to the Society, especially those members whom the author has accused of being involved financially in the institute. And, of course, to Dr. Haverstock. But this place does not exist.

ming? Muttering to herself on the other side of the room? Eventually I realized that Hilda was laughing. A horrible snickering.

The tapes degraded still further. She didn't often say anything, and when she did it was more disturbing singsong refrains, talking about blood and flesh, about tearings and shatterings.

The final week's worth of tapes contained just static on both sides, and this gave me pause. She hadn't used both sides of the early tapes and now, when she did, she said nothing at all. I didn't know what to make of this.

I wiped a hand across my face, surprised to find that it was wet. No. Not surprised. How could I have been surprised?

But at least now I knew. Hilda had been through intense physical and psychological torment. I wondered what Rosemary had gained from the process. What she had ever gained from these kinds of processes.

She had achieved our one stated goal, however. Hilda didn't remember her brother. She wouldn't break the law again.

She wouldn't do anything again.

# Thirty-One

AFTERWARD, I SLEPT. I DON'T KNOW FOR HOW LONG. SLEEP WAS a welcome escape, but of course it was only temporary.

When I awoke, I was faced with the need for decision. For action.

I had evidence. For the first time, I had real evidence. And now I knew, now I knew for sure, that Rosemary had to be stopped. I had to stop her from harming anyone else the way she had harmed Hilda.

But I had to be careful. Rosemary had spent her entire career establishing contracts, forging alliances. She had created for herself a web of complicity and indebtedness. All the officials named in the files knew that if she went down, she would bring them down with her. And they would not allow that to happen.

Rosemary would be protected. I would go down instead.

But I had prepared for this, to a certain extent. After Rosemary had indicated that she knew I was keeping files in my home, after she had indicated that Teresa was talking to her, I stopped keeping files in my home. It had taken a bit of thought to put this in place—if I couldn't keep things at the institute and I couldn't keep them in my home, where else was there to keep them?

I knew where there was and really I'm only delaying now, at the end, because, well, it's my story and I'll tell it how I want. Is it cheap of me, do you think, to try and insert some dramatic tension to my life story? More tension, I should say, because I was tense enough while living it. I'm tense still.

Anyway.

Irrelevant.

The other place there was for me to keep things was a safety deposit box in a bank on the other side of the country registered to an Ewa Keith.[1] I'd had it for years. It was one of the first things I set up, when bureaucracy started to assert itself in the world again. It was easy, in those days, to claim a new identity, to create a false persona, to give yourself a fake name.[2] Well. This name wasn't fake, of course. It was real. It was an amalgam of my parent's names. It was part of me. They were part of me, even if I remember little more of them than how they died.

What's important is that—as the world started to piece itself back together, as it started to make records of the pieces—it was easy to claim a little extra piece. And so Ewa Keith had a birth certificate, which meant that she could get as many identifying documents as she needed. And plenty of new identifying documents were brought in and phased out and reestablished over the decades. Each time, I took a small holiday alone. I liked to travel alone. And while I was travel-

---

1 Dr. Gregory does not name the town, but there are records of an Ewa Keith having lived in Salt Lake City.

2 It may have been easy, but it was still fraud.

ing, I could apply for certain things. And so Ewa Keith had a safety deposit box.

I didn't really have any plan for her, when I first brought Ewa Keith into existence. There was no reason for her. No pressing need, and no expectation of one. I suppose I just didn't trust the . . .

I just didn't trust.

I had never told anyone about her. I think I always assumed that it was a normal thing to have done. I would have been surprised if Teresa and Rosemary and everyone else hadn't done something similar. It's just preparation. If you live in California, you store water and flashlights in case there's an earthquake. If you live in Australia, you build firebreak fences and water reservoirs in case there's a wildfire. If you live in the world after it has torn itself apart, you give yourself an escape route in case it does again.

And you see, I was right to do so. I didn't know when or why I would need it, but I was right that I would. So you can take from that what you will.

As I became less secure in my position, after I ceased to trust my old friend, after I ceased to trust my wife, I started sending things to the safety deposit box. Slowly. Carefully. Just a couple of things at a time shoved into a pile of outgoing mail, or tossed in my bag to be dropped in a mailbox on my way somewhere. Dropping things in mailboxes now and then, I reasoned, wouldn't appear suspicious in the least, if anyone happened to be watching.[3]

---

3 Delusions of being followed are generally considered to be a sign of an unstable and unreliable mind.

By now I had shipped off most of what I'd found. But there were a couple of things still in my office at the facility, waiting to be sent: some patient files and a list of guests from a benefit dinner Rosemary had held earlier in the year. There was also one more file of the initial plans for the building that I wanted to have another look at.

And I wanted one more thing to make sure all the evidence could be tied together: photographs. Photos of the buildings, of the patients, and, if I could manage it, a photo of Rosemary. I wanted to put her there beyond a shadow of a doubt.

So when I woke that morning—with a crick in my neck after sleeping on the couch in my study—I may have been scared. I may have been so terribly, terribly sad. But I knew what I had to do next.

I packed the cassettes in some padded envelopes—it took three or four—wrote out the address on each, and dropped them in my bag. I stepped out of my office with hesitation and listened for a moment. The house felt still. Dead. Teresa wasn't home.

I took a quick shower and brushed my teeth. It would not do to turn up at work looking like I'd had no sleep, due to being neck-deep in uncovering a dangerous conspiracy. I grabbed Teresa's old camera and left.

The house was still empty as I walked out to my car. It felt eerie. Permanent. Or maybe I just remember it that way because I know now that it was.

Is it strange that I can't remember the last time I saw my wife? What she was wearing, what I said to her?

Anyway.

I got in my car and headed to the post office. It was a good half-hour drive out of my way—a small gas station with a drop-off counter, in the middle of the highway—but the detour felt worth the extra time. I wanted to see my last few parcels stamped and put in delivery sacks with my own eyes.

And then I got back behind the wheel and turned to face it.

I turned to face the end.

IT WAS TEN THIRTY BY the time I pulled up outside the institute. I glanced around, but there was no one near the parking lot. I pulled out the camera and took a few shots of the outside of the building.

"Calm down, Miriam," I told myself. "No one can tell how scared you are." I almost believed myself.

Rosemary was one of the first people I saw as I entered the building.

"Good morning, Miriam," she said, a slow smile seeping across her face. "How nice to see you."

"Is it, Rosemary?" I said. "You see me almost every day. From a distance, maybe."

"Hmm," she said. "For some reason I wondered if I would, today. I wondered if maybe you wouldn't be here."

"Why wouldn't I be here?"

"Oh, I don't know," Rosemary said, an eyebrow cocked, her head tilted. "You've seemed off recently. A little pale. I wondered if you were coming down with something."

"Well I'm fine," I said. "As you see."

"If you're sure. If you are coming down with something

of course, if you are not feeling entirely yourself, you should stay away. You don't want to run the whole facility into rack and ruin just because you think you're strong enough to overcome whatever you've got on your own."

"I don't have anything, Rosemary. I'm perfectly fine."

She looked at me for a moment. Appraised me. "All right, then," she said. "If you're sure." And she turned and walked away.

I took a deep breath, my heart pounding, my fingertips tingling, and raised the camera. I pressed the shutter button a few times, knowing the photos would be useless. What good was a picture of someone's back?

I sighed and headed in the other direction. I unlocked the filing room and went in, locking the door behind me. I took a quick look through the filing cabinets to check if there was anything I hadn't found yet, pulling out one or two last documents that might be a bit suspicious. I piled them in with the files of some of my ongoing patients and left the room.

Once in my office, I sat down and caught my breath. I was torn as to what to do next.

I wanted to take everything I had and run, right then. As fast and as far as I could. But that would stand out. I didn't know how Rosemary would or could come after me. She had a lot of influential friends. And I was sure she'd be willing to spin whatever stories she needed to come out on top.

She could claim that I was dangerous, that I was a secret dissident—that I was actually opposed to the Age Ten Protocols, that I was working to dismantle them rather than shore them up. She could say anything and make it impossible for me to prove her wrong. All the evidence of my real work was in this building, and the building was hers. It had always been hers. I'd been wrong, I'd been stupid to believe it was mine.

The best idea I could think of was to put in a normal day. I had some sessions with patients scheduled for the afternoon. I had treatment plans to go over. I would get through the day as if it was any other. Then when I left, I would just . . . not go home. By the time Rosemary realized I was gone, it would be too late.

EVERY MOLECULE IN MY BODY wanted just to sit in my office with the door closed. Every molecule that wasn't crying out to run, that is. But I didn't. It wasn't how I usually behaved, and so I could not behave that way.

I left my door open as I looked over the files of the patients I was scheduled to see. I sat there with a pen moving over the pages of a treatment plan. When I went to the treatment room for my 11:00 A.M. appointment, I switched off the light and closed the door but didn't lock it. This was my usual practice—I wanted patients to know that they could always come to see me. If I wasn't there, they could let themselves in to wait. Anything important or confidential would be locked in cabinets, but the room itself I left accessible. To avoid suspicion, I left it accessible.

I went through the planned session with my patient, who was nearing the end of his program. Everything was progressing more or less as it should. I actually relished the distraction, which surprised me. But I was sad as I treated him as well. It had suddenly come home to me that today's appointments were the last I would ever keep. This rote, textbook treatment session was my farewell.

When I realized this, I took pains to note the details. His name was Miguel. He was one of our older patients—around fifty-three or fifty-four. It was uncommon for us to treat people older than their mid-thirties, because it was unusual for the Age Ten Protocols to be broken later in life. If they hadn't worked, it would show up earlier and be dealt with in whatever way.

Miguel was a sweet man. He tried very hard; he wanted this for himself. Not because he wanted to forget his family but because he wanted to go home. He didn't want to be in prison for trying to hide a granddaughter.

I had a moment of doubt. What was I leaving Miguel to, if I ran? What was I leaving all my patients to? If Rosemary had control of the whole facility, without my influence, what would she do?

I couldn't know, and that terrified me. But if I didn't go, I couldn't stop her at all.

I finished up the session and went to the cafeteria to get a coffee on my way back to my office. If I was here to seem normal, I was going to put in the detail work.

When I got back, the door to my office was ajar. This wasn't unusual. If someone was waiting inside, they might have left it open. Or if someone had come and then decided not to wait, they might have forgotten to close it. But given my state of my mind, it made me uneasy. I slowly pushed the door all the way open. The office was empty.

But as I stepped inside, I saw something waiting on my

desk. Just a single piece of white paper, but somehow it filled me with dread. I picked it up.

But before I could unfold it and read it, the phone rang.

I quickly picked up the receiver to silence its startling alarm. "Hello?" I said.

"Dr. Gregory. It's Meg." Her voice sounded breezily professional as always, if a fraction higher in pitch.

"Of course, Meg, what can I do for you?"

"I'm just calling to see if you have time for a meeting with Rosemary this afternoon at four thirty."

"Oh," I said. I felt as if a hole in the ground had opened beneath my feet. "Yes, Meg, that's fine. In Rosemary's office?"

"Actually she's asked to meet you in the south wing."

"Okay," I said. "That's fine. I'll be there."

"I sent a note to your office as well," Meg added. "With some information to help you prepare for the meeting?" Her professional tone slipped a bit, gliding up into a question.

"Yes, I see that. It's on my desk. I'll have a look over it before the meeting."

"Fabulous. Thank you, Dr. Gregory, I'll let Rosemary know the meeting can go ahead."

"Thank you, Meg," I said. "Thank you."

I hung up the phone and opened the note. It was handwritten—scrawled, really—in large capital letters.

It read *DO NOT COME TO THE MEETING*.

# Thirty-Two

MY HEART WAS RACING. DID MEG MEAN THAT I WAS IN DANGER? Was the meeting a pretext to get me into carpentry? There was no way I could follow up without putting her in danger too. I could either believe her or not.

If she was right, was I safe even now? If Rosemary was determined to take me below, then she would have put measures in place to prevent my leaving. Would she have people keeping an eye on me? What would they do to me if I tried to get away?

I don't know how long I stood there, frozen. Eventually something moved in the corner of my eye, and I looked up. Through my office window, I saw Rosemary walking across the parking lot toward her car. She looked up and noticed me.

She smiled and gave me a cheery wave, and it felt like my heart stopped dead. She got into her car and drove away. She must have a meeting, I thought. A lunch, perhaps, with some official or other. Something sketchy.

And then I saw someone else. A security nurse. Not just any security nurse—the one who escorted me from the cell-block when I discovered the basement levels. Anjelica.

She was standing in the parking lot smoking a cigarette.

Suddenly, my mind felt clear. If Rosemary had someone watching me, surely it would be her. I quickly unlocked a cabinet and searched through my medical supplies for what I needed. I went back to the window.

She was still there, and no one else was around.

I pushed up the window and waved her over.

"Anjelica," I called. "Sorry to interrupt your break—can you come over for a moment?"

She eyed me for a moment and walked slowly to my window.

"What?" she said. Just as sullen as I remembered.

"Oh, it's nothing important really. I'm just hoping you could help," I said, babbling a bit, trying to seem like the doddering old woman Rosemary had no doubt painted me as. "I need to clarify a few things regarding some patients. And I need to check Rosemary's files on them, because I'm sure something's missing from mine, and I don't want to accuse anyone of stealing, of course . . . But, you know, I don't know what else could have happened, and I need to clear it up as soon as possible, but I just saw her leave, and I know you're one of her most trusted security nurses, so I wondered if you have access—"

And I brought up my hand as swiftly and fluidly as I could, plunging a needle into her neck and pumping her full of morphine. She dropped to the ground, her cigarette still dangling from her mouth.

I DIDN'T TAKE ANY TIME to think about what I was doing. I locked the door of my office, grabbed everything I needed, and clambered out through the window. I wish I could say I did so with ease and grace and what-have-you. But I was not as young as I once was.

I dragged the nurse—Anjelica—I dragged Anjelica around the corner of my office, into a small space between the buildings. I quickly swapped my clothes for her nurse's scrubs, coiled my gray hair under her hat, and took her keycard just in case.

I thought about heading to my car—but if it was missing from the parking lot, it would give me away. I took a moment to be thankful for whatever instinct had told me to mail the tapes before I came to work. I snuck around the sides of the building until I got to a place where the trees pressed in close. Then I struck out into the woods.

I wanted to put distance between myself and the facility before I tried to get help, but I knew the longer it took, the greater the chance that Rosemary would be the one to find me. I did not want to be walking away from the facility while she was driving back toward it.

I did not want to think about what would happen if she found me.

I walked through the woods for ten minutes or so, before I let my path curve toward the highway. It wasn't a busy stretch of road, and for a while I worried that no one would come by. I think it was around half an hour before someone did. When I heard the engine approaching from behind, I was almost too scared to look—but it sounded too throaty, too loud to be Rosemary's compact sedan. I stuck out my thumb, glanced behind me, and saw a battered little truck approaching.

It pulled up beside me, and the driver leaned over and opened the door. "Need a little help?" he asked.

"Thank you," I said, climbing into the passenger seat.

He pulled back out into the road.

"I take it you ran into some trouble?"

"I did, yes. A tire blew out on my car, and I lost control. Ran it off the road."

"You want to go back and check it out? Call a tow truck?"

"Oh, that's okay," I said. "When I get to a pay phone, I'll call my assistant and have her sort it out. Right now I just need to get to the airport."

"Okay," he said. "It's a bit out of my way, but we can do that."

"Oh, don't worry—you don't have to take me all the way. If you drop me in town, I'm sure I can get a shuttle."

"Nonsense," he said. "It's no trouble. To be honest, I always love an excuse to go out there. Something about watching a plane take off, you know."

It was one of those strange moments that happen more and more often as you get older. Things you've always taken for granted mean something different to someone else. This man was around twenty-five or thirty. Planes, in his world, had only ever been for transportation. In mine, they'd been used to drop bombs.

"By the way," he said, holding out a hand, "I'm Blake. Nice to meet you."

"Elsa," I said. I shook his hand. "Thank you again. Let me pay you for your trouble."

"Come on now. Just being neighborly. You'd do the same."

He gave me a sidelong glance. "You sure you're okay? You look a little winded."

"It's just the shock, I think. And I was walking for a while before you happened along. I'm not as young as you—things hit a bit harder."

"You sure you don't want to see a doctor or something before you go to the airport? You might have whiplash."

"Don't worry, Blake," I said. "I'm a nurse. I'd know if something was seriously wrong."


I'M VERY TIRED NOW. BUT I'm close to the end. There's very little left to tell you.

Whoever you are.

Blake dropped me at the airport. He insisted on walking me inside to make sure I was okay, but I wouldn't let him come to the ticket counter with me. An abundance of caution, perhaps, but I didn't want to give anything away.

I told him I would call my assistant for help, and waved a decisive goodbye to him from the pay phone. But I wasn't calling for help—at least not the kind he thought I needed. I called Lupe Alvarez, the reporter I'd talked to months earlier. I didn't want to say much on the phone—I was still afraid of being followed—but I told her about Hilda, and that I had evidence.

"I don't think you believed me—did you, Lupe?" I said. "But now you'll know. You'll know I was right."

I got on a plane, and I flew west. I kept a low profile while I was there, and I didn't stay long. Just long enough for my last delivery to arrive and to develop my photos. I cleared out Ewa Keith's deposit box, sent copies of everything to Lupe, and left the continent.

I started poring over every newspaper I could get my hands on.

I still do. I never used to read the news. I never had a head for politics, never cared about scandal, but now I read

the papers from Washington, from New York, from London—
every single day.

Every day I hope to find something. I hope a little less
each day, but it's been twenty years, and I still haven't quite
given up. I looked today, and I'll look tomorrow.

I'm still here, farther north than I have ever been. Despite
this region's capriciousness—generous summer days and unre-
lenting winter nights—it's a nice place to be, even if the room I
live in is dingy and depressing. I can hear the roar of the waves
and smell salt in the air and, if I had the energy, I could be
walking along the edge of the sea inside of ten minutes.

I do not have the energy. I am using the last of it—I suspect
the last drops of energy I'll ever have—to write these words.

I found a place to stay. A bedsit. It's not the nicest option,
but they don't ask questions. Including questions regarding
identification. I gave my name as Elizabeth and left it at that.

So I'm sitting here now with files and cassettes piled
beside me. I wonder why Lupe's story never came out. Did
someone get to her? Prevent her from writing it? Rosemary
had so many people in her web.

I've barely left this room in two weeks. The landlady
leaves food outside my door and leaves me alone, which is
about all I can ask for at this point.

I'm starting to wonder what I was hoping to gain by
writing all this out. If Lupe wouldn't tell my story, I guess I
wanted to do it myself. But I could have done it in an easier
way. Found another journalist.

I could have just sent the files and tapes to someone else
on their own. I could still. Or with a short letter explaining

how it all ties together perhaps. But I locked myself away and wrote out my entire life story.

Why?

Is it just because I've never really told it to anyone? Not everything. I've told stories from it; I've shared anecdotes. But no one knows everything about me. Not Rosemary. Not Teresa. Not even you, not really—but you're the closest I have now. And that's all anyone can have, really. No one can share all of themselves. No one can even know all of themselves, not even me. Especially not me.

Was I hoping to write my way to absolution? I don't think I even believe in absolution. You live your life, and then at the end you have to look back on it. You can either accept it or you can't, but either way, you die with it behind you.

I think I just want to be able to believe that someone, somewhere, someday will understand. And the only way to understand is to know everything, or as close to that as possible—which isn't really very close.

It's not a confession, though I have regrets to confess to.

I wish I'd been able to see Teresa one last time. I wish I'd been able to explain to her why I was going. I didn't even leave her a note, and now she'll never know what happened to me. I'll die here and be found with a birth certificate saying "Ewa Keith" and no one will ever connect that with the woman she was married to.[1]

So I regret that.

---

1 Teresa Moyo died of breast cancer in 1982. It is not clear if Miriam ever tried to contact her again.

I wish I could see Rosemary's face as she is brought low by my work. She thought she was too far ahead of me; she thought she could stop me. She was sure of it. And I haven't come out the winner—I'm dying alone in a dusty room under someone else's name—but she hasn't either and I want to see the knowledge of that on her face.

So I regret that.

I wish I'd seen who she really was. Back at the start. Early enough to save Edgar. I wish I could have seen who he would've become, if it wasn't for Rosemary.

So I regret that.

I have a lot of regrets, it turns out.

Anyway.

Irrelevant.

Everything is irrelevant.

Everything is important.

Everything is important, until it is irrelevant.

Breathe in. Breathe out. Until you cannot.

Memory is malleable. History is mutable. All I can do is try to make sure my story isn't lost. I have saved what I can, so you will understand what we have become. The institute—I believe it still exists. It is still functioning, and no one knows. But you know now.

Whoever reads this, whoever you are—you are responsible now. You must do something. You must see it destroyed.

I'm not sure you will agree.

Perhaps it doesn't matter.

Perhaps all I can say is goodbye.

# Epilogue

As might have been predicted, there is no evidence that Dr. Gregory ever contacted Lupe Alvarez, or any other journalist, about her claims. We have verified that no story was ever published in any newspaper on the continent of North America, and we have found no evidence of it being published elsewhere in the world.

The files and cassettes she speaks of have never been found. If she really did send them out, the recipients never released them, and they certainly were not with the manuscript or with the doctor's body. No identification document at all was found with her, let alone one naming her as Ewa Keith. The room was registered to an Elsbeth Morton.

Like the author, we have not managed to put together a compelling theory as to why she wrote this manuscript. Given how much of it is clear and proven fabrication, her purpose seems murky at best. Was she trying to destabilize the Society? Or was she suffering under some kind of delusion? For all we know, she was simply trying to write a work of fiction, presented as autobiography.

There is no way to know, and it does not seem productive to guess.

It does seem prudent for us to remind the reader of our hesitation in publishing this manuscript at all. Perhaps you already believe that we should not have done so, and that all copies should now be destroyed.

Our chief concern lies in the possibility that, if overly credulous readers were to stumble upon this book, they could be taken in by the author's conspiracy theories and attempt to spread her erroneous claims. There is a danger that, if the claims spread too far, they would lead to violence against the Society and those who support and rely on it—which is to say, everyone.

We would like to stress that our reasons for establishing this press were not to undermine the Society's laws. Yes, we operate in defiance of some of them, but that is only because we disagree with them on one issue.

We believe in the power and importance of freedom of information. We do not support censorship and secrecy, though we acknowledge that the General Council might believe it has good reason to use both. We are not opposed to the existence of the Society, and we do not support or endorse any actions against them.

We wish to stress the importance of keeping this book to yourself. If it is in your hands, it is because we have vetted you and ensured that you can be trusted with incendiary material such as this. You have been authorized to read this because we know you to be capable of critical thought and unlikely to be swayed by the author's propaganda.

Now that you have read it, we request that you either return this copy to us, burn it, or take responsibility for its safekeeping yourself.

The one thing that must be avoided at all costs is the widespread distribution of this manuscript.

We thank you for your understanding and for your support of Yuriatin Press.

### SERMO LIBER VITA IPSA
*Free speech is life itself*

# Acknowledgments

Bless you, Mary Epworth, for making beautiful music with us. And thank you to EHG and to Amherst Books in Amherst, MA, for inadvertently introducing us as colleagues and friends.

Thank you to Jillian Sweeney, Jamie Drew, Emma Southon, Conor Sally, Joseph Fink, Meg Bashwiner, Cecil Baldwin, Gennifer Hutchison, Joella Knapp, Adam Cecil, Christy Gressman, Bettina Warshaw, Leann Sweeney, Ellen Flood, Karen Hall, Helen Zaltzman, Martin Austwick, Sarah Maria Griffin, Sarah Dollard, Caroline O'Donoghue, Ella Risbridger, Sarah Perry, Alice Tarbuck, Anna Scott, Amy Jones, Sharron Denekamp, Peter Matthewson, Christy Greenall, Joyia Kelly, Philip Thorne, Eli Matthewson, and Tineke Matthewson.

Thank you to those who have worked with us on our podcast *Within the Wires*: Rima Te Wiata, Lee LeBreton, Mona Grenne, Amiera Darwish, Norma Butikofer, and Will Twynham. And of course to all of our listeners who have supported our show since we began in 2016.

Thank you to our fantastic editor, Amy Baker, and to our agents Jodi Reamer and Claudia Young, and Holly Faulks and Alisa Ahmed.